T0274534

MIDNIGHTS WITH YOU

MIDNIGHTS WITH YOU

CLARE OSONGCO

HYPERION

Los Angeles   New York

For the diaspora kids, for the daughters

Copyright © 2024 by Clare Osongco, LLC

All rights reserved. Published by Hyperion, an imprint of
Buena Vista Books, Inc. No part of this book may be reproduced or
transmitted in any form or by any means, electronic or mechanical,
including photocopying, recording, or by any information storage or retrieval
system, without written permission from the publisher. For information
address Hyperion, 77 West 66th Street, New York, New York 10023.

First Edition, November 2024

1 3 5 7 9 10 8 6 4 2

FAC-004510-24241

Printed in the United States of America

This book is set in Adobe Garamond Pro/Monotype

Designed by Marci Senders

Library of Congress Cataloging-in-Publication Data
Names: Osongco, Clare, author.
Title: Midnights with you / Clare Osongco.
Description: First edition. • Los Angeles : Hyperion, 2024. • Audience:
Ages 12-18. • Audience: Grades 7-9. • Summary: Seventeen-year-old Deedee
longs to escape the stifling world her Filipino mom has created since
her husband died, so when Jay, the boy next door, offers to teach her to
drive it seems like a way out—but both of them are haunted by family
ghosts and traumas that force them apart.
Identifiers: LCCN 2023048546 • ISBN 9781368101936 (hardcover) • ISBN
9781368102025 (trade paperback) • ISBN 9781368101981 (ebook)
Subjects: LCSH: Teenagers—Juvenile fiction. • Mothers and
daughters—Juvenile fiction. • Family secrets—Juvenile fiction. •
Filipino Americans—Juvenile fiction. • Automobile driving—Juvenile
fiction. • CYAC: Filipino Americans—Fiction. • Teenagers—Fiction. •
Mothers and daughters—Fiction. • Family secrets—Fiction. • Automobile
driving—Fiction. • LCGFT: Romance fiction. • Novels.
Classification: LCC PZ7.1.O845 Dr 2024 • DDC
813.6 [Fic]—dc23/eng/20231116

LC record available at https://lccn.loc.gov/2023048546Reinforced binding

Visit www.HyperionTeens.com

SUSTAINABLE FORESTRY INITIATIVE
Certified Sourcing
www.forests.org
SFI-01681

Logo Applies to Text Stock Only

This story contains on-page depictions of a parent being emotionally abusive, slapping, depression, grief, and racism. It also mentions the off-page death of a parent and off-page domestic violence, and contains a brief scene of on-page sexual harassment.

ONE

Across these sleepless nights, I've memorized the view out my window. A slice of moon against the dark, peeking through the tree branches. The roof of the house across the street, slanting through the frame.

Headlight beams shine through the glass, sweep the ceiling. My eyes follow them as I'm lying in bed, limbs tangled in the sweaty sheets. It's always too quiet here, and my thoughts are too loud.

I reach for my phone and take a picture of the light bending. A photo is something to keep me in the moment, away from my spiraling thoughts.

But Mom's voice tears through my mind, sharp-edged, glinting. The fights we had yesterday, last week, every week, for years. The crushing disappointment in her voice when she says, *What is wrong with you, inside there, Deedee? Are you missing a part? It's like God is punishing me, leaving me stuck with you.*

We haven't been to church since my dad died, but she'll probably keep saying that for the rest of her life.

Ever since the ambulance drove away, it's just been me and Mom against the world, but we're not a team, exactly. I'm her dead weight, holding her down while she fights everybody.

Mom has a lot of rules, and I discover them by breaking them. Something left out of place, my shirt untucked, my expression too sour. All the little things that might set her off, buzzing around me, penning me in.

That panic, when Mom is yelling—can't get enough air, can't ever explain this feeling, hot and sticky and filling up my veins. Reminding me that I'm contaminated, incomprehensible to anyone outside this house. Only Mom really knows me, and what she sees is rotten.

Just fix your face! she said tonight, wiping the tears under her eyes. *It's unfair to me, having to look at that all day. Who's going to love a face like that?*

I overheard a white girl at school talking about her mom once. *God, she's such a drama queen,* she said, with a swish of her ponytail. This girl might as well have shot lasers out of her eyes or made doves fly out of her sleeve on command. I couldn't stop staring at her.

I don't know how she can dismiss her mom so easily. Mom's words are always there, knocking around in my bones, asking me who's going to love a face like mine.

Telling me, *You don't know what real suffering is, living this comfortable life.*

And like water circling a drain, my mind keeps pulling me back.

To the ambulance driving away with my dad inside, disappearing behind the trees at the end of the street. I was small then, straining on tiptoe to see out the window.

To what Mom said, later, after his funeral. Her words float up in the dark, making my blood run cold in the August heat. I'm tossing on the mattress, burying my face in the pillow—*can't think about it, can't go back there!*

But whenever I make a mistake, I'm right back there again. Everything is ruined so easily, and real suffering is still out there—crouched, waiting, like the creatures in her stories. The tales of ghosts and monsters she tells after we fight, the kind she must have heard growing up. All of them set in the Philippines. The place she never wants to talk about.

After we fight, Mom doesn't say *I'm sorry*, or that I'm okay and she forgives me. But she knows I'm obsessed with her stories, and when she shares them, it's the closest thing.

They always start kind of the same way:

Your Lola Ines heard the strangest thing from a lady at church, or, *Your Tita Lena heard this from some friends she meets for mahjong*, or, *Your Tito Andoy told me he saw it floating above the fields late one night.*

She'll tell me about ghosts of women all in white, roaming in the road, looking for revenge. About sinister kapres, smoking cigars that glow red from the trees at night. About the tikbalang, half man, half horse, a demon who'd help you plant your crops if you got on his good side. *(Tito Roger swears this really happened!)*

And then there are all the different kinds of aswang—shape-shifters and things that go bump in the night. But when she says *the* aswang, I know the one she means.

By day, she looks like a beautiful woman. And at night, her top half detaches from her body, and she flies around, terrorizing people, while

3

her bottom half just lies somewhere, chilling. *(Tito Andoy swears he saw her, right before she split herself in two!)* I could just picture how her entrails would dangle loose behind her, blood dripping, leathery bat wings going *ffff ffff* as they accordion open and shut. Flying through the night to suck people's viscera with her long, awful mosquito-straw tongue.

I always hear the word *viscera* the way Mom says it, so carefully, precisely, in her crystal-clear English. Like she beat her speech against the sink, handwashing it, scrubbing it, putting elbow grease into getting all the Filipino out.

She doesn't like talking about her family, most of the time. But with these stories, it's like she's telling me about her world as a kid and the people in it, whether they ever really existed or not.

I met some of her brothers, a long time ago—the ones who came to the States before her, who live on the other side of the country, in California. We haven't talked to them in a while, and it hasn't gone so well when I've tried to ask why. *If you keep asking questions like that,* she'll say, *I won't tell these stories anymore.*

Our family is basically just Mom and me now, though the internet tells me that's unusual. That Filipinos all have giant families, that you grow up never being alone. That's what it sounds like Mom's life was like in the Philippines. I tried to tell her I was lonely once, and she said, *Do you know what a luxury that is?*

My eyes travel across the white walls I'm not allowed to put anything on, bare except for some framed awards. The desk that has to stay free of clutter, nothing on top but the loose-leaf paper Mom leaves out for me to write letters to my grandfather.

Outside of her stories, Lolo Ric is the only one in our family Mom still talks about. How he built his own construction business, how big the family home is, how he got invited to the president's cousin's wedding one time. Details that are supposed to mean something to me, but just leave me feeling hollow.

She's had me write him every other week, going back years now. *He wants all your news*, Mom says, *trust me*. But he's never once written back.

It doesn't make sense! I've been talking back like that more and more in my head lately (not *out loud*, oh God, could you imagine?).

The restless feeling in my gut has been building and building. The one that pushes outward, wants more than this. The one that's going to get me in trouble.

I have to get up out of bed, cross the room in my bare feet, open the window to let in some air. Looking out onto the quiet road, and the light still on in the second floor across the street. That house was empty for the past few months, up for sale. Someone must have moved in during the day when I wasn't paying attention.

TWO

IF I COULD DRIVE, I COULD FIX IT.

The thought keeps pushing its way up, insisting on itself. It doesn't even make sense. Mom would never let me anywhere near her car.

But I'm still replaying the scene from earlier tonight in my head for the millionth time. How furious Mom looked when she realized I was crying. The harsh light in the kitchen, emphasizing her cheekbones and the hollows beneath. The pale brown skin she frets about, the broad nose she complains about when she looks in the mirror.

The way the light from the setting sun caught the vases clustered around the living room, on the table, the counter, the top of the cabinet. Curved shapes, soft colors, always empty, never flowers. Her weird collection of objects that are meant to hold things but never do.

If I could drive, I could have gone back to the store and gotten the right cut of chicken, replaced the one that made her burst into tears when she saw it in the fridge.

When she threw it on the counter and cried, *What is this shit! I asked for skinless and boneless!* I almost wanted to say something, out loud this time.

Mom let me get my learner's permit, but then she changed her mind. *It's too dangerous*, she said, no further explanation. Like when she taught me to ride a bike, even though she doesn't know how to herself—pushing the back of the seat, running behind me, helping me balance until I could do it and she let go. Then she took the bike away, a few years later. She gets stressed about things suddenly like that.

Did Suzy drive you? Mom demanded. *Were you having too much fun to pay attention?*

Riding with Suzy is the only way I can get to the store! It was almost a physical sensation, the urge to talk back straining against the rest of me.

You spend too much time with that low-class family! She pointed a trembling finger at me. *Friendships always fizzle out eventually. Family is the most important, remember that.*

And I got so scared, everything turning the color of dirty dishwater, picturing my life without Suzy Jang in it. The girl who found me reading on the side of the elementary school playground. Who looked at all the other kids running around, sweaty and happy and normal, and decided to come sit with twisted me instead.

Then Mom grabbed my phone out of my hand, shoulders tense as she swiped through my photos, deleting them all: the blur of trees on the side of the highway. Suzy doubled over laughing in the frozen-food section. Cars glittering like shiny beetles in the parking lot outside.

I should have expected it, because Mom does this all the time. Should have emailed them to myself, but I forgot. I don't have a password on, because she'd kill me if I did.

Go to your room, she said, thrusting the phone back at me. *I don't want to look at you anymore.*

I breathe deep and focus on the night in front of me. Cooler air coming into the stifling room, through the open window. My heart rate slowing a little, staring at the dark sky and the light on across the street, for so long, I lose track of time.

Finally I look at my phone, glowing in my hand, Suzy's texts from hours ago on the screen. Dispatches from another planet.

> **Suzy Jang:** oh my god deedee
> **Suzy Jang:** you won't believe what happened at work
> **Suzy Jang:** hiii are you there

I saw them earlier, but I try not to talk to her when I'm too sad, in case I won't be the version of me she likes.

And out of the dark, a pair of headlights appears again, coming around the corner, shining in my eyes.

Tires crunch as the car pulls into the driveway across the street.

The headlights turn off, but the moon is full and bright overhead, against the inky sky. The metal grooves pinch my elbows as I lean into the window frame.

The driver gets out, and an automatic light over the garage comes on. It's a boy about my age, maybe. Looking at the stars, lingering. His hands meet behind his head, elbows raised, stretching out his back.

The bad feeling retreats for a second, the way it does when I'm thinking about composing a shot. Picturing how I would capture this lone figure, under the big sky.

If I had a real camera, anyway. My phone won't do shit in this light.

Something prickles under my skin, looking at him. Envying that ability to come and go. To decide things for yourself.

Why can't you? that restless feeling asks, in a voice that sounds like Suzy's. *You could come and go, if you want. Step outside for a minute. Walk around the block.*

Like in elementary school, when I wouldn't go on the jungle gym because Mom said not to.

What, you think she's going to know? Suzy's face lit up, all mischief. *What do you think is going to happen?*

Mom always knows, somehow.

I've never sneaked out, by myself, for no reason. But that restless feeling has me pulling on clothes, heart pulsing from the tips of my fingers to my neck. I grab a flashlight and move down the stairs, slipping on my shoes and slowly opening the front door, on high alert for noise.

Then I'm on the other side of it, closing it so gently. Laughing quietly, like I just pulled off a heist.

The silence is so loud. I'm bracing myself, waiting for an alarm to sound, or for Mom to run out screaming.

But there's nothing. Just crickets chirping, wind moving through the pines, the fresh smell of dew.

Our town looks like it's asleep pretty much all the time, but something is different about the stillness at night. Everything a little strange, colors and passions of the day drained away.

I feel lighter, just breath and a heartbeat, floating in the middle of the street. Like I'm the ghost in the story, not the one who has to be afraid.

I loop the block just to prove I can. And when I'm close to home again, something about the house across the street catches my eye.

There's someone there.

The upstairs window is open, and—oh shit!—*that boy* is out there, sitting on the stretch of roof that sticks out over his porch, soft yellow light glowing behind him. The way he's backlit, it's hard to see his face, but there's his outline, his wiry frame and dark hair. He's sitting with his feet planted, elbows on raised knees and hands dangling between.

Goose bumps rise on my arms. I didn't expect him to be out here.

Apparently he didn't expect me either, because he almost loses his balance. He actually lets out a little undignified yelp as he braces himself, trying to recover.

I scared *him*? I'm doubled over laughing, distracted from my own frightened heart for a second. Not like at home, always clenched and waiting for the next bad thing to happen.

So I turn the flashlight on my face from below, like I'm about to tell a scary story.

"Boo!" I say, and he laughs—a sound with a low center of gravity, a sound like warm fresh laundry and crisp autumn leaves. One that says I added to his life for a second.

His shoulders shake. "I thought you were a ghost!"

"Oh, whoops." The way I say it makes him laugh again. It's addictive.

He rubs the back of his neck with one hand and leans forward, like he's trying to get a better look.

Who's going to love a face like that?

I turn off the flashlight, hiding in the dark.

"What are you doing out here?" he asks.

He looks so mysterious, a shadow framed by his bedroom light. I wish I could take his picture.

You better not start thinking you're some kind of artist! This phone is for safety, it's not a toy!

And I know better. Being an artist is for other people.

I just want to save things, all the warm moments already sliding through my grasp. To have something to hold on to, later. I only have a handful of photos of my dad.

"Hello?" the boy on the roof says. I guess I was quiet too long.

"Hi!" I laugh like it's the funniest thing. Is this even real? The part of my brain that's always watching and worrying is too sleepy to care.

Fuck it, why not? I take his picture.

"Hey!" He's laughing so much he can barely get the words out. "Don't make me come down there."

"I was inspired!" I'm always trying so hard to sound normal when other people are around. Being this bizarre is kind of a thrill.

He stares at me, and the silence gets too long, him up there, me down here. I can hardly stand it.

"Okay, well," he says, like he came to a decision. "Good night, little ghost."

He waves, and I wave back. The warmth drains from my cheeks as he climbs inside and shuts the window behind him. It's funny how disappointed I am to see him go.

THREE

THAT BOY'S LAUGH IS STILL RINGING IN MY EARS THE NEXT DAY, WHEN Suzy pulls into my driveway. I've been waiting for her all morning in our empty house, with my circling thoughts and the drone of cicadas for company.

The sun glints on her ancient white Honda Civic. She bought it off her mom earlier this summer, and it's Suzy's pride and joy.

"Did you eat?" she asks as I plop down into the passenger seat, her eyes glued to the sun-visor mirror. She takes a tube of concealer from the makeup bag on her lap and dabs lightly under her eyes. It's hot enough today to melt anyone's face off, but her winged liner is still crisp and intact.

"Dad said to bring this for you," she says, reaching into the back seat for a container of kimbap. Her mom makes them to sell in the refrigerator cases by checkout at the store. *Jang's Hardware—a legacy brand*, her dad likes to say, *that sells more than hardware*. It's his spin on the original store his father opened, a few years after coming to the States.

"He's still thinking of us little people," Suzy adds. "Fame hasn't gone to his head yet."

She thinks it's hilarious that he's become an extremely minor internet celebrity, after a TikTok from the store account went viral. People have started recognizing him at H-Mart.

I think it's his contrasts. Full sleeve tattoos under his Respectable Businessman button-downs. Stern resting face and salt-and-pepper buzzcut, but when he talks, his voice is gentler than you expect. This charm radiates off him, even when he's just doing mundane shit, lip syncing to the store radio while he uses the forklift. He always corrects me when I call him Mr. Jang, insists I call him Charlie. *Mr. Jang is my father*, he'll say, like the thought makes him stressed.

Suzy yawns and takes a bite of kimbap.

"You had to open today?"

She nods, massaging her temples. "You're so lucky you don't have to deal with the public."

I nod, even though I'm kind of jealous.

When I was younger, Mom used to say that she wished I could *get a job and stop being such a burden*. But when I was old enough to work, she switched. *After how hard I worked to give you this life, the idea of you serving other people—!*

So I stay at home in the summer, feeling like a bag of rocks.

"I saw this makeup look I want to try on you," Suzy says, glancing over at me. "It would work so well with your skin tone."

"Mmm . . . hard maybe."

Suzy laughs and nudges my arm. "What does that even mean?"

She's always trying to share the joy of makeup with me, but I have a thing about my face. I just don't want to deal with it.

I know my face is confusing because random people have questions—*what are you, where are you from, what are you mixed with?*—and when I get in front of the mirror, I start picking it apart, until I can't see myself anymore. I just see fragments of strangers I know from photos.

Nose and freckles from my dad. He was white, from here—not *here*-here, but he was American. Cheekbones and full lips from my grandmother in the Philippines, who looks so sad and glamorous in the grainy old pictures I have of her. Skin from who knows where, darker than my mom's somehow. Maybe it's just because she avoids the sun.

Everyone has guesses about what I could be—Chinese, Japanese, Mexican. I got asked if I was Korean once, and I felt this weird little glow inside, like I tricked someone into believing Suzy and I have something else in common. I don't think people really know what "Filipino" is around here.

Suzy makes a sound with her lips like she's deflating and tosses her makeup bag into the back seat.

"Want to go somewhere?" she asks. My love language.

The usual options run through my mind. Getting coffee at the diner. Watching a movie at the old theater in town. Taking her little brothers to the park, where they'll tear around like they're possessed—Ben and Jake are eight and ten, and they're basically always in motion.

Everything we usually do feels flat and tired. There's this pressure in the air, like I don't want summer to end, even though the days are kind of excruciating.

"The beach!" I'm obviously joking. It's like an hour away, and Suzy's barely ever driven on the highway.

She grins. "Genius."

"Seriously?"

14

"Obviously." Her face is all mischief again as she puts the car in drive.

We zip down two-lane roads winding through the woods, past clapboard houses and trees with their lush leaves rippling in the breeze. Suzy turns up the volume as she curves onto the highway, and harsh chords crash from her speakers. She accelerates and looks over her shoulder nervously—once, then again, until she's in the far left—and forces a strained laugh.

"Not as scary as it used to be!" she says, knuckles white, gripping the wheel.

The song changes, GBH now, and Suzy turns it up even more so we can shout along to the chorus of "City Baby Attacked by Rats." We're not city babies and we're more likely to be attacked by squirrels around here, but I guess it's aspirational.

I love moments like this, speeding through space with her, in between places. When our voices break and blend together, screaming along to her dad's old mixtapes, and it doesn't matter how ridiculous we sound.

Her glove compartment is full of them, with track lists we know by heart. The punk shit he used to listen to at his middle-of-nowhere Midwestern high school. I kind of hope she never gets a newer car, without a tape deck.

Overpasses and green-and-white road signs whip by under the bright blue sky, and the light glints off the cars flying by on the other side of the median.

Mom wouldn't like that I'm here right now. She always says not to go too far, and this is probably breaking some more rules I don't know about yet. But she won't be back until late tonight. She doesn't have to know I was gone.

I roll the window down a crack, warm air on my fingertips. It feels like life is out there, just waiting for us to find it.

"Would you teach me how to drive?" I blurt out.

Suzy pushes her bangs back with one hand. "I don't—" She hits the horn as another car comes into the lane ahead of us, too close for comfort. "I don't think I can? I can still, like, barely do this."

I shouldn't have asked. It was too much. I'm skirting close to the point where she'll get tired of me, like Mom says everyone will.

I check my calendar app for a distraction, to see who I have lined up for tutoring this week.

Mom didn't like the idea, when I told her there was a hole in the market for non-cheating essay help. *You should focus on your own studies. Don't I do enough for you? Don't you have enough?* But I needed to feel like I could do something for myself.

"In two miles, take the exit . . ." Suzy's phone declares from the cup holder. She leans way forward as she gets over to the far right.

And then we're winding through the empty streets of a seaside town, with its narrow streets and gray-shingle houses. The parking lot by the beach isn't as full as I'd expect. Suzy pulls into a spot and slumps over the steering wheel.

The ocean smell hits as soon as we get out of the car. On the sand, we pull our shoes off and run into the water's edge, yelping at how cold it is. Arms crossed, we stand in the surf, water rushing in around our legs and receding again.

"So when's the next Sunday dinner?" Suzy asks.

Mom insists on having Suzy over once a month. *We have to reciprocate*, she'll say, shaking her head. *You're always over there. You eat so much of their food.*

I used to look forward to it, this tradition that made Suzy part of our lives. But lately it seems like it's just an opportunity for Mom to interview Suzy and talk shit about her after.

"Probably soon?" I say, trying to keep my voice light. "I have to ask."

"How's your mom doing, anyway?"
What did I do to get stuck with you, ha?
I must be cursed.
You're so unlovable.
You're missing something everyone else has.
I can't explain it to Suzy. My toes dig into the sand, salt air on my tongue.

I've tried before, but it didn't seem to register. She assumes everything has to be a misunderstanding, like we're just a different version of her and her mom, at the heart of it.

I don't want her to know it's my fault. What I did to deserve this.

So I try saying it like a joke. "She hates me."

Suzy laughs. "I know what you mean, my mom was so pissed at me the other day. . . ."

I force myself to laugh along, checking to see how normal my voice sounds.

When we learned about the social contract in history last year, I thought about how everyone at school must have agreed to be extremely casual and chill about everything. And I'm always trying desperately not to violate it, to hold myself in. But sometimes my mouth gets ahead of me.

"Like you know how she has me write letters to my grandfather all the time?" The beach is so open and sunny, curved to embrace the waves. It feels too exposed, suddenly, painfully bright. "Even though he never responds anyway."

"Families, man. My grandfather's the same, he's totally emotionally constipated."

Her grandfather who she sees a few times a year, who shows up frowning on her Instagram, her dad with an uneasy arm around his shoulders.

I've never even seen a photo of mine.

"What's that thing you wanted to tell me?" I ask. "That happened at work."

Something is off now, the way she hesitates. There's a sour taste in my mouth as she shakes her head. "It wasn't as funny as I thought."

The water runs out and the sand is getting softer under my feet, shifting little by little. The sun dazzles my eyes, the way it reflects off the waves, and I know I should feel good, with the warmth on my skin and the glittering sea ahead of us. Maybe if I take a picture, I'll be able to feel it later. I lift my phone, and Suzy sticks her tongue out, posing for the camera. So I take a few of her instead.

I almost want to tell her about the boy on the roof, but my stomach clenches. Remembering the time I told her a story about a boy, and she said something when Mom was there. And Mom panicked and pulled me out of the debate team, right when I was starting to make it my entire personality.

It was last year, and Mom was driving us somewhere. She used to do that, before Suzy got her car. We were talking about the debate trip coming up, and Suzy said I must be excited Matt Gilbert is going. Teasing me the way Mrs. Jang, a self-described romantic, might rib her at dinner.

Mom didn't react right then—she has an instinct for company— but she heard. She noticed. She called the school the next day and said I wouldn't be participating, not in the trip, not in the team.

"What are these people thinking? All these teenagers, traveling together, *staying in hotel rooms*?!" She shook her head in disgust and pointed at me. "Remember this. Women's bodies are ticking time bombs. You have so much more to lose than he does. There's a lifetime's worth of consequences, waiting to explode."

She's talking about you. You're her lifetime of consequences. You exploded everything.

"These Americans have lost their minds," she said. "You're not growing up like that."

There were so many things I wanted to say. But if I'm not American, then what else am I? Do I belong to the place I only hear about in your ghost stories?

But I figured it out then. That lots of things aren't up for debate. That there was no point, and it was better to stay quiet.

I smother the little flame of anger licking its way up my spine—because *what will I do* if I'm mad at the one person in the entire world who's most on my side? Be alone? And when Mom stops yelling and leaves the house in icy silence again, I won't even have some text messages from Suzy that I can ignore?

I try to remember that boy's laugh, but it gets swallowed up in the rushing of the waves.

FOUR

I DIDN'T THINK THROUGH HOW LONG IT WOULD TAKE TO GET THERE and back. We're cutting it close to when Mom gets home.

Suzy's humming along to the stereo, in the driver's seat beside me. My nerves are frayed, but I don't want to say anything. Once, a little while ago, I kept telling her I was stressed about getting home on time, and she cut in, laughing. *Girl, you need to relax! It's just your mom, it's fine. You're being kind of a lot.*

Suzy thinks she knows her because Mom is nice to her face at dinner. So I stare out the window, silently calculating how much longer it will take.

But when we're a couple miles from my house, Suzy exclaims, "Oh! I forgot," and pulls into the parking lot outside the 24/7 convenience store. "I promised Ben and Jake I'd get them Hot Cheetos."

There are some boys standing around the parking lot, in a clump between the cars. It takes a second, but I recognize them.

"There's Alex," I say.

When I look at him now, I don't feel anything. Which is a relief, considering Alex Lavoie had my heart doing backflips for most of last year, when we got paired up for chem lab. Everyone is kind of obsessed with him—he plays football in the fall and lacrosse in the spring and has these soft green eyes that make him seem sensitive. There was a period of time last year when I couldn't shut up about him. I hadn't learned my lesson yet, after the Great Debate Team Incident. And back then, talking to Suzy about having a crush was more fun than having the crush itself.

Suzy starts coughing when she sees him. "Oh fuck!" She laughs and slides down in her seat.

I know that look, when her nose turns a little pink. She's embarrassed.

Suzy glances over at me, cheeks flushed. "Do . . . you still like Alex? You said, um—a little while ago, you said you were over it, but . . ."

Oh my God, does *she* like him now? Is that what this is?

"Yeah," I say. "I'm over it." And I mean it, so why does this make me so anxious?

"Uh—" Suzy looks away, into the woods, fingers running through her hair. "You know the funny thing I was going to tell you? That wasn't so funny. He, um—" She sits up straight again and clears her throat. "He came into the store. A few weeks ago."

A few weeks ago?

We used to give each other every micro-update about our crushes. Every run-in and possibly meaningful glance.

Why wouldn't she tell me about that? It feels like something is slipping away, sand melting under my feet as the tide runs out. And instead of flailing in this murky feeling, I just need to do something.

21

"Let's go talk to him, then!" I say, hopping out of the car.

"What! Wait—" But I close the door on her answer.

She catches up and tries to pull me back by the arm. "Who *are* you today? Since when do you like talking to people?"

But it's too late, because we're basically in front of him already.

"Deedee!" Alex exclaims. "Didn't see you around this summer."

Then he looks at Suzy, and—is it my imagination, or does he seem nervous? "Hey, I looked up that movie you were talking about. The one where the piano eats someone?"

Oh. Okay.

They've definitely been talking.

And that's fine, whatever, but—the fact that she didn't tell me?

"Who is that?" a boy off to the left says. Kevin Harper. I've vaguely known these guys since elementary school, but most of them probably don't know I exist.

"Oh, that's the girl who helped me fix my English paper," Ted says. He's a repeat tutoring customer. Not the best, not the worst.

Kevin snorts. "Can't believe you paid someone to do that when AI can do it for you."

"Hey, I don't know! Teach a man to fish . . ."

"Dude," Suzy pipes up, annoyed. "She's right here. We can hear you!"

That's the Suzy I know, always standing up for everyone. The way she almost punched a bank teller who made fun of her mom's accent. Or the way she barely missed a beat when some guy in eighth grade wouldn't leave me alone.

"Hey, Indonesian girl!" he'd called.

We just kept walking. Honestly, I was surprised he knew Indonesia was a place.

"What, you think you're too good for me? You and your *fat lips*?"

Suzy whipped around, that come-at-me-bro energy in the set of her shoulders, the I'm-sick-of-your-shit expression that might be her natural resting face.

"At least she *has* lips, unlike you, fucker! Who'd want to kiss that lipless mouth?"

I have to hand it to her, he left us alone after that.

"Sorry, ma'am," Ted says now, snickering.

"Ignore these clowns," Alex says, and asks Suzy something else about that movie I haven't seen.

All these conversations are going on around me, laughter rising upward, like the heat, and I'm receding into the background. And whatever, that's fine. I can enjoy the scenery. The convenience store's neon sign, letters glowing bright blue. The dense pines on the edge of the parking lot, mounds of dark green where the woods begin. The clouds tinged blush pink as the day slides into evening.

But then something closer to Earth catches my eye.

Someone is coming across the parking lot toward us, a boy with a wiry build and messy dark hair.

The other guys notice him, too.

"Heyyyy!" a few of them exclaim simultaneously.

"This fuckin' guy!" Ted says, giving the mystery man one of those hand-slaps that turns into a vigorous handshake.

"Jason, you piece of shit," Kevin says, as affectionately as a person possibly could.

Wow, who is this? I've never seen him before, but somehow he knows everyone already.

Maybe he does look kind of familiar. I shift around to get a better look at his face.

Thick brows, broad nose, moody full lips. There's something in the shape of his features, the warm shade of his skin. This feeling of recognition hits me all at once. It's hard to pinpoint exactly how I know, but—*he's like me.* Asian from most angles. Asian enough for people to comment on it, ambiguous enough for questions. In my little life in this little town, I've never met anyone else like that.

And suddenly he's looking right at me, and I feel like I'm jumping on the trampoline in Suzy's backyard, at the top of the arc, weightless for a second, about to come down.

Josh Dean claps him on the back. "Jason, my man, haven't seen you in forever."

"Dude, it's Jay now, I told you," Alex says.

"Ohhh, a rebrand," Ted says. "Why the switch-up?"

"Quarter-life crisis." Jay's voice is low and bouncy, sardonic edge baked into it. "You know, like when you shaved your head last summer."

I guess that must be an in-joke, because everyone bursts out laughing.

"Hey," Ted says, putting his hands up, "my head is just naturally bumpy, all right!"

"Yeah, new year, new me, I guess?" Jay grins. "I live here now. Surprise."

"No way!" Josh says. "Man, I haven't seen you since that party last summer. That shit was wild."

Suzy and Alex are chatting up a storm now, on the other side of me, and I'm nervous again, checking the time on my phone.

When I look up, Jay's watching me, across this circle of people. Like he thinks I look familiar, too.

Is he . . .

It doesn't matter. I don't have time to think about this.

"Hey," I say, touching Suzy's arm. "I'll get the Cheetos, okay? I'll be right back."

Inside, the lighting is harsh, washing everything out. When I get to the chips aisle, the door pings. I look up to see Jay walking in and tug my shorts down slightly so it's more obvious I'm wearing a crop top.

He goes to the refrigerator cases glowing in the back of the store and takes his time making a selection.

Finally he approaches the counter, and I line up behind him with the Cheetos and some chips for myself. I almost want to laugh at the sheer number of energy drinks the cashier is bagging right now.

"Jay, man, what's up? How's your mom doing?" the clerk asks between boops of the bar code scanner. "Everything good with the house?"

He really does know everyone.

"Yeah, the thing you suggested with the duct tape worked great."

"Hey, any time, glad to help. She's lucky she has you helpin' out. You take it easy, all right?"

Jay turns again and gives me a slightly confused look. He takes his bag and hovers there, waiting while the cashier rings me up, and falls in step beside me as we head for the sliding doors. I point to his bag, trying to ignore the soft pins-and-needles feeling in my chest. "Are you pulling an all-nighter?"

He shrugs. "Gotta keep up with these guys."

Jay stops just outside, so I do, too. He's standing tight in the shoulders, like he just had a growth spurt and hasn't gotten used to life at that altitude.

I kind of don't want to go back to everyone else clustered on the other side of the asphalt. Suzy's gesturing with her arms, getting really animated about whatever she's telling Alex.

"What'd you get?" Jay asks, leaning over to look.

My cheeks warm up as he takes the bag from me and peers inside. "Hot Cheetos, solid choice," he says, head bobbing. His eyebrows go up. "Salt and vinegar? *Interesting.*"

"What's that supposed to mean?"

He just smiles and shakes his head, handing the bag back to me. His fingers brush mine as I fumble for the plastic handles, and it sends a little jolt down my spine.

"So, uh . . . you just moved here?" I hope I don't sound flustered.

"Yeah. From Maine." Jay shifts his weight from foot to foot.

"But you know these guys already?"

"Long story. Hey, this is going to sound weird, but . . . were you . . ." His brows knit closer together. "Do you live around Grove Street?"

"What!" My shirt feels too tight around my armpits suddenly, sweat blooming there. "Why?"

"Holy shit." He's grinning like he's made an amazing discovery. "It's Ghost Girl."

What he's saying hits me slowly, a drop of dye changing the color of water. Fitting the lines of his face to what I could barely see in the half-dark.

His face that, from this angle, is stressfully handsome.

"Wow, okay. Sorry." The corners of his mouth turn down like he's trying so hard not to laugh. "Just realized how creepy this must sound, if I'm wrong."

"No, uh, I remember. On the roof, and—" I wave my hands vaguely. *"Boo!"*

His eyes flit downward, mouth stretching into a quick smile. Then he glances back at me, like he's squinting into the sun. "I'm Jay. Hi."

"Deedee." I reach out a hand, and he gives it a firm shake.

"You can't just go around scaring people like that. Girl with long black hair, appearing in the dark, suddenly? You're going to give someone a heart attack."

"Wow, sorry." I can barely get the words out for the laugh jostling my chest. "How's your heart now?"

"Fine, thanks." Jay's doing this fidgety thing with one hand, pressing down on the tops of his fingers with his thumb, one after the other. Like he's an athlete warming up, but his sport is competitive typing.

His eyes turn skyward, and he sighs. "There's a lot going on."

I want to ask him about that, but the words stick in my throat, so I stare off in the same direction. The clouds are so gorgeous right now— without really thinking about it, I lift my phone to take a picture.

Jay leans over to look at it. "You have a good eye."

"I don't know." I feel hot and prickly all over, suddenly. "This is, like, the most cliché thing to take a picture of."

He laughs a little at that. "Remember when you took a photo of me for some reason? Kind of rude, honestly."

"I—"

"Do you have an Instagram I could follow or something?"

"Oh, uh—" I have a private one I rarely post to, that Suzy gently bullied me into starting. I don't really like other people seeing my photos. And I don't have that many friends, anyway.

The sun is behind the trees now. Fuck, I'm going to be in so much trouble.

"Not really. Um—I should go." I jerk my head toward Suzy. "I'll, uh, see you around?"

"Seems likely." Jay blinks a few times, like he just remembered where he was. "Stranger things have happened."

I run up and grab Suzy, linking arms from behind. "Hey, I have to get home!"

"Oh, right, sorry!" she says, frazzled. "Bye, boys."

I glance over my shoulder as we're walking arm in arm back to her car. Alex is standing with Jay now, telling him a story. But Jay's still watching me go.

FIVE

OH GOD, MOM'S CAR IS IN THE DRIVEWAY. THE USED BEIGE MERCEDES she's so proud of.

After Suzy drives away, I stuff my shirt into my shorts—they're high-waisted enough that I can satisfy the rules in a pinch, if I slouch. And I tie the plastic bag with the chips shut and tuck it under a bush by the front door. I'll come back for it later.

Mom is waiting for me on the prim gray living room couch, back stiff like the cushions.

"Where have you been, ha?!" The voice Mom uses most of the time is like a radio announcer's, carefully molded into her ideal American accent. But there are times when her real voice peeks out a little more. When she gets really into a story, when she's beside herself with laughter. When she gets mad. "Why were you out so late?"

Every light in the open-plan kitchen-living-dining area is on, illuminating the bare white walls and glittering, empty vases. It feels like an interrogation is about to take place.

"Um." Panic is rising in my throat. Can she tell, somehow, that I've been with *boys*? "I was with Suzy."

"I asked *where*."

Does it show on my face? Do I have an instant tan? She's always saying messed-up things about what will happen if I get darker.

"The beach," I mumble.

"The beach?!" She hops up and crosses the room. I'm a few inches taller, but it still feels like she towers over me. "You went so far away without telling me?"

At least I remembered to hide the chips, or it would have been worse.

Mom sighs like all the air going out of a tire. "You're spending too much time with Suzy. It's your senior year now. Time for you to get serious. Do you want to end up working in some *store*, like her?"

What is that supposed to mean? I want to say something, defend Suzy, but my thoughts are all trying to rush out at once, and there's a bottleneck by the exit.

"Have you even written to your Lolo yet? Can you imagine what you'll say to him if no colleges accept you?"

My head feels too hot, thinking about those letters.

"My college essays are basically done." Multiple versions written and rewritten, YouTube videos consulted, spreadsheets made.

People act like I should be looking forward to college, but it just fills me with dread. Either getting in debt to a bank—Suzy's dad says they're still paying off his student loans—or adding to my debt to Mom. The impossible debt I can never pay back.

There's another option, but it means I'll probably keep living here:

going to Eastleigh, a little over an hour away. My test scores could get me a full ride because I'm in-state.

"Then reread them again!" Mom exclaims. "I'm sorry, is this too much *work* for you?" She draws a wide circle with her hand, like she's gesturing at my entire life. "You know how hard I work for you? Everything I do, I do so we can survive. You have to start thinking about that for yourself, too. Start making some good decisions."

I want to circle the word *survive*, write, *Not the best word?* next to it in pencil.

What does survival have to do with not seeing Suzy? Why is it always the thing Mom says to explain everything that doesn't make sense? *Survive survive survive.* It feels like something else is the issue, but I don't know what to call it.

"And your head is all over the place!" Mom's voice gets nasally, mocking. "Thinking about art, thinking about boys!"

"I'm not thinking about boys!" I say, knee-jerk, as Jay's laugh rings in my ears.

I'm trying not to think about his eyes in the golden afternoon light.

Or his hands, the way they do that nervous flexing thing.

Or his mouth when it curled into a smirk.

"You better not be!" Mom clicks her tongue. "Ay, you're so exhausting. Just draining the life out of me." She closes her eyes and makes a swatting motion toward the ceiling. That's my cue to go to my room.

I run up the stairs, away from her voice shouting, "Door open!" As if I could forget that I'm not allowed to close it.

Curled under the covers in bed, I pull up the picture I took in the middle of the night. You can't see Jay's face, but it's still comforting. The feeling of the moment is there, somehow.

My mind wanders back to the way he looked this afternoon, and I bite my lips, thinking about how I always feel self-conscious about them. His lips are fuller than mine, but on him it doesn't seem like a flaw.

There are footsteps outside, suddenly, coming closer. So I panic and delete the photo.

The bed dips as Mom sits on the edge, and I poke my head out from under the covers. She really does look exhausted.

"Your Tita Loleng told me this story," she says. "About the White Lady."

This ghost is in her stories all the time, a woman in white who roams around, long black hair obscuring her face. The details change—the locales, the causes of death. Mom riffs on it, adds to it. I think she just makes things up when she gets bored.

Kuya Manny swears he saw her in the middle of the road, where she died in a car crash.

Ate Tricia saw her in the bathrooms at the university. They said she hanged herself, after her lover refused to leave his wife.

Tito Jesse spotted her on the side of a winding mountain pass, where she'd thrown herself off a cliff.

Mom calls her the White Lady, but I get embarrassed when I say it out loud. Rosemore, Massachusetts, was 95 percent white as of the last US census. There are lots of white ladies around here. You'll have to get more specific.

"This happened to a man Loleng's husband knew from work," Mom says, ironing wrinkles out of the blanket with her hands. "Cars kept crashing into a tree outside his house. People said it was because a woman's spirit was trapped inside. She died there, driving recklessly after she found out her husband betrayed her."

Mom raises her eyebrows meaningfully at me. The weight seems to lift from her shoulders when she's telling a story, in gossip mode. Her inner tsismosa doesn't really have anyone to talk to around here.

31

"What did she want?"

"*Revenge.* They said she would make any man who looked like her husband swerve into that tree." She leans in for dramatic effect. "So one day, Loleng's husband's friend thought to himself, *I'll just cut it down.* He took an ax to it, but the blade cracked. He borrowed a chainsaw from a friend, but the motor died. And then, that night, he developed a mysterious fever."

Mom is so absorbed in the story now, her accent peeks out. The *k* sounds come from deeper in her throat, and the stress on her syllables falls a little differently, a sharp landing on the end of *fever.*

"He was thirsty, but he couldn't make himself drink. He was hungry but he couldn't eat. He tossed and turned, unable to sleep." She's leaning into each sentence, more and more, a wave about to crest. "After three days like that, he passed away. Any scratches or dents he'd made in the tree had faded.

"It still stands today," she adds with a creepy flourish. "Completely unscathed."

Mom nips at my arm with two fingers, like the weakest pincer. "Isn't that scary?" She smooths the blanket some more. "It's funny you liked these stories so much when you were little. They would always make you fall asleep right away."

She turns off the light and gets up.

"Mom," I whisper, and she stops in the doorway, tense frame backlit. "Do you want me to stop hanging out with Suzy?"

She hesitates, a hand on the doorknob.

My whole body is clenched in terror, waiting for her answer. I asked, but I'm not sure who I'll be on the other side if she says yes.

She sighs, and her hard edges soften, rounded off by exhaustion. "No. It helps. To know you can go over there. It's fine."

Mom leans a hand against the doorframe and turns back to me. "Did I ever tell you about the time I saw an aswang?"

There's a weightless feeling in my gut, like when Suzy takes a corner too fast in the Civic. Mom always tells these stories like they happened to someone else.

"I was in our backyard. Late at night once. And I saw her." She gives me a pointed look. "I was almost your age."

There's something accusatory in her voice that's almost funny. *When I was your age, I saw an aswang,* the distant cousin of, *When I was your age, I walked fifteen miles to school.*

"It was right after my mom died," she adds, so quietly I almost don't hear.

A chill runs through me. She never talks about her mom.

"I saw a lady walking in the road. I wondered what she was doing out so late. And then, the next thing I knew—wings erupted out of her back! Her top half lifted off, and her intestines came spilling out!"

Her phone starts ringing, and she scrambles for it. I know that ring tone by now, the one she only uses for her boss at work.

"Yes? I thought I sent that to you. What did he say? Huh, okay. Interesting."

Her voice is different now. *Huh?* with that deep, calm *u*, like she practiced it. Not the *ha?* I know—sharp and terrifying sometimes, sure, but others it's inquiring, warm, boisterous. Full of life. A reminder of who she used to be, maybe.

Head bent to keep the phone pinned to her shoulder, Mom disappears from view, slippers shuffling quickly down the hall.

I'm alone again, in the dark.

I can't believe I deleted that picture. Didn't even email it to myself first, like usual.

I've started so many new email addresses over the years, because Mom doesn't look there and then they get full. All these old accounts just floating in the ether, full of random photos, screenshots of Suzy's texts, things I wipe from my phone before she can find them.

Why do I want to cry right now? It's just a shitty, blurry photo that doesn't even show his face.

But what if we don't talk again?

That lightness I didn't expect, that strange moment in time. I want to remember it happened.

I open the drawer of my nightstand and slowly detach the photo I keep taped to the top, where it's hard to see.

The one where we're all together, me and Mom and Dad, in front of the New York skyline. The place where they lived, before I came along. When she was happy. We all took a trip back, for nostalgia's sake, when I wasn't old enough to remember. Before he got sick.

Mom probably wouldn't like knowing I have this. When I ask about my dad, she'll say, *It's self-indulgent, making yourself miserable on purpose.* Or, *That's private. I don't have to explain myself to you.*

I lie there for a while, but I can't make myself sleep. When I finally give up and look at my phone, it's just past 2 a.m.

I get up and go to the window, and there Jay is again. On his roof, staring into the night.

SIX

OVER THE NEXT COUPLE WEEKS, I CATCH GLIMPSES OF JAY OUT MY window. Bringing groceries inside, mowing the lawn, chasing a little girl—must be his sister?—across the grass, arms raised like a cartoon monster. He catches up and tickles her, and their laughter filters faint through the glass. And at night, when I can't sleep, I see his headlights, hear his car leave and return, get up to see him on the roof again. But somehow now I'm too scared to sneak out.

Then school starts, and all through the first week, I'm trying not to notice, heartbeat pulsing under my skin, whether Jay is in my classes. Trying not to react when he sits a few rows ahead of me in English, or when he walks into US History late and stares at me for a second, before choosing a seat far away. I catch this look on his face some-times—like he's haunted by something, maybe.

At the end of the week, I sit right behind him in English and spend too much time staring at the place where the back of his neck meets his shirt.

Mrs. Johnson writes out a quote on the board. "'History doesn't repeat itself, but it rhymes,'" she says, reading slowly to match the speed of her writing. "Mark Twain."

I'm close enough to hear Jay say under his breath: "Mark Twain didn't actually say that."

He leaves quickly when class is over, and we don't talk, after.

I'm sure the things that haunt us wouldn't be the same. But I kind of wonder if they'd rhyme.

When classes get out, Suzy and I head to the bathroom so I can change.

It's our routine. In the morning, I left the house in jeans with a safe T-shirt tucked into them, no possibility of a midriff showing—Mom-approved—and clothes I bought with tutoring money in my backpack. A short floral dress and an olive canvas jacket, plus Suzy's combat boots. I dressed to capture my mixed feelings: I want to look cute, I want to disappear, I want to be strong.

Now I'm changing back, because I'm eating dinner at Suzy's, and I don't want her parents to wonder why I switch outfits at the end of the night. I want them to think I'm a halfway good kid, even if it's not the truth.

I'm in the stall, balancing on one leg getting back into my jeans, when Suzy says: "So Alex wanted to go to the diner with his friends! It's the one day he doesn't have practice."

It's a Thursday. We always have dinner at her house on Thursdays. There's that sinking-sand feeling again.

I stare at the chipped green paint on the inside of the stall door and think longingly of her dad's homemade burgers, the ones he serves bun-less with rice and kimchi on the side.

"You should come!" Suzy says brightly. "It'll be fun."

My stomach lurches. *Is Jay going to be there?*

"Deedee?" Suzy says. "I want you to come, this doesn't . . . have to be a big deal."

God, I can just hear her feeling sorry for me.

"Yeah! Yeah, that's great," I say, pulling on my shirt, leaving it untucked. "It'll be fun."

We drive past the town common, the old colonial meeting house rising up next to it, puritan-white steeple scraping the vivid blue sky. Some kids from school are sitting cross-legged on the grass, soaking up the sun.

"What is . . . going on with you and Alex, anyway?"

"Oh, I love this song," Suzy says, turning the music up and singing along.

Why doesn't she want to tell me? Did I do something wrong?

But after the chorus, Suzy sighs and turns the music back down again. "Are you sure it's okay?"

"It was a stupid crush. Ancient history."

Suzy leans back against the seat, arms stretched to the wheel in front of her. "He came in to get a new cutting blade for his lawnmower.

A few weeks ago. And he was wearing this shirt—" She can barely get the words out because she's already laughing. "It had the poster for *Killer Klowns from Outer Space* on it."

This is her favorite kind of movie. The sweet spot of spooky and ridiculous where I can join her, because I'm too chicken to watch horror movies most of the time. And we have watched some *painfully bad* ones together. We did a marathon one summer of the worst-ranked on Rotten Tomatoes, eating popcorn and making jokes in the humid dark.

"So I notice it and burst out laughing. And he looks at me like, *What is happening right now?* And I point at his shirt and say, 'Wow, a man of taste.'"

She's laughing again, and talking like things are normal, so why do I feel so on edge?

"And then we just couldn't stop talking about terrible B movies. I almost got in trouble. I wasn't even on break." She sighs. "He made me feel . . . fascinating."

"You are fascinating."

"I mean he made me feel like *the most special girl on earth*, instead of *that girl who works at the store*." She glances at me sideways as she takes the turn toward the diner. "What about his friend—Jay?"

"What about him?" I try to sound disinterested.

"He's half, too, right?"

Of course I know what she means. The same thing I thought, the first time I saw him in daylight. But the way she always says it—half, not *full*, not a complete, whole thing. Like I'm a fraction of a real person. Like I'm—

What's wrong with you, inside there?

"I hate saying *half*, it sounds . . . like I'm missing a part."

"He's cute, though."

It stings, sometimes, how she just breezes past things. When she doesn't see me, like on the beach.

But how much can an unlovable person like me expect? Mom's voice is in my head, saying, *Just be grateful for what you have.*

What I barely still have, maybe.

"We had one normal conversation. It happens sometimes. Did you want me to stand quietly by myself?"

"Yikes, fine, sorry I asked," Suzy says as she maneuvers into the diner's giant parking lot.

Her best friend and Alex's friend—it would be so convenient for her. She doesn't understand. It's too neat, and I'm a fucking mess.

"Oh," Suzy says, and reaches for a plastic bag in the back seat. "Mom got this for you."

Inside there's a small glass jar, and I turn it around in my hands. *Bagoong,* the label reads. Salty fermented shrimp paste, *Product of the Philippines. Ba-go-ong,* to my ears one of the most beautiful words in any language. The soft percussion of the double *o*'s, the air between them, the way they hit after the throaty *g.*

They carry it at H-Mart sometimes, the one outside Boston that Suzy's parents trek out to a couple times a month. They always look for it because they know it's one of my favorite things, eating it with sliced mangos. And I'll try to pay them back, but her dad will wave me off and say, *Walters, your money's no good here.* The way he calls me by my last name, like I'm another kid he's coaching in Little League.

I unzip my backpack and put the jar gently inside. "Here," I say, pulling out some bills and handing them to her.

Suzy shakes her head. "Not a chance."

We came to the diner a lot two summers ago, when Suzy had the clos-ing shift and she'd get off work craving pancakes. It has a name, but we always just call it the diner. It feels appropriate—the neon sign outside just says FOOD.

I feel so nostalgic for those nights, warm air and dark sky and the comfort of drinking diner coffee, staying up later than we should. I'd tell her some of Mom's stories. She loved them—exactly her kind of horror shit. And she'd give me a dramatic retelling of the movies I'm too scared to watch.

Though I'm pretty sure nothing in those movies is as scary as the moment we walk in, and Jay's eyes immediately meet mine, from the corner booth where Alex's friends are sitting.

I have to look away, at the chrome detailing on the long counter, the Pepto Bismol pink of the booths.

He's going to talk to me. Suzy's going to see him talking to me.

But we get closer, and he's not looking at me anymore. It seems like they're talking about something that's stressing him out.

"Is Candace at school already?" Alex asks.

"I wouldn't know. We're not really talking right now."

"Oh yeah Candace!" Ted pipes up. "What's she doing now? She was a babe."

"Ted, please," Alex says.

"Haven't seen her this summer, actually." Jay sounds annoyed.

Alex notices us then and scoots in to make room.

"Oh—" Suzy puts a hand on his shoulder. "My mom wanted me to bring home a pie. Come help me pick?"

She shoots me a little grin, because when Alex gets up, that leaves an empty space next to Jay for me to slide into.

I'm lightheaded, mind running ahead, trying to game out how risky this might be.

How one thing might lead to another, and what I might lose, at the end, like when Suzy got me pulled out of debate. I was starting to really make friends on the team, at least I thought. Staying up late, making obscure jokes in the group chat, riffing off the things we were reading to prep.

But after Mom took me off the team, I stopped getting the jokes, and they said it didn't make sense for me to be in the group chat anymore. After they removed me, I scrolled back up through the old messages, rereading the times people laughed at things I said.

All the sounds in the restaurant feel amplified, suddenly, grating. The laughter erupting from a booth behind us, silverware clinking on plates, cooks shouting out orders that are up from the kitchen.

"You okay?" Suzy says, touching my arm. "You look kind of pale."

"Um, you know, I don't feel so good. I think . . . maybe I need to go home."

Her face falls, and she glances at Alex, hovering next to the table, eyebrows raised. I'm ruining this for her. She wants to stay.

"I could take her," Jay says, and everything slows down, the voices and laughter and ambient sounds, as I turn back to look at him, a neglected coffee in front of him full of creamer.

"Oh! Are you sure?" Suzy says.

I feel too many things at once. Stressed about what she's thinking and what the consequences might be, but under that, another feeling shimmers through: *He wants to drive me home.*

"Yeah, I have to go get my sister anyway," he says, standing and leaving some dollar bills on the table. "And it's not like it's out of my way." His eyes meet mine again for a second. "We're neighbors."

SEVEN

THERE'S JAY'S CAR IN THE PARKING LOT, THE ONE I'VE SEEN DRIVING around late at night. A blue sedan with a raised vent in front and a little fin in back, like it's on its way to race. Older, but well cared for, like he puts work into it.

"Are you okay?" Jay's peering at me with concern. "Do you need some water? Or, um . . . juice?"

"Juice?"

He opens his trunk, gesturing with a flourish in a way that makes me laugh. There's a forty-pack of apple juice boxes nestled there, like he just came from Costco.

"They're for my sister. She's kind of a nightmare if she goes too long without something sugary."

I'm trying not to smile too wide. "Thanks, I'm good."

He shrugs and closes it, jogs around to the driver's side.

Mom would be mad that a stranger is driving me home. But she shouldn't be back from work until, like, seven at least.

Inside the car, it smells like old plastic and artificial pine, maybe an air freshener he hung at one point. The color scheme is wild in here—royal blue accents on the seats, the door panels, the carpet, contrasting with the black and gray of everything else. I guess it's supposed to be sporty, but something about it feels like the inside of a middle-school boy's bedroom.

Jay's so close, suddenly, beside me in this small space. There are so many things I want to ask him, my head feels full of bees. Like: *Who is Candace?* And: *Why aren't you talking to her anymore?* And: *Why can't you sleep, either?* But the social contract weighs on me. I can't think of anything that wouldn't be very not-chill to ask.

Then I notice the pink letters printed on the center of the steering wheel.

My mouth twists, and I point. ". . . STI?"

His cheeks flush a little pink to match. "Subaru Tecnica International," he says too fast.

"Oh, okay," I say with a weak laugh. "That clears it right up."

Jay seems agitated as we get onto the road, chewing on his lip and drumming his fingers on the wheel. He's driving one-handed, left arm outstretched while he shifts gears with the other. I kind of wish I could take a picture right now, the way his face looks in profile, blur of green filling the window behind it.

There's a smudge of ink running down the side of his right hand, along his pinkie. Like he was writing something—or drawing? I almost want to ask about that, but I don't want to seem too obsessed with him.

The muscles in his forearm tense as he makes a turn. His gray T-shirt is a little frayed around the neck, and his hair is chaotic in the back.

The way his lips look extra pouty from the side . . .

Oh my God, stop that. I need to survive this whole car ride home. *Survive survive survive.*

Somehow I don't think this is what Mom was talking about.

"Why did you change your clothes?" he asks, glancing over at me.

Heat rises in my cheeks. I'm flattered that he noticed. And instantly mad at myself for being flattered.

"Wow." I laugh too loud. "It's like you're obsessed with me." Then the blood drains from my face as I realize what I just said. "I mean—"

"You're the one who took a photo of me."

"I deleted it, okay!"

His eyebrows go up. "Why would you do that?"

I can't answer him. Maybe he's not even really asking. We're at an impasse again.

"What's the story with this car? Do you, like, race or something?"

"There has to be a story?" he says flatly, eyes on the road again. "It's a car."

God, he's kind of frustrating.

My fingers tap my knee. "So how do you know those guys?"

"Um." Jay glances at me again, dark eyes that make my chest hurt, for a second, before he looks back at the road. "I knew Alex before. We were pretty close. When he lived in Maine."

I do remember that, Alex showing up at the end of elementary school. That there was a time when he was shy and new.

"And after he moved away, I'd come visit. Spent a bunch of summers here, actually."

"You guys must be really close? If you stayed all summer."

"Yeah. Our parents were, too. And after he moved away, I got kind of . . . difficult, I guess. I'd just sit on the computer all day and never go outside." He laughs abruptly, like he remembered to be uncomfortable.

"My mom was at her wit's end, basically. So they sent me here to be someone else's problem. Put me into lacrosse camp with Alex."

Alex's dad is the sports director at the middle school, and I'd vaguely heard about the camp he runs, people looking forward to it at the end of the year.

"So why were you wandering around at one a.m.?" Jay asks, and the skin on the back of my neck prickles.

Maybe he won't get it. Like Suzy on the beach.

He glances over at me, waiting for my answer.

"Just wanted some fresh air, you know?"

"Really." He looks back at the road with a skeptical smirk. "Fresh air, super healthy."

"Why were *you* out there?"

"Oh, same, same." His head bobs up and down.

"Your light is always on, though." Something about the look on his face makes me want to challenge him.

Jay sighs and changes his grip on the wheel. "I have to pick up Gemma." His tone is flat, closed off again. It doesn't seem like he wants to say more. "You good? Think you'll hold up for a bit longer?"

"I think I'll live."

We turn down the driveway to the elementary school and stop in front of the familiar, tired-looking building in yellow-orange brick. A girl with dark hair is barreling down the concrete steps.

She wrenches the passenger door open and frowns when she sees me. "Who are you?"

"Gemma, be polite!" Jay says. "Deedee needed a ride home."

"Hi," I add.

"You're in my seat."

"Gem!"

"It's okay!" I unbuckle my seat belt and clamber out. "I can move."

Gemma bounds in next to Jay while I slip into the snug back seat.

Jay's eyes meet mine in the rearview mirror, the look in them a mix of apology and relief.

"You won't BELIEVE what I had to deal with on student council," Gemma says as he starts to drive. "It's like no one can do math!"

"I believe it."

"Oh! Oh look at this!" She's waving a piece of paper between the seats, trying to get his attention.

"Can't look right now, Gem Gem."

"I told you not to call me that!"

"Gem Gem, Gemmy Girl," he singsongs.

"IT'S GEMMA, OKAY? I'M NOT A LITTLE KID ANYMORE!"

"You're, like, seven."

"EXACTLY."

"Whoa! Okay, don't worry, I respect you."

Gemma twists her head around to look at me, little hands clinging to the seat. "I'm bored! Tell me something?"

"Okay, well, did you know . . ." Mom's stories cycle through my mind, but I feel self-conscious about them for some reason. "That there are a lot of haunted buildings in this town?"

"Oh yeah?" She looks skeptical.

I make something up on the fly, about a creepy old house where lights kept turning on after the people who lived there went to sleep.

"Did they call an electrician?" Gemma asks impatiently.

My stomach shakes, trying not to laugh. "They did! And he couldn't find anything wrong."

"Typical!" She seems genuinely mad on their behalf. "That's what always happens when you call for help!"

Jay snickers, and our eyes meet in the mirror again.

I fumble along, but I'm not sure how to end it. There's something unsatisfying about Mom's stories. They don't resolve; they just are. Maybe Gemma deserves a resolution.

"And from then on, they always made sure to leave a light on when they went to bed. They've lived with the ghost peacefully ever since."

"Sounds fake," Gemma says, just as Jay pulls into their driveway. She bolts out of the car, overfull backpack bouncing behind her.

His mom comes outside, arms crossed tight over her chest, her black hair swept into a loose, messy bun. The family resemblance is strong—Jay has her eyes, and there's an echo of her in his mouth and nose. She looks a lot younger than my mom, but frazzled, like she's had some sleepless nights lately, too.

Jay gets out of the car, while I hesitate inside, not sure what to do.

"You didn't answer my calls," she says, voice muffled through the glass. "Did you go to the bank?"

"Um, I forgot," he says, voice lower, his back to me. "I was with my friends."

"Jason. I need to be able to count on you, okay? Especially now. Why wouldn't you answer the phone?"

"I was driving." His posture is tense. "I can go back now."

"Candace used to—"

"I'm not Candace, Mom."

That name again.

Jay glances back at me, over his shoulder, and his mom notices I'm there.

"Oh hello!" She waves as I get out of the car and nudges him in the arm. "Jason, why didn't you say something? You have a girlfriend already?"

"*Mom.* She's not my girlfriend." The way he says that, like he's spitting out something that tastes bad—I kind of hate it.

"Thanks for the ride!" I give them a stiff little wave and run back to my side of the street.

EIGHT

I'M TRYING TO STUDY AT THE KITCHEN TABLE, BUT WAVES OF DELAYED embarrassment wash over me. Thinking about the things I said on that car ride. Playing back how quickly Jay said I wasn't his girlfriend.

It's different for him. He's obviously allowed to have one, the way his mom asked, all excited. He just doesn't want it to be me.

Suzy texts me a row of eyes emojis, and I bite the side of my finger. She just wants to push us together so she doesn't have to feel bad about leaving me behind.

I send back three red question marks.

> Suzy Jang: did you have a good trip home
> Deedee Walters: jay is annoying lol
> Deedee Walters: i don't think he's a big fan of me either

Suzy Jang: what the fuck

Suzy Jang: want me to kill him?

That actually makes me laugh—right in time for Mom to come out of her home office, down the hall.

She went straight there after work, papers peeking out of her bag, big due date for an important project coming up. Now she locks the door behind her, like she always does, jiggles the handle to double check. I wonder what's in there, sometimes. What she needs to keep locked up inside an already locked house.

"What's so funny?" she asks.

"Nothing." Phone under the table, I delete those last texts. "Funny math problem."

She rolls her shoulders to release the tension. "Remember to finish your letter to Lolo Ric."

Those letters! It makes my blood boil suddenly, the idea of wringing out another fake positive update. *I'm studying hard. I'm taking part in a debate. I'm preparing this project for the science fair.* Except Mom pulled me out of debate, and she says I *clearly have no aptitude for science, if I keep bringing home grades like that.*

I laugh, sharp, like a bark, all that back talk in my head pushing its way out.

She slaps the flat of her hand on the table, and my stomach contracts. *Oh shit, oh shit, shut up!*

"Is something *funny?!*"

A little voice somewhere inside answers. *It's funny that you think anything I can say will make him answer! It's funny you think I could fix this relationship when he obviously wants nothing to do with us!*

"Might as well be writing to myself," I mumble.

"What was that?!"

I flinch, thinking maybe she'll slap me.

"*Does Suzy do that?* Talk back so disrespectfully."

I actually try to think about it. The way Suzy and her mom bicker, and Mrs. Jang calls her *Soo-jin-ah!*, affectionate and reproachful at the same time.

The way Suzy rolled her eyes when her dad said they were introducing a skincare section at the Eastleigh store, for the college kids. *I don't know if halaboji would have pictured you selling snail mucin*, she said, laughing. And he pinched her side, so she had to wriggle away, and said, *We're iterating for the next generation.*

It feels different. But I'm quiet, too scared to talk again.

"I don't understand you." She sighs. "Growing up here, you can be anything you want. Why do you have to—" She makes a vague gesture.

"Have to what?"

"Associate with immigrants!" Oh God, the way that comes out, like a trapdoor opening in the floor.

My scalp prickles and my mouth feels like it's stuffed with cotton. The guilt about talking back pushes up against something else now, the feeling that I'm letting Suzy down by staying quiet.

"Mom. You're an immigrant."

She closes her eyes, like I'm *so tiring*. "I can be anything I want. I don't feel Filipino. And you have even less reason to be."

She speaks slowly, with detachment. Pronouncing each word carefully. Once when I was little, upset, talking incoherently between sobs, she said in her radio announcer voice, *You need to enunciate.* I was so confused, I stopped crying.

"There are—there are just some things—" My voice sounds shaky and weak, swallowed by the tense stillness in the room. "They're just *there*, whether I like it or not. Like the way I look." This has to be an all-time record for the number of words I've ever said out loud to contradict her.

Mom scoffs. "I know what Filipinos look like. You don't look like that."

Why does it feel like she's taking something important away from me, sending me to a nowhere place? Too American, but I always feel different. I'm *something-else* enough to notice, but I have no right to be Filipino.

I'm a nothing. I'm like the ghosts.

"We have bagoong," I say in a small voice.

Mom gets up, moves around the counter, and opens the fridge. She starts slicing a mango for us to share, the sound of the knife heavy against the cutting board.

We eat in silence, using the mango slices to pick up the bagoong she scooped onto the plate. The taste makes me remember the first time I had this, right before she started making me write the letters.

We were visiting my uncles in California, back when we still did that, a little while after my dad died.

I was running around the backyard with my cousins while one of our uncles grilled chicken barbecue skewers, tangy from the Sprite in the marinade. There were aluminum trays of pancit and lumpia out on a table, and we crammed our paper plates full. I watched the way my aunts ate it with a spoon and fork and tried to copy them, pushing the noodles on top of the rice.

Then suddenly there were voices raised, but I didn't know what was wrong, because I don't speak Tagalog. Mom was gesturing, looking upset.

And we left suddenly, and she drove for a while, without direction, just drove to drive.

When I asked what was wrong, she didn't answer, so we just sat in silence. Palm trees went by out the window, and I thought it was so funny, that palm trees are a real thing.

We stopped at a Seafood City. I don't think Mom even likes Filipino food—she doesn't make it or talk about it—but it seemed like she wanted something in particular. She got two plastic bowls of sliced mangos with little containers of bagoong, and we drove to the beach, waves crashing muffled outside the car.

I felt a little special, parked by the ocean with her, like we were on an adventure together.

She started eating the mango slices dipped in the bagoong, chewing like she was mad at them.

"Eat," she said, pointing at the unopened container in my lap. So I did, and the savory, fishy taste of the bagoong with the sour mangos was addictive. I pictured the other kids at school seeing this dark brown paste and thinking it was disgusting. But my God, it was *good*.

And as we ate, she said the most she's ever said to me at once about her family. She told me about her mom, the food she would make, and how much she looked up to her. How she and her mom would sit outside for hours on a hot night, gossiping and listening to people going by. They would hear street vendors calling out, selling balut—*What's balut?* I asked, but she just kept going—and they would eat mangos her mom had sliced up, straight from the tree in their backyard, with bagoong on the side.

We were eating mangos, too, but she said they weren't as good, they were too ripe, and the bagoong wasn't the same, not the spicy kind she likes. To me, the mangos were somewhere between crunchy and tender, and the bagoong cut through the acid taste in this way that balanced it, enhanced it, made it warm and full.

Even though what I was eating was just a poor imitation of her memory, it became my memory, a flavor I crave. Something we could share.

And when we have it, I think about the woman who looks so sad in those old photos. But we haven't been back there again. And up until this week, Mom hadn't talked about her since.

I've been lying in bed for hours, tracing the shadows on the ceiling.

I miss my dad, but it's not exactly like missing a person you remember. All I have are little flashes of him. A glimpse of a face, unstable, hard to see. A hand holding mine while I teetered on a curb. The smell of his scalp lingering in a baseball cap he used to wear, that somehow still hangs in the hall closet.

But that's not really what aches right now, dull and hollow inside my rib cage. It's the absence he left behind, and the wondering that fills it.

How things might have been different, with him here. Whether I would be less lonely. Whether he might take my side.

Suddenly there's a sound—an engine starting, strangely close. I pad over to the window in time to see Mom's car pulling out of the driveway. Her taillights glow red, moving down the street, disappearing around the corner.

My phone says it's 11:47 p.m.

What?

She always makes a big show of going to bed at a *reasonable hour*— 10 p.m. at the latest. I'm the one who lies awake for hours, thoughts spinning, muscles clenched.

Where could she be *going*?

I scramble to get dressed, fumble on my shoes, and run outside.

But she's long gone. There's just the empty street, the wind making a creepy sound as it blows through the trees.

It makes me think about her stories again, all set in a place with winding mountain roads and sudden cliffs, imposing pines and fog. These places I've never been, that live in my head.

Where would she have gone? What is happening?

I put the hood of my sweatshirt up as I hurry past Jay's house. But he's not out there, and his window is dark.

Good. He's the last person I want to see right now.

I want to walk until the sky dotted with stars makes me feel small and insignificant again. But my heart doesn't calm down, and for some reason I'm crying.

And then there are headlights over my shoulder, shining onto the trees, and— Oh shit, oh fuck, is that him? I don't want him to see me!

I'm running, crying, hair wild, probably looking like something from my mom's stories come to life.

But I don't know where I think I'm going. Because there's just this one straight road, and of course the car catches up to me. The familiar blue sedan, with its absurd little fin.

It slows to a stop next to me, window down.

"Deedee?" Jay says. "What's wrong?"

"Why would something be wrong?!" I exclaim, hackles up.

"Whoa, all right." His hands are raised, palms out. "You're just . . . crying while you get some *fresh air.*"

I laugh so loud, he looks startled. "It's kind of rude to just point out when someone is crying, okay!"

Jay laughs, too, but quietly. It comes out like a wheeze. "Never heard that one before. Guess neither of us is great with manners."

He bites his lip, drums his fingers on the wheel. "Want to go for a drive?"

"Get into a car with a strange man at night? Textbook thing not to do, right?"

Mom would kill me. Or I guess, to be precise, she would tell me that *he's* going to kill me. But she would, if he didn't get there first.

"I mean, I'm not a *strange man*, though." He looks down at his hands. "You know where I live. I'm in your classes."

For just a second, an image flashes into my mind: I'm getting in beside him, yelling *Follow that car!* and driving off after Mom, like this is an old movie.

I know that can't happen. I know.

But with part of my brain looking on in surprise and my heart beating loud in my ears, I walk around to the passenger's side and get in.

NINE

I SHUT THE DOOR AND JAY LETS OUT A LITTLE LAUGH, LIKE HE CAN'T believe I actually did it.

"So where are we going?"

"Um." He glances at me. "Where were you thinking of going?"

"Nowhere."

"Great," he says lightly, putting the car in gear. "Then we'll go there."

"Strange man," I say, and he scoffs.

Outside it's all shades of black, dark branches against dark sky. I think about the White Lady again, long hair hiding her face. How she would appear suddenly in the back seat of a taxi and ask to be taken to the cemetery. How a driver lost on a desolate road would see her pop up in his rearview mirror, and he'd be so scared, he'd crash.

"Did someone . . . do something to you?" he asks with a nervous glance my way. "I mean, like—if your dad, or someone—"

"I don't have a dad," I snap.

"Oh! Fuck, I—" He laughs uncomfortably. "I should shut up."

"I mean, I did. But he died when I was little."

"I'm sorry."

"It was a long time ago," I say, crossing my arms and settling back into the seat.

Jay moves the gearshift with one hand while the fingers of the other drum the wheel. The numbers on his instrument panel glow red.

"Are you sure you weren't an extra in a Fast and Furious movie or something?" I ask.

He snorts but doesn't answer. Outside, the insects caught in the beams of the headlights look like stars hurtling toward us as we fly through space, discovering new worlds.

Then he talks again suddenly, like he was debating it in his head the whole time. "My dad used to like cars. It, uh—" He seems embarrassed at the sound of his own voice. "It was basically the only thing we had in common."

That past tense stands out to me. I'm sensitive to it, since I also use it.

"Does he . . . not like cars anymore?"

"No, he probably does." Jay readjusts his grip on the wheel. "He left, though."

"Shit, I'm sorry."

"I'm not," he says, like it's an effort to keep his voice steady. "He's an asshole."

The way he says that, so plainly, after holding back—it feels like there's a shift in the social contract between us. The one that says I have to pretend to be more okay with things than I am. Maybe he would understand, in a way Suzy doesn't. Maybe I could tell him about things with my mom.

I need to know more to be sure. He seems like he's done talking, but now I want to know everything about him.

And—it's a little mortifying, but—I desperately want to ask what kind of Asian he is. Then I hate myself for wanting to ask anything in the neighborhood of *what are you*, the question that makes my skin feel like an itchy sweater, so I get too in my head and don't say anything.

We curve through the woods, near-full moon to our right, criss-crossed by the power lines we pass.

He takes a side road and parks in a lot by a pond. There's a picnic area next to the asphalt, a dirt path down to a small beach framed by trees, dark water lapping at the sand.

Suzy was confused about ponds when she moved here in fourth grade. "A pond is a tiny thing in a backyard! This is a whole lake."

Her dad laughed and said, "That's what they call them here."

But I didn't even know this pond existed. It's surreal, this new kid taking me to a place I've never been.

We're parked in the harsh orange glow of a light post, and it outlines the curves of Jay's nose and mouth.

He motions with his head toward the picnic table and pops his door open. "Let's go over there for a bit."

Jay sits on top—feet on the bench, elbows on knees, chin resting on his hands. So I climb up next to him.

We're quiet for a while, just breathing beside each other, looking at the moon. I would take a picture, but I don't want Jay to comment on it again.

"This is nice," I say, near-whispering. "I can see why you like it."

"Hey, so . . ." He hesitates, and the silence fills with the sound of water sloshing against the sand. "We're both up at this time.

Maybe . . . you should be able to reach me? In case, you know—you need a ride to nowhere again."

My throat is tight, but I hand him my phone and watch him bite his bottom lip in this cute way as he puts his number in.

He gives it back, and I text him a ghost emoji. The way he smiles when he gets it makes my heart grow a size.

Jay pokes me in the ribs. "You're really not going to tell me what's wrong?"

"Um. You know. Just family stuff."

"Like . . . what kind of stuff?" His voice is careful, pushing but not too hard.

"There are just . . . lots of things at home that don't make sense. That my mom won't talk to me about."

He nods seriously. "Can you give an example?"

"Like . . . she tells me these stories. About ghosts and monsters." I shake my head. Why did I start there? "I'm not even making sense."

A smile spreads across his face. "I love ghosts."

I can't tell him. I can't ruin this.

So I nudge his side instead. "Why are *you* up every night?"

Jay breathes out sharp, the world's briefest laugh. His knee jiggles, shaking the table. "I work late."

Of all the things he could have said, somehow I didn't expect that. "Doing what?"

He makes his voice exaggeratedly deep, like he has to make it a joke to tell me. "I'm a full-stack developer."

"Developer like . . ."

"Coding."

"What?"

He laughs and hunches forward. "Um, I found this guy on a message board, a few years ago—a developer at a big company." Jay hesitates, probably wondering how much more he wants to say. In the distance, a frog croaks. "He wanted to farm out some of his workload, something about *better work-life balance*. So he sends me everything he doesn't want to do at close of business, and I send him my commits overnight."

"Your what?"

"I do computer stuff."

"Don't talk down to me!" I shove his shoulder, before my brain catches up. *Shit, that was flirty.*

"Okay, I won't." He's grinning.

"Don't you need to go to college for that?"

"I'm self-taught."

"Get the fuck out," I say, yawning right in the middle.

Jay laughs so hard, he leans sideways into me—*hello, heart-rate spike!*—and I can feel the shaking in my ribs.

"So you have a full-on corporate job. On the side."

"I'm an independent contractor," he says dryly.

"Kind of sounds like this guy is taking advantage of you."

He shifts back, palms flat on the table behind him. "I guess it depends. Like, yeah, I do most of his work and get a cut of his pay. But it's more than I could be making, doing anything else. Especially when I started. When I was, like, fourteen. Anyway." He nudges my foot with his foot. "I don't really like talking about it."

"Why not?"

"People's opinions are annoying. What they think is normal."

Am I being *people* right now?

"Why did you want to work for this guy?"

"Honestly?" He scrubs both hands through his hair and laughs like it's mortifying. "At first I wanted to save up for this car. But yeah, now it's different. Now it's to pay the bills. Help my mom out."

And here I thought he was just up late brooding. I didn't realize he was busy being a productive member of society. The literal opposite of me.

I squeeze the fingers of my right hand with my left. "You do a lot to help your mom."

"Um, yeah, she's really stressed right now. With work and school. She's going to Eastleigh like four nights a week."

"Aren't you also doing work and school?"

He lets out a sharp little breath. "Yeah, but. It's not the same. She wasn't working for a while—my dad didn't want her to. So it's new for her. And I kind of owe her."

Shame prickles under my skin, thinking about what I owe. "So shouldn't you get some sleep?"

Maybe it amuses him, because he laughs again. "I kind of love being up at this time." He glances around, like he's worried someone will overhear. "This is the one time of day . . . it's just for me, you know? I want to be awake for it."

I'm quiet for a minute, working through how he must feel about every other time of day. And then worry sours in my gut, thinking about how late it is. We must have been here for hours, now.

"Why don't you ask your mom about those things?" he says. "The ones that are bothering you."

Because she'll remind me again how I ruined her life. But I don't want to tell him that.

"I just can't," I grit out. "It doesn't work, when I try."

"Your mom probably grew up in a really different situation, right?" I can almost feel him wondering how similar we are. "Maybe you should try to see it from her perspective."

That takes the wind out of me. Somehow, I thought the rules were different in the world we're inhabiting right now. The 3 a.m. rules, the in-between place rules, for when everything from the buttoned-up daytime comes undone. Bringing the gravity of family guilt back here feels like he shoved me with both hands.

"I'd love to consider that situation," I say, voice hardened, like I'm talking to a stranger—which, I guess, I am. "But she won't tell me about it."

"Maybe you could try different questions?"

"What's the point?" I'm burning inside, and my voice sounds like Mom's. "You can't change the past."

"Yeah." Jay's voice gets careful. "But it can help you understand why people are the way they are. Help you accept things."

I just want to escape, forward movement for its own sake, like when Mom left the family party. *Accepting things*—I try it on for size and feel like I'm suffocating.

"Okay, or think about it another way," he says, when I've been quiet too long. "What are your options? The things you could do?"

"Oh wow, *a man of action*."

There's his wheezing laugh again. "I mean, I always ask myself, *What can you do about it*, you know? And if there's nothing—" His hand kneads the back of his neck. "Try to accept it and move on."

This level of emotional maturity is *extremely irritating* right now. It is way too late—too early?—for this shit.

I'm bursting with all the things I want, and it's suddenly hard to think of a single one I could say out loud. But the sensation of being on the highway comes back to me, wind in my hair and music on the speakers. The lightness of going somewhere, open-ended. Noise and movement and an escape from my spiraling thoughts.

"I want to learn to drive," I mumble. "My mom doesn't want me to."

"Why not?"

"Umm, I don't know." I regret saying anything now. "She thinks it's dangerous. She has a lot of rules."

Jay's looking down at his fingers as they trace a groove in the wood. "I could teach you."

"No thanks." I don't want to accept anything from him. I can barely stand being here, in this moment with him, right now. How is it possible to be this fascinated and this annoyed with a person at the same time?

"Okay, well," Jay says. "You know where to find me, if you change your mind."

I hop off the table and turn away from him. "Can you take me home now, please?"

On the ride back, my shame balloons out, thinking about the difference between us. He's practically a saint, working into the night to support his family. I'm a useless leech draining the life out of my mom.

"Here is fine," I say, before he's about to turn onto our street.

He slows to a stop and looks at me, uncertain, while I unlock the door and scramble out.

"Hey, wait—" he starts to say, but I slam the door and take off before he can finish.

TEN

Tires crunch outside, Mom's car returning. I roll over, tangled in the sheets, pretending to sleep for an hour before I have to get up for school.

What do I even know about her perspective?

That she works too much. That she likes to collect vases, beautiful objects to remind her of the beautiful life she's achieved. But she says flowers are a waste of money because they just die anyway.

That she's thrifty. That she's nervous. That she says feeling sorry for yourself might be the worst sin. And focusing on the past is just another way to feel sorry for yourself. Eyes forward, always straight ahead.

That it's impossible to ask her about the past without a reminder—

I'm tossing in bed, thrashing, like I'm having a fever dream—of *how much I took from her.*

That I don't really know anything about what she was like, before what happened to my dad.

That of all the creatures in her stories, the aswang appears the most. But the word *aswang* can mean a lot of things: witches, weredogs, vampires that stay in one piece. It has another name, the manananggal—the one that tears itself apart, puts itself back together, drains you of everything you have.

And then the sun is up, and Suzy is texting me, and it's time to act like a person again.

For the next few weeks, I avoid Jay at school.

In class, two rows up and one to the left, he draws something and obliterates it with furious cross-hatching, shoulder blades moving under his T-shirt.

It's not like I *want* to look at him. I have to keep an eye on him to avoid him.

While I'm at it, I get curious. I sharpen my pencil when I don't need to, just so I can walk down the aisle and peer at whatever he draws in his notebook. But Jay always closes it before I can look.

I notice other things, while I'm *avoiding* him. How intently he stares out the window when he's not drawing, faraway look on his face, lips slightly parted.

How he hangs back on the edges of his circle of friends and leaves to answer his phone.

I overhear him talking to his mom, while he's standing by the doors to the parking lot.

"What do you mean?" he says, shoulders hunched, leaning against the wall of concrete blocks painted white. "I put money in the account, though. I thought I paid— I know, Mom. Sorry. I know."

He's dealing with so much more than me. And he manages to be so mature, while I'm a barely functioning mess.

At night, Mom and I fight—*it's oppressive*, she cries, *having to see your sad face all the time!*—but I keep my brooding indoors.

What Jay said knocks around in my head, making me feel like shit. *Maybe I don't want to see things from her perspective! I'm barely on my own side as it is!*

And as I'm so focused on avoiding him, Jay starts disappearing. He's not in History, but he's in English. The next day, the opposite. Then he's missing in both.

It's annoying, when worry creeps in. Is he sick? Did he drop out to focus on his job?

My mind wanders to him more often. I catch myself wondering where he goes.

Late at night, there's the familiar sound—Mom's engine starting, tires crunching. I get up to see her red taillights disappearing at the end of our street.

I start keeping track with cryptic notes in my calendar app. Once, twice a week, she goes somewhere—leaving just before midnight, coming back before sunrise. It nags at me, all through the bleary days that follow, that I have no way of finding out where or why.

ELEVEN

Dear Lolo Ric,

I hope this letter finds you in good health. My mom says hello. She said you appreciate these letters, even though you're very busy and can't write back, so I'm writing you again.

I've started senior year and I'm studying hard. I'm applying to several good schools.

Even though I'm set on going to Eastleigh.

But yeah, sure, Lolo Ric can think there's a chance I'm going to Yale if he wants.

I stare at the copy of *As I Lay Dying* that I've been reading for

English, under the harsh light from my desk lamp. My thoughts churn, waves crashing against the inside of my skull as I watch the sky outside turn dark.

I want this to be over. I'll just write like myself.

> We're learning about the way the past haunts American literature. How it comes back, again and again.
>
> I wonder about our family's past.
>
> I wonder why I've never met you? Why you don't want to talk to us? Why I've grown up hearing about our family in the Philippines from my mom's ghost stories, but I don't know anything else about them?
>
> Just that Lola Ines chewed betel nut to ward off demons, and Tito Bobby would see the ghost of a decapitated Spaniard in full armor wandering in the garden at night, searching for his head?
>
> It's funny, right?
>
> Maybe you can tell me—what happened? What did we do?
>
> Or really, tell me anything. What did you study in high school when you were my age? What did you like to read?
>
> Or tell me about the Philippines? We don't really learn about it in school. There was one paragraph in our textbook about the Philippine–American war.

It's sad, but most of what I know about the Philippines comes from random articles and Wikipedia. Centuries of colonization—nearly four hundred years under the Spanish empire, half a century under the Americans following a bloody war. The Japanese occupation. Independence that—from what I've read?—was like being an American colony all over again.

There's an itch in my head, like I want to ask about that.

Maybe you should try to see it from her perspective.

But I can't think of how to phrase the question, and anyway, it's not like I would get an answer. Instead, I say:

> I'd like to visit sometime. Could we do that?
> Mom is working hard all the time. She seems
> stressed. I'm sure she'd love to hear from you! I
> hope you can write to her.
> Sincerely, your granddaughter,
> Lourdes Zamora Walters

I stare at the signature that feels like a stranger's.

Deedee is the name my aunts and uncles decided to call me, back when we would see them. A lot of my relatives go by nicknames, like Loleng is for Dolores (I googled it) and Andoy is for Andrew. The way I have a Tito Boy and a Tito Dingdong and a Tita Pepper.

Deedee is based on my baby talk because I couldn't say my own name.

"Lour-des, Lour-des," Mom said.

"Dee dee dee dee," I said back.

The rest, as they say, is history.

"Aren't you finished yet?" Mom calls from downstairs.

"Almost done!" I fold the composition paper in thirds and stuff it in an empty envelope.

But before I get to her office, I hear her voice through the open door. It sounds like she's on the phone.

"Yes. Of course, I'm so sorry. Yes, you're right, it was thoughtless. Yes."

She's bent over her desk, phone to her ear, like she's trying to make herself smaller.

"Certainly. I won't. All right. First thing. Okay." Someone is talking over her, audible from here, tinny and grating.

Guilt washes over me, red-black and sticky. Like I caused all this, somehow.

Mom steps into the hall, carrying her giant work tote, and wedges her feet into her shoes.

"What's going on?"

"It's all hands on deck on this, or we'll lose the client." Her voice is different than it was on the phone, anger surging up, accent peeking out. She shakes her head, jaw set, tense. "And I left something I need at work. God, I'm so stupid."

"You're not stupid." I want to reach for her, but she makes an annoyed sound deep in her throat that holds me back.

The front door closes, and the house is quiet.

The door to her study is still open. It must be really bad, if she forgot to lock it.

The light is still on. She wouldn't like that, the way she's always saying, *Turn that off, that's not for free, you know.*

I step inside, hesitating in front of her desk. There is probably something in here that would tell me about her perspective.

My throat is dry, every part of me humming. The room feels like it's holding its breath.

I open her top desk drawer.

Papers. Office supplies.

What was I expecting? I close it, open the next one, and the next one.

In the bottom drawer, there's a shoe box. Battered and old, not like the polished things she likes.

You shouldn't open it, you know how she gets when little things are out of place! When you touch what's not yours!

But she deletes my photos, takes what's not hers all the time. I lift it out and remove the lid.

On top there's an envelope, with our return address in my handwriting on the front. The letter I thought she mailed, a few weeks ago. The space for Lolo Ric's address is blank because she always says she'll add it before she sends it.

It's opened. Like she read it.

And underneath, there's another envelope, exactly the same. The floor underneath me is shifting, tilting slowly.

Underneath that, another. And another. All the letters I wrote to him. Opened, too.

My heartbeat pulses in my mouth, metallic and sour. They're all here. All unsent. Every one I ever wrote.

I drop the box like it's suddenly filled with writhing maggots, and the letters fan out across the hardwood floor.

TWELVE

MY KNEES WON'T LET ME STAY STANDING, SO I SIT ON THE FLOOR, rifling through the shoe box. Reading the letters back, throat tight. Did I ever say anything real in these? Something I wouldn't want Mom to read?

The recent ones sound bored and distant, safe.

> You'll be pleased to know I won an award for public speaking. Mom said you always emphasized diction when she was growing up.

> We're performing Macbeth at school this week, I've been cast as one of the witches.

> We're keeping you in our thoughts and hope to
> hear from you.

But the deeper I go into the box, the more earnest they get. My handwriting gets more looping and childish, traveling back to when I took it seriously.

> I don't really get along with the other kids at
> school.

> I had a school project about our family tree,
> Mom told me about all the things she's proud of
> our family for, it made me wonder about you.

> I miss my dad, I cried at recess.

> Hello, are you all right? I haven't heard from
> you. Did you get my last letter?

I'm so dazed, the blush of humiliation under my skin, like someone took something important from me when I wasn't paying attention.

I can't accept this. The words in my head match the rhythm of my thudding heart. *I can't. I can't.*

I rush down the hall, jam my feet into my shoes and lurch outside.

It's dark and I'm alone. The sky above is blue-black with a dusting of stars.

I can't ask Mom for an explanation, any more than I can talk to her about our family, or why I like taking photos, or why she hates Suzy so much.

My head is spinning, and I sink into a crouch in the middle of the street, clutching my phone like an anchor to the parts of my life that I understand.

I want to call Suzy, but she's with Alex right now—she video-called me for an outfit check before she left. And how could I explain this in a way that won't make her think less of me?

"Hey!" a voice cuts through the dark. It's Jay, sitting on his roof.

Why does he have to be out here right now!

I scramble up, ready to run inside. And my phone starts vibrating in my hand.

He's *calling me.*

He's sitting up there, phone to his ear, looking right at me.

It rings and rings. So I answer.

"Dude. Who *calls* people?"

He laughs quietly, a light gust of wind. "I don't know, I made a lot of phone calls this year. House hunting, moving. Kind of wish I didn't know what escrow was."

He's saying everything like it's a joke, but shame scratches under my skin. Jay's all the things I find it so hard to be. Helpful, responsible. A good kid.

I put on a prim voice, doing my best to channel my mom. "And may I ask what your call is regarding?"

That gets a real laugh, full-bodied. My heart is still racing, hasn't stopped since I dropped the box, but being funny for him is a nice distraction.

"You seemed . . . upset," he says.

"I'm fine."

"You know, I'll just go out on a limb and say I don't believe you." We're quiet for a bit, listening to the dead air between us. "Just stay there, okay? I'll come down."

"No, that's okay! I'm going for a walk."

"Um, well . . . stay on the phone, though? So I know you got home okay."

Jay waves, and I start walking. I'll loop the block.

He's out of sight, but his voice is with me. "What made you run outside like that?"

He's just going to say something about how I need to work harder to understand my mom.

"It seems like something is going on?" he presses. "I noticed you were . . . getting less fresh air lately."

He noticed?

"I don't want to talk about it," I say.

"Okay, sure! Whatever you want." The breeze picks up, rustling the tree branches. "I like talking to you, though."

Warmth spreads through my whole body. Suddenly, I feel like I could run five miles.

"Okay," I say, fighting to keep my voice flat. "So talk to me."

"Um, okay. What can I tell you . . ." His laugh rumbles low in my ear. "You know I got in trouble?"

"For what?"

"I'm failing English. And History." There's the sound of movement, in the background, like he's going inside. "I just hate writing essays?"

He says the past can help you accept things, but he's failing History?

"My mom is really sweet, but when she gets mad, she gets, like, scary mad." Jay sighs. "She wants me to get tutored now."

"So, what are you—"

"Tell me a ghost story," he cuts in.

My cheeks tingle. "How weird do you want to get, here?" The moon winks at me through the tree branches, like it knows something I don't.

"As weird as possible."

75

"So this isn't exactly a ghost. But you know, similar vibe. A tale of the uncanny."

"Great. Perfect."

"My mom talks about this monster, a shape-shifter. An aswang. The ma-na-nang-gal." It feels strange, trying those sounds in my mouth. "From the Philippines. Where she's from."

Why did I tell him that? I don't think I've ever told these stories to anyone but Suzy.

"In the daytime it's lots of things, incognito. Like a random person, or a sinister dog. But usually a beautiful woman. Then, at night, her top half detaches and grows wings. And her bottom half lays around, waiting for her."

"Whoa, sick," he says so sleepily, it makes me laugh. "Go on."

"And she flies around with her intestines hanging out, all gory. And her tongue is like a mosquito needle, and she punctures you and sucks up your essences."

"Wow, get to know me first."

"Shut up!" I'm laughing so hard, I have to stop walking for a second.

"Okay, so what else?"

"To defeat her, you have to find the bottom half. And put salt and vinegar on it." Or something like that? I kind of forget.

"Your chip choices make more sense now. It's all coming together." He's quiet for a bit, and my nerves rattle, rounding the last corner. "These stories are just to get people to behave, right?"

"Behave like how?"

"Like: Don't wander around at night!" Jay says with such sudden energy, I have to laugh.

"I'm so bad."

"Come back." The soft way he says it almost knocks me over.

But I am almost back now. And he's standing in the street, phone to his ear, waiting for me.

"I'll think about it." I walk up, heart pounding, and stop right in front of him. Standing maybe a little too close.

We stare at each other for a long minute. Over his shoulder, the blinking light of an airplane makes its way across the sky.

Jay looks away first. "So, uh—are you okay?" he asks, voice low.

The timing makes me laugh. "I don't know."

"Do you want, uh . . ." He sounds like he wishes he had some apple juice to offer me. "A hug?"

"Yes," I say, suddenly hoarse.

Jay steps closer and wraps his arms around me, pressing my face into his shirt. He smells like he just showered, with soap that claims to be like an ocean breeze.

His body heat warms my closed eyelids. His hand rests on the back of my head.

This is a bespoke hug. The best. Who knew he gave such good hugs?

It feels like being cracked open, warmth and pressure building behind my eyes. It's terrifying, because it's not what I deserve, and it's just a matter of time before he sees what I'm really like.

But there's also part of me that wants things, more insistent all the time. Wants more of him. Wants answers. All the things Mom might not want me to have.

And in my head, I see it: I'm sitting behind the wheel of his absurd car, following Mom wherever it is that she goes.

I take a step back, out of his hug. "I changed my mind!"

Jay laughs. "What?"

"When you offered—right?—to teach me how to drive. You said I could change my mind."

"Oh, uh—I said that, but . . ." His hand works that spot at the back of his neck that always seems to bother him. "It's just—my mom is pissed at me now, and things are . . . different. Than I thought."

"What about at night, after you get off work? You like driving around then anyway. And, and—I could tutor you! Your mom wants someone to tutor you, right? I could do it. For free, in exchange for driving lessons. I charge good money for that, usually."

He scoffs and looks over his shoulder, back at his house.

"During lunch! I could tutor you then, while we eat. You have to eat anyway, right? And English and History are my best subjects, I won this prize—" I cringe, thinking of the letter I wrote Lolo Ric about it. "I could, uh . . . put you in touch with some references."

Jay shakes his head, pinching his bottom lip between two fingers. I can't tell what he's thinking.

"You know the car's a manual?" he says. "Stick shift."

"That's . . . fine?"

He laughs like he doesn't believe me.

"Okay," Jay says, finally.

"Okay?" I'm stunned.

"Yeah," he says, looking me in the eye in that unnerving way. "Okay."

"W-when can you start?"

He shrugs. "Tomorrow?"

I nearly burst out laughing. I have to leave right now, before he can change his mind.

"Great, I'll text you!" I exclaim, running back inside.

When I get back to my room, I rip up the letter sitting on my desk. Grab a pencil, write something new, that restless feeling in my gut in overdrive.

Dear Lolo Ric,
I have written to you for years without a response. I'm not going to keep writing these letters anymore.

Then I feel guilty, remembering Mom's pained expression earlier, how she was folding herself up small.

So I rip that letter into pieces, too, tearing and tearing to get my anger out.

And I start on a fresh sheet of paper:

Dear Lolo Ric,
I hope this letter finds you well.
Mom works so hard and her coworkers really respect her.

THIRTEEN

THE NEXT NIGHT, AFTER DINNER, I FIND JAY'S NUMBER IN MY CONTACTS. *Jay Hayes*, it says, and underneath: *From the picnic table at 1 a.m.* This has been there the whole time?!

My back goes rigid, thinking about all the chances Mom had to find it. And another feeling glows under the wave of delayed panic: *He actually thought my life is interesting enough that I might forget who he is.* With trembling fingers, I write:

meet me at midnight?

I know Mom is going to leave by then, and this way, there's less chance she'll notice I'm gone. *And maybe*, a faint voice in the back of my mind adds, *we'll run into her out on the road.*

Then I immediately get nervous, staring at those words on the screen.

Deedee Walters: if you're done then, i mean

Haha! No pressure!

My stomach clenches as those dots pop up that show he's writing back.

Jay Hayes: yeah i should be
Jay Hayes: see you then

What does that mean? Does he hate this? Does he hate me? It takes all my strength to pretend to sleep for a couple hours, instead of rereading his texts every few minutes, searching for hidden meanings.

As soon as I get outside, I see Jay, standing in his driveway. There's something funny about it, the world so still, our houses dark, just him and me. My heart rattles with every step that closes the gap between us.

"Hey," Jay says, raising one hand in a little wave. He opens the passenger door for me. "After you."

When we're both inside, he hands me one of those energy drinks. I crack it open and take a sip.

"Sorry, I guess it's an acquired taste," he says, grimacing at the face I'm making. "I kind of live on this stuff."

He plucks it out of my hands and takes a swig. "How do you take your coffee?" The engine rumbles to life, and he twists to look behind him as he reverses into the street. "Can't have you falling asleep on me."

"Um. Just black."

The world feels smaller, tunneled down to what we can see in his headlights: yellow and white lines on the road, tree trunks, reflective signs flashing into view. And, at the same time, life feels more expansive than before—traveling through the night, vast and mysterious, Jay right there beside me. Just a few weeks ago, I would have thought this was impossible.

He parks in the convenience-store lot, facing the street, neon sign casting a blue glow into the car from behind.

"Be right back," he says, running inside, and I'm alone, staring out at the empty road, the dark sky over the trees.

Then he's getting in again, handing me a can of cold brew.

"Thanks," I whisper, taking it in both hands. I think this is the first thing a boy has ever given me.

"All right, let's do it," he says, and starts the car again.

He turns onto the empty highway, stars winking at us overhead, moon peeking through the trees. We don't go too far before Jay takes an exit, makes a couple turns, and pulls into a big parking lot, attached to the mall that no one goes to anymore. I vaguely remember coming here as a kid, and it's technically still in business—a struggling Macy's, a couple random stores. But it's pretty dead, even in the middle of the day.

The main building sits lurking like some kind of slumbering animal, long and white and glowing from the exterior lights. Jay drives deeper into the giant parking lot, through the overlapping pools of harsh blue-tinged light from the posts stationed across the asphalt.

He parks underneath one, top halves of our faces still in shadow from the car's roof.

A little laugh squeezes out of my lungs. "Wow, prime murder spot."

"Hey, you asked for this," he says. "Uh, that came out wrong."

I snort.

"To be clear—not going to murder you." He takes another drink from his can. "This is where I learned to drive, actually. Alex's dad taught me."

Being in this big empty space with him, ringed by woods where the light fades—it feels like normal life turned on its head.

"It's funny how you have your own version of this town." I sip from my coffee, the buzzing of the light post low in my ears. "How many more secret spots do you have out here?"

Jay shrugs. "We'll have to drive somewhere, I guess. I could take you around. Show you a few more." He smiles at me, and a little jolt of electricity dances up my spine.

Then he's getting out, coming around to my side. He raps his knuckles on my door and offers a hand to help me out. When I take it, his palm is warm and soft, brushing mine. There's this feeling like soda fizzing in my chest, over-shaken, opened too soon.

I ease into the driver's seat, and my hands look strange on the wheel.

"So," he says, beside me again, "are you ever going to tell me why you ran into the street like that?"

In my mind, the letters scatter across the floor, on loop. An itchy heat builds in my chest. He's not going to understand. I don't know how I'll survive it, if I tell him and he thinks it's not a big deal.

"Why were you even out there?" I ask. "Wasn't that a little early for you?"

Jay leans against the window, elbow propped under his head. "The guy I work for—he keeps sending me articles about work-life balance. Like, how perfect? This tech bro, offloading his shit work onto an eighteen-year-old, sending me articles about *work-life balance.*"

"Wow." I'm disappointed in myself for not having something funnier to say.

"But I took his advice. Set a timer to take regular breaks, drink water."

"So how are you feeling now?"

Jay laughs and sits upright again. "So balanced."

He says his mom gets mad at him, but he sounds so upbeat about it. He's working himself ragged, but he can laugh it off. The way he carries things lightly, talks about everything like it's a joke—I wish I could be more like that.

"What's his name?"

He blinks, like it's strange I would ask. "Phil."

"Phil should give you a raise," I say, fingers tapping the wheel. It feels cozy, sitting next to him in the half-dark, like when I sleep over at Suzy's and we talk for hours after she turns the lights off. "You work really hard."

"I mean—a lot of people work harder. Like . . . my mom when she was my age. Her parents owned a convenience store and she'd pick up double shifts, work overnight." His right hand fidgets, thumb pressing down on the tops of his fingers in turn. "Then my dad didn't want her to work, which was a relief, I guess? But he was a dick, so that was, like, work in itself."

He stops himself, eyes darting over to me. "Sorry. I guess I do this nervous-talking thing when you're around."

When I'm around.

It's a good thing it's dark, because that makes me feel flushed all over, from my cheeks to the tips of my toes.

Maybe it's because we're not looking at each other, facing straight ahead, but I work up the nerve to finally ask. "Where . . . did your mom grow up?"

"California, mostly."

He's quiet for a second, and the ocean rushes in my ears, light glinting off the waves at the beach where Mom parked, while she sat next to me in tense silence.

"But her family's from Vietnam," Jay adds. It sounds like he doesn't want to say more about it.

I clear my throat. "So are we going to drift? Do some donuts?"

"Are you going to buy me new tires?" Jay clicks on the overhead light. Suddenly, it feels smaller, closer in here. "We're going to do some nice, boring driving."

It's funny how serious he sounds. Like if you give him a task, there's no way he'll half-ass it.

"Left foot on the clutch, right foot on the brake," Jay says. He shows me how to wiggle the gearshift to check it's in neutral, how to start the car and shift into first. The rumbling of the engine cuts through my gut.

"Okay, look," he says. "You'll need to ease off the clutch while pressing on the gas." He demonstrates with his hands like they're the pedals.

He's explaining the engine, why you have to change gears. It feels like a lot of information to get from Point A to Point B, but okay. It seems important to him.

Jay leans closer to show me something about the gauges behind the wheel, and his face is suddenly very close to mine. I must breathe in too sharply, because he glances at me and leans back again. He clicks the light off, and the darkness hides my glowing face.

Then I have to try it, and it goes badly. We jerk forward and the engine stalls. I can't get the timing right. I restart the car, go back through the steps, and it stops with a jolt, again and again.

Oh my God, I'm disappointing him, I'm testing his patience! Why did I think this was a good idea? My hair must be frizzy and wild from the humidity of my own stress radiating off my body.

"Hey," he says, putting a hand on my back. Oh no, it's so sweaty right there! "It's okay. It takes time, you'll get it. Keep trying."

I laugh so desperately, I'm a little winded.

"You have to go slow and steady, find that spot where it catches." His voice is so calm, it's kind of infuriating. "Listen to the engine. Do you hear how it's—"

And then I get it, somehow. The car rolls forward.

"Ah!" Jay claps.

We're still rolling. "What now?!"

"Okay, relax. Just go straight. Give it a little gas and try switching to second."

I speed up, press down on the clutch, and—*oh!*—his hand covers mine on the gearshift, warmth and pressure over my knuckles as he moves it along with me. I can't think about steering, or gears, or what pedal does what. Holy shit, I'm going to crash this car.

"Okay, good, now—" He laughs and takes his hand away. "Turn so we don't go into the trees."

I panic and brake suddenly. We lurch forward, and the engine dies.

My heart is beating so loud in my ears, staring at the tree trunks lit up by the headlights.

"Great!" Jay says. "Let's do it again."

So we do, again and again, until I get the car stopping and going more smoothly, looping between the light posts. Even when it doesn't seem like he needs to, he puts his hand over mine through every gear change.

When Jay finally tells me to park, I slump over the steering wheel. He rubs my back briskly with one hand. "Good job."

I almost expect him to call me "champ."

This means the night is over, and I don't want it to be yet.

I would really love to make him do some more nervous talking.

"So why did you move here, anyway?" My head turns his way, still resting against my folded arms. "Like, why would anyone move here? Instead of anywhere else."

"You hate it that much here?" He sounds amused.

"Mm, I guess—I don't have that much to compare it to. But I dream about leaving."

"Where would you go?"

I open my eyes again, and he's leaning forward, looking at me like he's actually interested in the answer. "I didn't really think that far ahead."

Jay lets himself fall back against his seat. "I guess . . . I didn't love it at first, getting sent here." He looks at his hands and squeezes the fingers of one in the other. "My dad was like, 'You need to get out of this house full of women.' Kind of a bullshit reason to banish me."

"House full of women? What, because of your mom and Gemma? That's like . . . equal numbers."

"Um . . . and Candace." There's that edge to his voice, again. "My older sister."

The mysterious Candace.

"But I liked who I was here, after a while," he says. "It was like I could be someone else, a few months out of the year. Get away from myself."

"Is that how it feels now? Being here."

"Not exactly. It feels like . . . I'm in the place where something is supposed to be, but I can't find it." He turns his head toward me so his cheek rests against the seat, and the corner of his mouth turns up. "Like I lost it between the couch cushions."

That makes me laugh. He has a funny way of expressing himself sometimes.

"Anyway. My mom didn't want to stay in Maine after my dad left. And she didn't have anywhere else she wanted to be, so. I got to pick." He looks out the window, lamplight highlighting the curve of his neck. "It's good that we came here, though. Alex's dad pulled some strings and helped her get a job at the middle school, working in the office."

Jay's head turns back my way, but his eyes are looking down. "Hey. I thought about it later. When we went for a drive that time, and you were upset." His hands play with the seat-belt buckle. "I should have listened better. Instead of telling you what to do. I know I hate that—when people tell me what to do and they don't know what they're talking about."

"Thanks," I say quietly, suddenly stressed, because it means so much to me that he said that, and I don't know how to show him. My feelings are too big for my body, and what I might want to say is too big for my brain.

We switch seats and don't talk much, the whole way home. My thoughts spiral out weeks ahead, trying to sort through the ripple effects.

What if Jay tells Alex? And Alex tells Suzy? And—

"Hey, um—could we not tell anyone?" I blurt out. "About this. Especially Alex and Suzy."

I lose things when I tell people about them. And whatever this is, I want more of it.

His face scrunches, like he smelled something bad. "What? Why?"

"She just—she might not get it."

Jay sighs, and he's quiet again for a long moment while we're stopped at a red light. "Sure, fine." His voice is short, distant again. "Whatever you want."

My anxiety spikes at the shift in his tone. "Does that . . . bother you?"

"Why would it bother me?" Jay stares at the road, flexes his fingers over the wheel. "I'm just teaching you how to drive."

There's a bruised quality to the silence, the rest of the way back. Maybe I already lost him without anyone else's help.

FOURTEEN

I wake up wrapped in the memory of last night—everything bathed deep blue, buzzing like the light posts, soft like Jay's hand over mine. It's not even fully light out, and I'm sick with how much I miss it already, burying my face deeper into the pillow.

He's just helping you learn to drive, he doesn't like you like that. You're too different. The way he's mature and responsible and talks like problems have solutions. Like you can do something about them or forget them. Why would someone like that—

And then the next thing I know, Mom is shaking me awake, and sun is streaming harsh through the blinds.

"What is wrong with you, sleeping so late!" she snaps. "Why haven't you written to your grandfather yet?"

My whole body tenses, and I'm back in her office again, watching the letters scatter across the floor.

I'm so mad, suddenly, I'm shaking, sitting up in bed.

"You should think about it without me asking," Mom huffs.

An echo of last night lingers under my skin—that feeling like more might be possible in life than I thought.

What would Jay do? You should do something about it, or forget it.

"Mom. Don't you think it's strange that Lolo Ric never writes back?"

She shakes her head. "You don't know how lucky you are. Just be grateful."

"But it doesn't feel right, writing to someone who never writes back."

Mom slaps the palm of her hand against the bed, so it shakes. "Oh, I'm sorry, is that too much to ask? Is that too much *work*? What is wrong with you? Asking questions, looking for a fight?"

"I'm just—I'm—I'm—" That restless feeling that's been building bursts out all at once. *"I'm not going to write these letters anymore!"*

She looks so stunned, like I slapped her. Mouth open, brow pinched, eyes full of reproach. I hurt her. Every time I let her down, I remember. That I have an impossible debt that I can never pay. That I took too much from her, too early, and I can never make up for it. It's always there, hiding in the shadows of every conversation.

I remember what she said after my dad's funeral, off to the side, in a corner where no one else could hear.

This guilt is a fleshy thing, visceral, in my organs.

"*Fine*, if that's *too much to ask*. You don't have to write the letters anymore. And I won't tell you those stories anymore, either."

The one thing that makes me feel close to her. There's a hollow feeling in my gut, growing, expanding.

Mom sighs and gets up gingerly, like her muscles hurt. She's almost out in the hall again before she turns back my way. "I'll give you some advice, okay? Listen close." She grips the doorframe, leaning in toward me. "Never have kids. They ruin your life."

It's not the first time she's said it, but it burns going down. Hearing it as her only child, the only one who can take the blame.

Mom's gone now, down the stairs and out of sight, but I keep seeing her face, the exhaustion etched there. All the times she's slumped down at the table, head in her hands. Because of me.

You're draining the life out of me.

Wings flapping in the night.

The way the aswang story usually goes, it preys on pregnant women, slurps up their unborn children. But everything is upside down now. Night in the Philippines is daytime here, everything turned around.

I'm like the aswang in reverse—a child draining the life out of her parents, one quick, one slow. It's not the traditional story, but these shape-shifters are tricky. They adapt.

Mom's office door closes from downstairs. She'll probably shut herself in there for hours, the way she does every weekend, always working hard.

This thing she said once gets caught in my head, goes round and round. I was little then, crying, after we fought. I asked if she loved me.

"*How dare you?* Do you even know what love is?" she said, low and steady, which is somehow more terrifying than when she yells. "Love is suffering. Love is sacrifice." She jabbed the counter with one finger to punctuate every word. "Love is how hard I work for you. The money I bring home for you. *That's* the kind of love that counts!"

I think about Jay working late, making money for his family. How he must be full of love.

FIFTEEN

Dear Lolo Ric,
I'm doing great in school, studying really hard, even at lunchtime. School is nice because it's one reliable source of positive feedback. And it's nice to study with friends. What was your favorite subject in school? Looking forward to your reply.

Kind regards,
Lourdes Zamora Walters

A couple school days pass, and Jay does exactly what I asked him to. When I see him in the hall, he doesn't look at me. When I glance at him in class, he's always drawing, and I can't catch his eye. When Suzy drags me to sit with Alex and his friends at lunch, Jay ignores me. It's what I wanted, but the thought keeps gnawing at me: *Does he just never want to speak to me again?*

Maybe he forgot about our arrangement. Maybe it's safer that way. I'll just never remind him, let it fade into the ether.

Kevin scoots his seat closer to me and bumps me with his shoulder. "Why are you so shy?"

"Um, I don't know. Why are you so rich?" I snap. I've seen photos of the parties he throws in his giant house when his parents are away.

"Wow, easy, tiger!" Kevin says.

I look up, and Jay's eyes meet mine. He's laughing into his hand, chest shaking. And I feel a bit lighter, for a second, because I did that.

During English the next day, my phone rumbles. We're not supposed to, but I check it under the desk.

Jay Hayes: should we go somewhere?

My stomach practically loses its center of gravity. I glance at him, across the room, and catch him looking away.

Jay Hayes: i mean since you don't want anyone to know
Jay Hayes: maybe we should leave campus for tutoring

My fingers shake as I write: *the pond?*

For the rest of the morning, I can't stop looking at the gray industrial clock, counting down the minutes to lunch.

When the bell rings at the end of French, I'm the first person out of the room. And Suzy's there, waiting to walk with me to the cafeteria. "Ready?"

"Uh, a-actually, I wanted to tell you—I'm going to be booked up with tutoring at lunch for a while." I manage a weak smile. "Just trying to save up before college, you know?"

Suzy looks disappointed, but she squeezes my arm. "Look at that work ethic."

She waves to me as I head toward the library. And when I'm around the corner, I go out the closest double doors and sprint around the side of the building.

His car is parked at the back of the lot, where the asphalt meets the trees, leaves burning orange and red behind it. I don't see him. Maybe he's running late.

But as I get closer, I notice him: behind the wheel, seat reclined. His closed eyelids flutter. One of his hands rests on his chest. His face scrunches, like something is troubling him in his dreams.

Oh. He cuts class. To sleep.

That's why he disappears, during the day.

My heart sinks. Am I hurting him? *Draining the life out of him*, like Mom says?

I knock on the glass, and Jay jolts awake.

He blinks and rolls the window down. "Shit, you shouldn't sneak up on people like that."

"Are . . . you okay?"

"Broad question." He runs his hands over his face. "Just, um. Tired."

Jay's grinning at me now like nothing could be wrong. Maybe I was imagining how pained he looked a second ago, in his sleep.

He gets out of the car and stretches. "Okay," he says with a yawn. "You're driving."

"What!"

"Think fast." He tosses me his keys, and I fumble not to drop them.

"But I can barely—"

The passenger door closes. Jay's already inside. So I dump my bag in the back and open the driver's door.

"Are *you* okay?" he says. "You seem kind of . . . off."

"It's nothing," I say, rolling my shoulders back, trying to push his sleeping face out of my mind.

I start to drive, and the car stalls before we even get out of the parking lot.

Jay's just smirking slightly, like this is a fun way to spend his afternoon. "What are you looking at me for? Try again."

So I set off down the street, with *actual other cars on it*. This metal box feels so unwieldy, a death machine I'm controlling with my clueless hands and feet. I can't stop thinking about how I'm one wrong muscle movement away from disaster.

Jay puts on some music—gauzy, fuzzed-out sounds with a droning guitar and soft vocals. He narrates everything I'm supposed to do, and somehow we make it through town, into the woods again. There's a cinematic quality to everything we pass, with this soundtrack on and my adrenaline spiked. The sun comes out and catches the crowns of the trees, fiery red-orange.

I'm shaking when we finally park by the pond. I don't realize how tightly I was gripping the wheel until I try to let go and my hands are slow to unclench.

"You okay?"

"Fine! Excellent. Just . . . give me a minute."

My heart is still racing as I get out, like I actually almost died, even though we went maybe a mile.

I arrange my things on the picnic table, and Jay's eyebrows go up, looking at my clear pencil cases sorted by type—pencils, pens, Mildliners in a rainbow of pastels—and three different sizes of index cards. "So what you're saying is, you like school."

I do, though. The brain part, not the social part.

"So why do you hate writing essays?" I ask.

"Writing them takes so much time, I wish I could just . . . talk to someone for an hour about it instead." Jay pulls a brown paper bag out of his backpack and gives me a questioning look. "Aren't you going to have lunch? I think your exact words were 'you have to eat anyway.'"

I usually skip it to save my lunch money, but I don't want to tell him that. "Um, I ate already?"

"When? In English? During passing period? Here." He hands me half of his sandwich, and I hesitate, staring at it. "It'll hurt my feelings if you don't."

My stomach bounces as I take it from him.

Why does he care so much about whether I eat or not?

I feel guilty stealing his food, but after a couple bites I actually feel a bit better. The bread is flaky and crisp, a perfect little baguette, and the vegetables and meat inside combine so well. "Okay, this is fucking delicious."

He looks so pleased with himself. "My mom hates the grocery store bread here, so we stock up at the Vietnamese bakery whenever we're in Dorchester, fill the whole freezer." He takes another bite and rummages in his backpack.

"Oh, and here—" Jay tosses me a mini bag of salt-and-vinegar potato chips. "You know. To ward off evil."

I can't believe he remembered that. My chest feels too snug around my lungs as I pull open the crinkly bag.

He tilts his chin up at me. "What's your favorite food?"

I pop a chip in my mouth. "Is this a personality quiz?"

"It's a thing I like to know about a person, okay?" Jay plucks the bag out of my hands and eats one, too.

"Mangos and shrimp paste." I don't usually tell anyone that, but, I don't know. It feels like I can tell him.

Jay nods. "Great answer."

"What's yours?"

"Eggs and fish sauce."

He has to be making fun of me.

"This is the VIP answer." He crunches another chip pointedly and turns the bag back toward me. "Not everyone gets this answer."

The silence settles between us again, as we're eating, books open in front of us. The bare branches of the trees around the pond are a haze of brown and deep red, and the water is still and dark, the color of sleep. It smells like someone's using their fireplace in one of the houses in the distance.

"How are . . . your college applications going?" I ask, searching for anything to fill the silence.

"Oh, you know. My mom wants me to apply to a bunch of schools I won't get into." Jay slaps his copy of *As I Lay Dying* against the table. "What even is this book? Does this make any sense to you?"

"Ummm, I thought it was beautiful. Haunting."

He cracks a smile. "You love a good haunting."

"When the mom speaks from beyond the grave, it was so raw. . . ."

Jay bites his thumbnail and studies me.

"What?"

He just shakes his head.

I feel like the entire surface of my skin is lit up, glowing, but I have to act like nothing is happening. "Give me your essay."

He takes it out of his bag, hesitantly, and I snatch it from him and lay it on the table. Jay moves to sit next to me while I go over all his topic sentences, highlighting the ones that don't build on what came before. "They should add up to something when you read them back. Your thoughts should go somewhere."

He yawns. "No one told me this job involved travel."

I laugh and tell him to write a note in the margin about the purpose of each paragraph.

I should probably be taking notes on the next history unit for us to talk about, but I keep sneaking glances at him, the way he leans on one elbow over his paper and pulls at his hair.

The wind picks up, and I rub my bare arms, goose bumps raised against my fingertips. I'm just wearing a short dress today, baby blue with little white flowers.

"Are you cold?" Jay asks, and starts to take off his sweatshirt. It lifts his T-shirt up a little, and for a second I get a glimpse of his bare back, the outline of his ribs as he stretches to get it over his head.

"Thanks," I mumble. I pull the sweatshirt on, and it smells like he did that time we hugged. It's so comforting, I could probably fall asleep right here.

The leaves of the tree behind Jay's head are vibrant yellow, and the way he's looking at me makes my heart feel full to bursting. His eyes are liquid amber and I'm the ant that will get trapped in them—scientists will find me in millions of years.

"Can I take a picture of you?" I ask, and laugh at myself. "It's just, the light right now—it would be a shame to waste it."

Jay covers his face with his hands. "I kind of hate pictures of myself," he says with a muffled laugh. "I mean, I guess it's better than the alternative? Really wanting to look at your own face."

Who's going to love a face like that?

"Oh! Yeah, I really hate my face." I think it's going to come out light, but it lands like a rock.

Jay drops his hands to look at me. "Why?"

"Um, it's just . . . awkward. This combination of features."

He looks serious, suddenly. Eyes roaming around my face, taking in all the details.

"Mm, I don't know." Jay smiles while his eyes flit down. "I checked, I didn't find anything awkward here. Pretty sure you're just wrong."

My face heats up and I have to look away. He goes back to studying like nothing happened.

My reflection in the mirror makes me jump—I forgot I'm still wearing Jay's sweatshirt. If I hadn't stopped in the bathroom, I probably would have worn it right into Calculus with Suzy. I pull it over my head in a hurry and shove it into my backpack.

After school, I arrange it more carefully: folded neatly with a textbook laid flat over it, like a false bottom. Mom doesn't tend to search my backpack, but it should do the job if she peeks inside. And somehow, even if I don't look at it, I like knowing it's there.

SIXTEEN

WE GO BACK TO THE ABANDONED MALL PARKING LOT A FEW TIMES OVER the next couple weeks. Jay pulls some traffic cones out of his trunk— "Where the fuck did you get those?" I ask, laughing, but he won't tell me—and sets them around the edges of the spot. I have to reverse into it, over and over, until I don't knock any of them down.

Then it's time for tutoring, when he's in front of me in broad daylight, and it hurts to look at him for too long. The way he'll ask me a question, and his lips part slightly while he waits for me to say something, and it takes all my focus to give him a normal-sounding answer.

The next time we meet at night, I hesitate behind the wheel. "You know, I looked it up. I'm only supposed to drive with someone over twenty-one in the car."

Jay folds his lips into his mouth and shrugs. "I drove my dad's car alone before I had my license. Back when I actually did donuts." The way he smiles, he looks different from the person I've known so far, and I wonder about the people he's been. "I think it's rural enough around here. We'll be fine. Calculated risk."

He tells me where to turn, when to shift gears, what to do with the pedals. Narrating everything, voice low and steady beside me. We stay out on the roads for longer, taking looping routes through the sleepy neighborhoods by the mall. And then we're back in the lot, parked under the buzzing lights, and soon we'll switch seats and he'll drive us home.

Jay nudges my knee. "Can I see more of your photos?"

"What?"

"The ones you're taking all the time?"

I have some trouble inhaling. And I don't actually have any photos saved on my phone right now, but—I can't believe I'm doing this—I sign into one of my dozens of emails.

He looks at the inbox that's just endless blank emails to myself with photos attached.

"You know there are better storage options out there?"

I thrust the phone at him, and my soul almost leaves my body while he flips through the pictures.

"You're talented," he says.

"You're full of shit."

He's studying the screen seriously. "Why do you like taking them?"

I'm too tired to make something up. "To hold on to things, I guess."

"But there's more than what was already there." He chews his lip pensively. "You're adding something. Like this one—"

Jay turns the screen to me, and it's the one I took when we were leaving, the first time we met for tutoring. The yellow leaves look lush, sun-dappled, next to the warm wood of the picnic table. There's something expectant there, the way the image is focused on the empty space where Jay had been sitting.

"I was there," he says, "but I didn't see it like that."

I'm pretty sure if it was light out, he could see me blush.

And I feel so anxious right then, like if I agree with him, something bad is going to happen. People take photos all the time. It doesn't make them *photographers*. It's not like I think that's a thing I can be.

"I'm tired." I take the phone back from him and open the door. "Let's go home."

I'm finally good enough to drive us a little farther at night, so Jay guides me to the sports field at the middle school. The parking lot is on a little hill, and there are steps to walk down to get onto the green—so from up here, the sky looks so big.

"You had lacrosse camp here? What was that like?"

Jay scoots back and leans his knees against the glove compartment. "Lots of running around in the sun until we were exhausted. Not really overthinking anything. Then they'd bring out a big box of those frozen ice things—you know, the tubes? And we'd sit around on the grass eating them."

"That sounds nice."

In the dark, the silence feels more like something to swaddle yourself in, less like a personal failing. So we sit there a while, not saying anything.

The field stretches out in front of us, empty space calling for something to fill it. I haven't really ever seen it like this—it might as well be a different place altogether, under the thin slice of moon. The rest of the world feels far away.

We're so different. Jay's not twisted like me. But he's always asking me things, and he seems so interested in the answers. Maybe he would want to understand.

"You wanted to know why I ran out into the street that night?" My voice sounds throaty, like it's out of practice.

"Yeah," he says, no hesitation. "I do."

"There's . . . this weird thing my mom does." I look down at my hands, seeped of color in the dark. "She has me write letters to my grandfather all the time. But I don't know what he looks like, and I've never heard back from him. She's been having me do it since I was little."

I'm scared now, looking at his blank expression. His eyebrows go up when he realizes I'm waiting for him to say something.

"Mm." He nods. "That's strange."

"It's just . . ."

I'm losing my confidence, getting to the part about what I found. Maybe he won't get it, after all. Maybe I'll come out looking the worst.

"I . . . told my mom I wouldn't write these letters anymore, because it doesn't make sense. And then she got mad and I immediately took it back. So I'm writing them again, just like . . . shorter and more passive-aggressive." A shaky laugh squeezes out of me.

"I get that. My mom and I fight, like, twice a day."

Jay's looking at me intently, in the dim light, waiting for me to go on.

"It's just . . . funny that I don't know most of our family. My mom doesn't want to talk about them, but they show up in her ghost stories. So in this one really specific, weird way, she talks about them all the time." My chest feels tight, like it's hard to fill it back up with air. "I've never met them, but they're . . . always there, somehow."

He's quiet again, but it seems like he's thinking about it. He tilts his head back and traces shapes with one finger on the gray cloth ceiling.

"My mom is kind of the opposite. She talks a lot about how she grew up. The same stories on repeat, kind of." Jay meets my eye, and I blink away. "That kind of reminds me of something she said, though—that there was a lot her parents didn't talk about. She really wanted to know more about our family, so she went to Vietnam for a bit during college." He sighs, like telling this story inflames his lungs. "But . . . my dad was there, taking a gap year, traveling to find himself. He ended up finding my mom instead. Would have been better for everyone if he just stayed home."

He folds his lips into his mouth, lets them go with a pop. "She got pregnant with Candace on that trip, actually. Dropped out of college. Her parents were so mad—they were all, *You're throwing your life away, the opportunities we worked so hard for . . .*"

Jay trails off, and the silence stretches out, punctuated by birds chirping in the distance. "I guess sometimes family doesn't talk." He says it like an afterthought, but the little hairs on my arms practically stand on end.

"What do you mean?"

"Um." He clears his throat. "Like . . . with my sister."

"What happened with your sister?"

Jay inhales sharply. "Oh. I don't know why I brought it up. I, uh—I don't really want to talk about it."

There's a wall up between us again, and I feel like if I push on it, I'll break something. So I try to make my voice teasing instead. "You're so mysterious."

"I'm extremely not mysterious." He laughs and sounds almost relieved. "I'm boring as fuck."

"I kind of want to know everything about you," I whisper. "Like, I would watch a documentary about you."

There's a short burst of air from his nose, and a smile stretches across his face, making his eyes crinkle. "You're so strange."

"You must just bring it out of me." I try to sound airy, detached, like I'm commenting on the weather.

"What do you want to know?" His arms stretch above his head, pressing his palms into the car ceiling. "Throw me a softball."

"What are you interested in?"

"Who has time to be interested in things?"

I was kind of hoping he'd talk about whatever it is that he draws. "Okay, um, what . . . is your job like?"

"You mean, what do I do?"

"What does it . . . feel like? In detail."

Jay scoffs, but I guess he decides to humor me. "It feels . . . like my body is slowly disappearing. Like I almost forget I have one in the middle of the night sometimes."

He seems to be listening to his answer, deciding it's not quite right, going at it again because he really wants to give me the best one. "Like my brain is just going to merge into the screen. Like I'm just some floating thoughts and pixels."

"Wow, if you brought some of this descriptive skill to your essays . . ."

His laugh sounds like he just went on a run, and he's winded.

"Seems like you put a lot of pressure on yourself," I whisper.

Jay takes a deep breath, then lets it go all at once. "I'm not *putting* it there, it *is* there."

"I mean . . ." The way I felt when I saw him sleeping in his car comes back to me. "But your mom has a job, right? You have a house in a nice neighborhood."

"Why shouldn't we have a house in a nice neighborhood?" His voice hardens. "How do you think we're making the mortgage payments? How do you think we'll ever pay down the principal? Do you even know how debt works?"

Do you even know how love works?

I thought I knew something about that. But I guess I don't know anything at all.

"Yeah, sure, maybe we could be on a tighter budget. Live somewhere else." His breathing is strained, like there will never be enough oxygen in his lungs to explain to me what his life is actually like. "But I *can* work this hard, and—why shouldn't they have this? And maybe this will make up for—if I can—"

"I shouldn't have asked!" I say too fast. "I'm sorry I asked."

He takes a few deep breaths, rolls his shoulders backward, looking straight ahead.

"Sorry I got upset. I actually . . . like that you're interested enough to ask." His eyes are dark pools, pupils big, fixed on me. "I'm just not used to it."

Condensation has collected on the windshield, blurring the world outside into abstract streaks of color.

"Oh, I, uh—I brought you something," he says, reaching behind him to the floor of the back seat for a plastic bag.

He pulls out a Polaroid camera and hands it to me. "It's old—it was my mom's. But it still works."

I take it in my hands, barely breathing.

"I can't fully give it to you, but you can borrow it for as long as you want. And I got you some film." He points inside the bag before handing that to me, too.

My eyes are too hot, my throat is tight. I have to stare at the steering wheel for a while to regain my composure. "Why did you do that?"

"I don't know, I wanted to become a patron of the arts?" He clears his throat. "Just knew someone who'd put it to good use."

"Thank you." My voice is small. "I'll take good care of it. Let me pay you back for the film?"

"I'm going to pretend you didn't say that."

I get out of the car and take a picture of the thin slice of moon over the field. Jay's already in the driver's seat when I climb back inside, the white edge of the Polaroid between my two fingers. He clicks on the overhead light. Heads bent toward each other, we watch the image emerge from the milky gray.

SEVENTEEN

SUZY COMES OVER FOR OUR MONTHLY SUNDAY DINNER—BURGERS Mom picked up on the way home from the office, because this project is eating up her off-hours.

I didn't hold up my end of the bargain, when I said I'd stop writing to Lolo Ric, but Mom stuck to hers. She hasn't told a single one of her stories since then. And she still goes somewhere at night, a couple times a week, so consistently I stopped keeping track in my calendar. She might not make sense to me, but you have to hand it to her—she really sticks to her guns.

All through the evening, my muscles are clenched, waiting for the other shoe to drop. What if Suzy says something offhand about Jay, and how cute she thinks we would be together?

There was one time Suzy came over for dinner last year. Mom

ordered pizza, and we sat around the kitchen table, surrounded by her empty vases in the dim light, eating from our greasy paper plates.

That was back when I was the one who couldn't shut up about Alex. When I thought dating him would fix the things about me I don't know how to fix. Because if someone like that chose me . . . someone everyone loves . . .

Suzy teased me about him while Mom was in the bathroom, and I started to sweat. But by the time Mom came back, Suzy had moved on, and there was only my beating heart in my ears for the rest of the night as a reminder.

But tonight, the conversation stays neutral, pleasant. Suzy talks about where she's applying to school, and Mom doesn't ask any awkward questions point-blank.

When it's over, I walk Suzy out. She's ahead of me, and once the front door is closed behind us, she turns back, standing on the step below.

"Hey, so—" She crosses her arms. "I might not be able to hang out on Thursdays anymore."

Mom was right. It was just a matter of time before Suzy got tired of me.

"It's just—it's the only day when I'm off work and Alex doesn't have practice, and—I mean, you could probably still have dinner at my house anyway, my parents love you—"

Oh my God, she feels sorry for me.

"It's okay!" I say more abruptly than I want, crossing my arms to match her. "I'm good."

Suzy looks pained, mouth half open. "I mean, look, I still want you to come to things—but you seem miserable whenever you do, and, and—" Her words are tumbling out now, a runaway train. "I'm, like, new to this friend group, and it's a lot to balance, and—"

I'm trying to ignore the pressure building in the corners of my eyes. She runs an agitated hand through her hair. "And sometimes it's hard to worry about what they're going to think, *and* what you're thinking, and—I mean, I love you, but you can be kind of *intense*, and . . ."

"*Suzy*, it's *fine*." I have to bite the inside of my cheek to keep myself steady. "I'll see you later!"

I manage to make it inside, back slumped against the closed door, before I actually start to cry.

Jay and I are out on the road again, waxing moon overhead and the steady tones of his voice, telling me where to go.

"Okay, there's a hill, you'll need to downshift."

Sweat sprouts under my clothes and my bones rattle as we climb, but we get there, to the top of the hill somehow. Jay directs me to make a few turns, and then we're in another parking lot by a rest area.

I reach into the back seat for Jay's camera and roll down the window so I can capture the clouds passing over the moon. They look lit from within, like floating lanterns.

While the photo develops, my eyes adjust. There's a sense of depth and texture, in the quality of the darknesses around us. Straight ahead, you can tell there's a drop-off. A sea of treetops unfolds below it, an indistinct, dark mass between us and the lights of town. Up here, to our right, there's a stretch of grass with picnic tables before the woods begin.

"So you just happen to know all the picnic areas in a fifty-mile radius?" I ask.

"Alex's dad didn't love having me over so much. Once I had a car,

I'd . . . drive around a lot. In the summers. So yeah, free places to loiter, I'm kind of a connoisseur."

The way the moonlight falls into the car, the top half of Jay's face is in shadow, and that draws my eye to his neck, his jaw and mouth. An image appears in my mind, too vivid: Jay leaning closer, pressing his lips against mine. How soft and warm they might be.

Focus, Deedee! That's not what we're doing here.

You're setting yourself up for heartache, thinking someone like him would like someone like you.

I'm glad that it's dark so he can't see how wildly I must be blushing.

The song changes on the stereo then—it's the same one he put on, the first time I drove during the day.

"What's this?" I whisper. "It's nice."

"Oh. It's old. My Bloody Valentine." He sounds embarrassed, for some reason. "Candace used to listen to it."

Jay takes a big breath in and holds it, not looking at me. It feels like the moment is a soap bubble, and if we look at each other, it will burst.

"She had these noise-cancelling headphones. . . ." He taps the door handle with his fingers. "They were her favorite thing, basically. When our parents were fighting, she'd act like she had some music discovery she needed to show me *this instant*. She'd put the headphones on me and say I had to sit through the whole thing, really listen and appreciate the music. It took me a few years to realize she was doing it so I wouldn't hear them yelling at each other."

Jay sighs and changes the song on his phone. It's something newer now, melancholy vocals with snares and hi-hat rolls. "She'd write to me all the time, when I was here, actual letters—she thought it felt more special than, like, texting or something. I wasn't great about writing back, but she'd just keep sending them, anyway. And she was the only one who visited. Came down for Fourth of July weekend."

"So you were close."

"Yeah. For a while."

"You must miss her."

Jay laughs, but there's no joy in it, now. "I'm just so mad at her, you know? For a long time, she was always trying to protect me. She's older, but just by, like, two years. But once I was in high school and I had this job, it was more like—I don't know, like we were a team." He scrubs a hand through his hair and shakes his head. "I'm going to get less fun if we keep talking about this."

"You don't have to be fun," I whisper. "If you want to talk about it."

Jay runs a hand over his face. "Um. She and my mom fought, I guess. They fought all the time, but then they had this one really bad fight, and . . . Candace went back to school and stopped talking to her. And I kind of had to pick a side."

You can just stop talking to your mom? The idea makes my skin prickle all over.

I have so few people in the world as it is—no dad, no extended family I talk to, Suzy barely, Jay maybe. Just thinking about it makes me feel like I'm spinning off into space. Who even am I without Mom?

"My mom's not perfect," he says. "We fight all the time. But . . . she's human, you know? She's just doing her best. I wish Candace could see that."

Suddenly, everything is too warm and tight around my spine.

How do you expect anyone to love you?

It's like you're missing something everyone else has.

Are you even human?

I know Mom is human. Does she know *I* am?

My muscles are all knotty. The space between me and Jay feels so small and so big at once. He picked a side, his mom versus his sister. He'll just be disappointed when he realizes I can't be like him, well-adjusted, persevering. That I'm broken and difficult and flawed to the core. That I can somehow never manage to be *grateful* enough to make it stop hurting.

But pushing against that thought, a little ember of something unfamiliar glows inside me, like spite is the oxygen that breathes it to life.

"Have you considered it from Candace's perspective?" There's something tart and troll-y in my voice now.

"I mean, I know how she grew up," he says, voice hard-edged. "I was there."

"Do you really know what it was like for her? Maybe you could try *asking better questions.*"

Jay tilts his head back, hands resting on his chest as he considers the gray cloth of the ceiling. "You . . . still haven't really told me why you need so much fresh air in the middle of the night."

We're not made of the same stuff. He's going to hate me.

"You said your mom is scared of you learning to drive. Did . . . something happen?" he asks, eyes darting over to me. "Was there an accident? With your dad?"

He's getting dangerously close to the things I never want to talk about. What I did.

"No. He had cancer."

"Oh. Fuck. Sorry."

"It's okay," I whisper, as the wind outside shakes the trees beyond the picnic tables. "You're fine."

"What about . . . your dad's family?"

"What about them?"

"Could you talk to them? About . . . whatever is happening?"

"I don't know them." There's so little to connect us, not even a handful of ghost stories. Just a person I barely remember. "They'll just be more people who can judge me for not getting along with my mom."

"Deedee," Jay says carefully. "You kind of hint at it, but—what is going on with your mom?"

"She just gets . . . mean," I mumble. "It's not a big deal. Other people have it a lot worse."

He's quiet, biting the skin next to his thumbnail.

"My mom is always saying I'm going to turn into my dad," Jay says after a while, like this thought traveled a long way to get here. "And I try to tell myself she doesn't mean it, but . . ."

He's keeping his voice light, but it's obvious it weighs on him. That he's extending something toward me, wavering there in the air between us. And I want to reach for it, but— *No, he's not going to be on my side, I can't trust it!*

My head is getting too hot, and I can't think about this anymore. My fingers fumble against the camera that's still sitting in my lap, and the words just burst out of my mouth: "Can I take a picture of you?"

I'm not sure what made me say it, but I'm relieved when he laughs again.

"Sure. Why not."

He gets out of the car, walks onto the grass, and I follow.

Looking through the viewfinder, I frame it so the moon is in the shot, above his head. The camera spits out the picture, and we get back into the car, Jay in the driver's seat again.

I kind of love the aesthetic. There are little light flecks floating around him, and his eyes are half-closed, a goofy grin on his face.

I smile and take a picture of it on my phone.

"Why don't you like the way you look?" I ask, still staring at it.

"I don't mind how I look in the mirror, but . . . photos never look like the person in my head, I guess."

"What does that person look like?"

"Less like my dad." He laughs at how blunt it comes out. "Maybe this sounds weird, but from some angles I look more like him, and it feels like photos only get those."

"I think you look nice in this one. Like, it's a 'bad photo,' but . . . it reminds me of you." I hold it out to him. "I can't keep this, though."

"Why not?"

"I'll get in trouble."

"I'd rather have one of you."

My heart flutters, but I pass him the camera and sit there, stiff and sweaty, waiting for the picture to pin me down.

Jay lifts it to look through the viewfinder, then lowers it again. "Hey," he says softly, "relax."

He reaches out and rests his hand on the back of mine. My heart is in my throat, and part of me wants to flip my hand over and lace our fingers together.

Instead, I give him a shaky smile, and Jay pulls back and takes the photo.

Slowly, it comes into view: I'm staring right at him, chin lowered a little, bracing for something to happen. There's a glare against the window behind me, where the flash went off.

My expression looks too intense, and I cringe, thinking about what Suzy said. Maybe Jay won't like it.

But the way he smiles, while he looks at it—

"Okay," he says, tucking the two pictures into the pocket of his jacket, over his heart. "They can live next to each other."

EIGHTEEN

Halloween arrives, and as is tradition, Suzy and I are watching horror movies and handing out candy. We've been riding to school together still, just not seeing each other much the rest of the time. But tonight feels closer to normal than things have in a while.

We're nestled on the soft blue couch in her living room, waiting for the doorbell to ring. You can barely see the warm yellow paint on the walls for all the shelves crammed with books. Mrs. Jang was an international student at Eastleigh, doing her undergrad thesis in nineteenth century English literature when she met Suzy's dad. Her books are all over the house, in unexpected places. I'll open the cabinet to get a water glass, and there will be a couple paperbacks nestling there, next to the mugs.

Ben and Jake come clambering down the beige carpeted stairs,

Charlie running after them. He's dressed like J. Jonah Jameson, with a fake mustache and an unlit cigar in his mouth. "Get me photos of Spider-Man!" he bellows while Ben and Jake shoot imaginary webs at each other, and Mrs. Jang films on her phone.

They'd been fighting for weeks over who would get to be Spider-Man this year. Eventually Charlie had to intervene, looking up from his email and clutching his forehead: "You're both Spider-Man, okay!"

Mrs. Jang plops down on the couch next to Suzy, exhausted by the boys already.

"Is this mine?" Suzy pinches the sleeve of her mom's flannel shirt between two fingers.

Mrs. Jang swats her hand away. "Who does your laundry? Consider it a tax."

My cheeks hurt when I smile and my skin feels too tight, trying to stuff my jealousy back where it came from.

All through dinner, Mrs. Jang couldn't stop grinning and asking questions about Alex. She launched into a dramatic retelling of how she met Charlie, and Suzy jumped in and completed her sentences.

Even I know the whole story by heart now: She went to see his band play on campus, and they spent the whole night on the roof of the student union building, talking until the sun came up. I joined in, too, finished Suzy's sentences for her. Everyone was laughing. I was in on the joke, almost one of the family.

A text comes in, then, and a picture of Jay appears on my screen.

Everyone is distracted, but I can't look at this here. I pop up and hurry to the bathroom. Sitting on the closed toilet seat, I peek at my phone.

I have to put it face down on my knee and collect myself, grinning at no one, before I look again.

There he is, leaning back in a black computer chair, wearing a pair of oversize glasses with that anti-blue-light tint. Flashing a peace sign, going a little overboard in his sudden embrace of the whole selfie genre.

I'm shaking laughing, hand over my mouth.

Jay Hayes: personal growth?

I can barely focus for the rest of the night after Suzy's dad and her brothers leave. I keep thinking about the picture and feeling a little burst of serotonin all over again.

"Hey. You're so quiet," Suzy says, bumping my side, resting her weight against me. "Come to Alex's away game next week? Please. Please, please, please."

She's just saying that because she feels guilty.

But I pat her on the shoulder and say, "I'll ask my mom."

More than a month into our agreement, Jay breaks protocol for the first time: He comes up to me in the library after school, when I'm cramming for the SAT. Maybe he also knows that Suzy and Alex are at his game right now, the one Mom ended up saying I couldn't go to.

"Thought you might be hungry," he says, dropping a mini bag of salt-and-vinegar chips on the table.

"You know we can't eat in here."

"Mhmm."

"So I'll just . . . have to casually go outside and talk to you."

"Damn, you figured out my schemes." He laughs and nudges my shoulder. "Too smart. You probably don't even need to study."

We go out behind the building together and sit against the brick wall, passing the bag of chips back and forth. It's weird—our first interaction in so long that's not organized around a task. Jay's quiet for long stretches, rubbing the back of his neck with one hand. When the chips are done, I stick my fingertips in my mouth to get the last salty, sour crumbs. I glance over at Jay, and he looks away quickly. Is he . . . *blushing?* Am I imagining it?

I get his camera out of my backpack and take a picture of our legs sprawled out on the threadbare grass next to each other. His arms are in the shot, his hand still holding the empty chip bag.

Jay laughs as it develops. "You really found my best angle."

"You should drink more water." I point to his hand in the photo, the raised lines of his veins. "You're dehydrated."

He smiles, and his nose scrunches. "Thanks for your concern, I'll work on that."

I'm not proud of this, but I've googled *How to tell if a boy likes you* a few times recently. People describing all these little signs in great detail, trying to read the tea leaves.

Maybe he just needed a tutor. And who do you think you are, anyway? Someone so hard to love, how can you expect . . .

But then . . . there's the way he listens to me, the way he touched my hand. The way he brings me chips.

Maybe someone like him could like someone like me.

A thought tumbles through my head for the next few days, edges wearing smooth. I want to write him a note, but it takes me forever, debating the safest, least mortifying thing I could say.

Then I remember what he told me on the phone, the night I found the letters and ran into the street. How my skin prickled all over when he said, *I like talking to you.*

So I write on an index card:

I like talking to you, too.

I slip it through his locker vents, along with the Polaroid of our legs. All day, I'm on edge, stewing in the silence that follows.

I can't sleep that night, staring at the ceiling, wondering what he thought of it. Worrying I made things weird. Remembering every bad thing I've ever done.

I dig his sweatshirt up from the bottom of my backpack and pull it on. It still smells like him, and somehow that helps me drift off to sleep.

At 5:45, I wake up in a panic, terrified Mom will find me in it. So I leap out of bed and put it back in its hiding place, before she's up again.

NINETEEN

"I'M GLAD YOU CAME," SUZY SAYS AS SHE RINGS THE BELL AT ALEX'S house. "I missed you."

A little pang of guilt runs through me. Maybe she means it.

"I feel like people are talking about me lately," Suzy says, idly playing with the strings of the sweatshirt she's wearing. It must be Alex's, gray with RHS FOOTBALL in green lettering on the front. "Yesterday when I went to the bathroom, these girls just quickly stopped their conversation and left in a hurry."

"You're famous now. So many heartbroken Alex admirers out there."

She gives me a sideways glance. Does she think I'm talking about myself?

"I mean, not me, though! I can't remember why I even liked him, honestly." Shit, that came out wrong.

She looks a little hurt, but then Alex answers the door, gives her a hug, and waves us inside.

It's kind of chaotic in the living room, magazines and unopened Amazon boxes on the coffee table, pea-green wall-to-wall carpet and furniture that looks like it's been here for decades. A bunch of people from school are spread out across two couches, some armchairs, the floor.

Jay's reclined in a La-Z-Boy, talking to Ted and half-watching an anime on the TV—something about car racing.

"Look who it iiiiis!" a blond girl calls from the couch, patting the empty spot between her and Alex. She leans over to nudge him. "Bro, I love this girl, don't mess this one up!"

"*Beth!*" Alex says, more stressed than I would expect.

Suzy makes her way over to them, and I'm still standing there dopily by the door, looking from her to Jay and back again. She's already deep in conversation, gossiping with this Beth girl like they've known each other for years.

The voices ebb and flow around me, adrift in this room with the two people I most want to talk to, too far from both.

You're missing something everyone else has!

I don't know where to go, but I can't keep standing here. So I force myself to an empty chair and settle in to observe everyone.

If I wasn't so self-conscious, these are the photos I would take right now:

Alex beaming next to Suzy, giving off golden retriever energy. Suzy laughing so hard at something Beth said, clutching her sides. Ted and Josh's animated faces, their arms extended, pointing at Kevin, as they argue about the details of a story they're all simultaneously trying to tell.

I wish I didn't have to be so aware of Jay off to the side, on the edge of my field of vision. He looks uneasy, leg jiggling. Not how I would expect, if this is his second home.

"My dad's always saying I need to get a job, that's my problem," Ted exclaims at the tail end of the story. "Suzy, what's that like?"

"What?"

"Having a work ethic! None of us would know."

Ted and Alex laugh, and I look at Jay, his blank facial expression. *Wait, so . . . do they not know about his job?*

Alex slides over and sits on Suzy's lap. "Oof, boy, you're heavy!" She pretends to struggle to push him off, and he wraps his arms tight around her.

I wonder if I could ever have something like that with anyone. It would hurt too much, maybe, thinking I could and being wrong about it. So I shouldn't let myself think about it at all.

I try actually watching the anime on the TV. This guy's engine blew out while he was racing, and he's sitting there by himself in the dark on the side of the road. Then a tow truck arrives, and—"Dad!" he calls, all surprised he showed up for him.

On the drive home, the dad says the engine is beyond repair, and I don't expect it, but the guy starts to cry. He must be really attached to his car.

The dad reaches over, puts a hand on his son's head, and says, "It's not your fault."

My face heats up, the way I always feel kind of teary, in this sudden, infuriating way, any time there's a moment of warmth between family members in movies.

I glance over at Jay, and his face is scrunched up like he just ate a lemon.

What—

He gets up and goes into the hallway. I wait a few beats, make sure no one is paying attention, and get up to follow him.

Jay's standing near the bathroom, head tilted back, blinking a lot. Definitely trying not to cry.

Oh.

This whole time, I've been thinking he's so much better than me. Stronger, more able to deal with everything. That life doesn't bother him, the way it bothers me.

But seeing the same thing get to him—

Maybe we're more similar than I thought.

Jay sees me then and covers his face with his hands. "Oh my God, please leave."

"Are you . . ."

He waves a hand at me, the other still hiding his face. "Nothing to see here!" he adds in a goofy voice.

I'm not sure what comes over me, but I get closer and wrap my arms around him, from the side. His body stiffens, at first, but then he relaxes into it, puts both hands on one of my arms and squeezes. Then he steps back, out of reach, and wipes his face impatiently with the heel of his hand.

It's like I can see the embarrassment wafting off him, the way he's holding himself. Coming in searing, from somewhere in his core.

Jay sniffs and forces a smile. "It's an involuntary physical response, okay?"

"What are you, pre-med?" I can just picture him, sitting at his desk late at night, googling for words he can tell himself to make crying sound clinical and safe.

He runs a hand over his face. "Don't judge me."

He's worried about *me* judging *him*? I spend so much time worried about the opposite, it's a strange thought.

Jay leans his back against the wall and slides down to sit.

So I do, too, facing forward together, like we're on the road.

"I . . . messed up yesterday. Got confused about what day it was and left Gemma stranded at school for, like, two hours by herself."

"You're doing your best," I say.

"You know what she said to me? *You're so unreliable!*"

"She's a little kid. And you're a good brother."

He's so stressed, and I'm making it worse. Forcing him to stay up late, driving in circles with me.

"Maybe we should stop!" I blurt out. "We don't have to . . . do this, anymore. If it's too much."

"What?" He sounds a little panicked. "Why? Is that what you want? You feel like . . . you don't need lessons anymore?"

"That's not what— No! Have you seen me? Terrible driver." I hug my knees, look at him sideways. "I'm just worried about you."

Jay sighs and leans his head back against the wall. And then he lets himself droop slowly sideways, until he's resting against my shoulder. My entire world tunnels down to that spot where his weight presses against me. He's so close, I can smell his scalp, hints of minty shampoo. Just taking deep, steady breaths fully occupies the last two brain cells I have.

We sit there like that in silence for a little while, staring at the old, flowered wallpaper and the framed photos crammed on the opposite wall. There's one of little Jay and Alex, standing on the field, afternoon sun low in the trees behind them.

"Look at you!" I point. "So cute." They must be about twelve here, smiling wide, sweaty, Alex's arm around Jay's shoulders. Jay's hair looks like his mom cut it with a bowl.

"You know, I guess I was surprised . . ." I say, voice dropping to a whisper. It's strange to talk when every word jostles his head. "It seems . . . like your friends don't know about your job?"

Jay scoffs. "What about you and Suzy?"

"What about us?" My voice sounds more defensive than I want.

"Just . . . you're kind of going out of your way not to tell her things."

"It's complicated."

"Okay. All right. Sure."

Then footsteps are getting closer, and I scramble to my feet, so he does, too.

Suzy emerges into the hall and sweat sprouts under my shirt as she looks between us, confused. "Is this . . . the line for the bathroom?"

"Um, yeah," Jay says, pointing to the bathroom door and looking at me, his expression clouded over. "It just freed up. Your turn."

"Yeah, thanks," I say with a tight smile, and lock myself inside.

TWENTY

ALL WEEK, I KEEP THINKING ABOUT JAY'S HEAD ON MY SHOULDER. My heart has been beating in time with this thought: *Something is going to happen. Something is going on here. It can't just be my imagination.*

Tonight, we drive farther than before. Jay gives me directions to another spot he'd go to in the summers, when he wanted to be alone and think. It's so dark, as we get deeper into the woods—just the slightest sliver of moon overhead, waning into nothing. If I didn't trust him so much, I'd think this was a terrible idea.

When we're almost to the old bridge on the outskirts of town, he tells me to pull off to the side and park.

Jay walks onto the bridge and sits down on the footpath running along the side, so I join him—leaning our arms against the cold metal guardrail, legs dangling off the edge. Below my swinging feet, there's nothingness. A long drop to the train tracks I know are there but can barely see.

Mom has a thing about bridges, like she never trusts them not to collapse. Every time she has to drive over one, she's tense, gripping the wheel hard, repeating under her breath, "I can do anything with Jesus who strengthens me." She'll probably never stop doing that, even if we don't go to church again.

She always has St. Christopher watching over her, from the medallion clipped to the sun visor. The patron saint of travelers. Fitting for her, the way she's in transit all the time, always going, never quite arriving. Eyes straight ahead.

Jay flops backward on the concrete, arms folded over his chest.

He pats the ground next to him. "Come on, you're missing the stars."

So I lie down, extremely aware of the inches between us, and we stare at the little points of light in the dark above.

"Do you ever feel like you just want too much?" Jay says out of the blue.

"What do you mean?"

"I guess . . . people are counting on me, and I disappoint them . . ." He trails off, and the silence expands. Off in the distance, an owl hoots. "And I want too many things I can't have."

I feel so agitated—close to him but still far, wondering what the fuck is going on.

I've been staring at the stars for so long, they start to blur, and *up* starts to feel like *down*. It's like I'm facing an endless stretch of dark water, and any minute I might fall in.

He laughs uncomfortably. "Sorry. Me and my littlest violin."

I have to ask him some more questions just to feel in control of myself again.

"Does Alex even know about your job?"

Jay lets out a surprised puff of air. "People are friends in different ways, okay? He . . . knew my parents fought a lot. After a certain point, I just—I didn't want to tell him things he might not get. But . . . he shows up, you know? When we pulled up with the U-Haul, he was right there, ready to unload."

He's quiet for a while, as the cold of the concrete seeps through my clothes. I wonder if I upset him.

Jay sighs. "You really want to know why I don't talk about it?"

"Yeah. Of course I do."

There's another long pause. "I was . . . kind of a shitty kid before Candace left for college." His voice is scratchier now, strained. "When she stopped talking to us, I had to step up, because she used to take care of a lot of things, at home. And I wanted to make up for everything. For how I was, before. For her cutting us off. For my dad. And this job is a thing I can do. While everything else is falling apart. I might hate it sometimes, but—I'm proud of it, too, you know? It's a thing I can do," he repeats, more firmly, like he's convincing himself. "It's a thing I understand. It means too much to me, I guess. I don't want to give anyone a chance to misunderstand."

It makes me a little dizzy, how much I relate to that.

He turns his head toward me. "That's why I don't like talking about it."

Our faces are so close to each other, now. All I can do is stare at him, wheels spinning, searching for the right thing to say.

"How are . . . things with your mom?" Jay whispers.

Why would he ask me that now?

I scoff. "Aren't you just going to tell me to try harder?"

"No." He sounds so serious, and his hand squeezes my arm, through my jacket. "I don't want anyone to be mean to you."

A bright, agitated feeling ripples through me, from my chest to my toes.

I can't look at him anymore. My eyes flee back to the stars.

"What are those things you were talking about, anyway?" I ask the sky. "The things you want but can't have."

Jay sits up abruptly, looking at me from above. Even though it's hard to see his expression, exactly, it's intense, how long he stares.

"Why do you *do* that?" His laugh sounds kind of desperate, in the quiet. "Keep . . . *asking* me things, like that? It's like you want to—to open me up, to see what's inside. Because you're bored, or, or—I don't know—"

I need to smooth it over, be funny for him again. "Like how people open the fridge just to stare inside?"

"Yeah! Like that." He laughs uneasily, looking up and away from me, working the back of his neck with one hand.

"I asked because I wanted to know the answer," I say flatly.

"Well, have you ever heard—" Jay leans back on his palms and laughs. "That you can't always get what you want?"

His tone is light, jokey, but a little twinge of anger sparks through me. "As if I'm always just *going around*," I grit out, "*getting what I want.*"

Jay huffs out a big breath. "Okay, fine, ask me . . . something else."

Cold sweat gathers under my clothes because I know exactly what I want to ask him. I've known all week, the whole drive over, every minute we've been here. All my muscles are clenched, like Mom going over the bridge.

"Do you like anyone?" I ask.

He laughs, and my heart sinks. "What?"

Shit. I need more plausible deniability.

"We're friends, right?" I ask, trying to keep it light.

"Um. Yeah." He sounds so stiff, now. "Yeah. We're friends."

"It's a thing friends talk about."

Jay lies back again, looking at the sky instead of at me. His breaths sound like they take more effort, now, every exhale almost a sigh.

"It's just—it's not a good time for me to like anyone," he says.

It's an excuse. He's too scared to hurt my feelings. I don't know why I thought he could like me back.

I start to get up, and he reaches for my arm.

"Deedee," he says. "I'm really glad we're friends."

It sounds like he's serious, like the words have weight.

There are so many things I want to say right then, caught between how much this means to me and how much more I want. But I swallow all of them, get up, and walk back to the car without replying.

TWENTY-ONE

WE'RE SKIPPING TUTORING FOR THANKSGIVING BREAK THIS WEEK, AND we don't have plans to drive.

It's late, and I can't sleep. My phone says 12:54 a.m.

Headlights shine through my window. I get up to see Jay pulling out of his driveway again.

One of Mom's stories comes back to me: floating balls of fire, appearing in the night sky to mislead you. That turn you around, make you forget your home and get lost just feet from your destination. *(Kuya Boboy got so confused, he ended up in the next province!)*

I'm not going to think about the past.

Anymore.

His hand on my arm.

His head on my shoulder.

His eyes in the afternoon light.

None of that.

I'll try to be more like Mom.

No more *making myself miserable on purpose*, thinking about things I can't have.

My birthday falls on Thanksgiving this year. Ironic, being *the most ungrateful child*.

It's always kind of lonely, everyone else with their families. But whatever, it's a bullshit problematic holiday anyway.

When Suzy picked me up yesterday, she had a cupcake with a single candle in it waiting for me on the dashboard, and I almost bawled.

"Are you okay?" she asked. "Are you depressed?"

"Why would you ask that?" I said, mouth full of frosting.

"I don't know, you've been kind of . . . different lately. I tried looking some stuff up about it."

Then she dropped it and started talking about how she's nervous to meet Alex's parents when she goes to their house for Thanksgiving dinner.

The day drags out, tense and silent, like always. I take a nap before dinner, and when I wake up, there's an envelope on my desk, Mom's handwriting in marker on the front:

Happy birthday. You're an adult now. I don't know what you want.

I want you to tell me the stories again like you used to! I want you to tell me I'm not so bad.

I peek inside, and there's cash nestling there.

It's supposed to feel like love, so why doesn't it?

I think I know what Mom would say. That if you were starving, this would feel like love. That *you have it too good*.

Try harder! Feel loved!

Mom's in the kitchen, reheating the rotisserie chicken she bought a few days ago, our Thanksgiving tradition. "Less work and it tastes better anyway," she would say when I was little, and I'd feel like I was in on an important life secret.

I set the salad I made earlier on the table, a recipe with cubed ham, peas, and pasta that I learned in first grade for a take-home exercise on Thanksgiving foods. The same year when Mom came in for Take Your Mom to Class Day and Take Your Dad to Class Day. Always working twice as hard.

Mom couldn't get enough of this salad, so I started making it every year.

She opens the dishwasher now and makes a disgusted sound. "I told you to prewash!" Her voice cuts through my brain fog, the way it could cut through anything. It could slice, dice, and flambé. They could market it on daytime television.

"Sorry." I'm trying to be good and not talk back. Or maybe I can't be good, but at least I don't want to make it worse.

"Better not do it at all if you're going to do it wrong!" She yanks the dishes out of the machine and piles them noisily on the counter.

"Let me—"

"You've done enough!"

She's agitated when we sit down to eat. "Don't look so sad like that!"

I force a smile, and she clicks her tongue. "And don't give me that fake smile either! I've been working so hard, I should get to *relax* now, finally, and then—" Mom waves a hand at me. *"There's your sad face, ruining it!"*

I'm so tired, suddenly, I don't think I could find the words to talk back if I wanted to. I just want to sleep.

"And when you have all this!" Her hand sweeps the room. "If this is hard for you, how are you ever going to make it out there, ha? What are you made of? How are you going to survive?"

Mom leaves the room and comes back a few minutes later with a hand mirror. She pushes it up in front of my face, and I wince.

"Really! Who would want to come home and see *that*? Not warm, not pleasant, just—*there*, all the time! All of my days, like punishment!"

The room is wavy, losing its shape. I'm crying, *why am I crying, what is wrong with me*?! *Stop stop stop stop stop!*

"Just like my dad, always feeling sorry for yourself," Mom says under her breath.

My head snaps up. "What did you say?"

Mom puts the mirror face down on the table, goes to the sink, and pours herself a glass of water.

"You said—"

"Drop it!" Mom says, shaking her head.

We sit down to eat again, but I must get too in my head, lost in the fog.

"Fine, you're not going to eat?!" Mom leaps up with my plate and scrapes the rest of my chicken into the trash. "*There*, you made me waste food, are you happy?"

There's a stabbing feeling in my gut because she raised me to know wasting food is even worse than feeling sorry for yourself.

"Just go to your room!" Mom says, so I rush upstairs.

Under the covers, I look at the texts I missed from Suzy, asking me if I want to come to some party at Kevin's house.

> Suzy Jang: we have to dress up for it
> Suzy Jang: it's this tradition kevin started
> Suzy Jang: his "formal winter party"
> Suzy Jang: i don't get it but alex is excited for some reason

I bury my head in the pillow, doubly jealous. Suzy with her boyfriend on Thanksgiving, holding hands, passing the mashed potatoes. Going home to her dad's leftover fried chicken in the fridge, her parents and brothers watching a movie together on the couch.

And here I am—tragic unrequited crush, a mom who hates me, half-eaten chicken leg sitting in the trash.

I open Instagram for a palate cleanser, and there's a photo Suzy posted earlier this week—Beth with her arm around her at a party, both of them holding up drinks, jostling, laughing.

Okay, that's enough of being awake for today!

I sleep for a while. I don't dream.

But I wake up again around one, when my phone rumbles.

> Jay Hayes: what are you doing right now

Oh my God. Sure, that's a normal friend thing to text at 1 a.m. Well. I don't have to impress him anymore.

> Deedee Walters: crying
> Jay Hayes: are you actually
> Deedee Walters: guess

Those dots pop up and disappear.

Jay Hayes: want to go for a drive?

This is not normal friend stuff, *Jason*!
But instead, I say:

Deedee Walters: sure

I slip out and meet him in his driveway. It's kind of surreal being out here with him again, in the stillness that swallows everything.

"You look sad," he says.

I want to yell, *No I don't!* or maybe, *What do you want from me!*

Instead, I cover my face with my hands and say, "Don't look at me, then."

"Come here," he says, and pulls me into a hug—which, I guess, technically can be a thing friends do? Sure, whatever. This is fine.

My face presses into the canvas of his jacket. It smells like the cold and something crisp and clean, like the first thing in the morning.

"You want to drive?" he asks.

"Fuck no."

The way a laugh bursts out of him almost makes me feel better.

We glide through the dark woods, floating specks in the road catching the headlights. And after a while, the way I felt during dinner gets further away.

"If you could go anywhere right now," I ask, "where would you want to go?"

"Is this a personality quiz?" he teases. But before I can reply, he answers. "New York."

That makes me think of the photo in my nightstand, and the way Mom clams up when I ask about her life before me.

"Why there?"

"I like how it feels. The chaotic energy. Everyone is so deep in their own shit, no one's wondering about you. It's like I could be whatever I want there."

I feel so horribly close to him, like this. In the dark it's like our bodies disappear, and we're just floating together. Spirits meeting for a chat.

We pass some houses with their porch lights on, breaking up the dark.

"You went to New York?"

"Yeah, last year. To visit Candace. That's—" He swallows hard, like he just remembered he shouldn't be talking about her. "That's where she lives now."

We take those familiar turns through the woods, into the lot by the pond. We're back to where we started, but it looks different tonight, with barely any moonlight. The orange glow of the light post is harsher, more pronounced. I can't see the trees on the other side of the water.

Jay lets out a big breath and stretches out his fingers over the wheel. "Hey, so—I didn't really answer your question very well, last time. When you asked if I like anyone." His eyes dart over to me before looking down at his hands, dark lashes like a skittish butterfly. "There's . . . something else I wanted to say. About that."

My skin prickles all over. "What?"

Some skeletal branches fall in our pool of light, reaching toward the sky. It reminds me of an X-ray of lungs I saw once, and I picture my own right now, expanding, contracting. Trying to seem normal and steady.

"Before we moved here . . ." He sighs. "I haven't really told anyone this. But it seems like you can keep a secret."

He takes a deep, gulping breath, and his words come tumbling out in a rush. "My dad was cheating on my mom. And . . . I knew, and I didn't know if telling her would make things worse. I just wanted to avoid it, not think about it. I tried not to be home a lot, I was spending a lot of time with my girlfriend.

"And I came home one day and—everyone said it was an accident, after. Her doctor prescribed something to sleep, I guess, but—my mom was just on the floor, passed out, and . . ." He swallows, with difficulty. "I've honestly never been more scared in my life."

The branches outside clatter as a gust of wind blows through.

"So I broke up with my girlfriend. I told myself I can't get distracted—I have to *be there*. Be *responsible*." His voice is ragged. "I guess that's why I feel like I can't afford to like anyone."

"I'm sorry that happened to you," I say, voice thick, too many feelings fighting in my chest. All at once, I'm so exhausted. It's like something just collided hard with my chest, and I need to lie down. "Jay, why . . . Why are you telling me this now?"

He looks frozen for a second, at a loss.

"I should probably get back," I whisper.

We're quiet the whole way home, like he's still trying to find his answer.

He parks in his driveway, and I'm halfway out the door when he exclaims, "You should come over for dinner!"

The pleading look on his face, and how breathless he sounds—I can't process what he's saying.

"My mom wanted to have you over," he adds. "To thank you. For getting my grades up."

What am I supposed to *do* with this now? I hate the way my heart leaps at the idea of going over to his house.

"I'll check my schedule," I say, and slam the door shut between us.

Back in bed, I look at my phone again, and there's a message waiting for me.

Jay Hayes: i told you because i trust you

This has to be the most intimate thing anyone has ever said to me.

I'm too scared to take a screenshot of it, so I read it ten more times before wiping it from my phone.

TWENTY-TWO

AFTER HOURS OF AGONIZING, I SETTLE ON WHAT TO WEAR TO MEET Jay's mom: black turtleneck, wide-leg orangey-brown pants. Something I could imagine myself wearing to a job interview, or a poetry reading, maybe. Then I spend the afternoon second-guessing my choice.

It's a Saturday, and I told Mom I'd be going to Suzy's for dinner. She wasn't really interested, busy in her office, waving me away with one hand.

But she'd kill me if she knew I was going to a boy's house. So I walk around the corner, like I'm going to Suzy's, and cut through other people's yards.

When I get there, it turns out Jay's backyard is ringed by a very inconvenient fence.

> Jay Hayes: where are you
> Jay Hayes: did you get lost
> Deedee Walters: i'm coming in the back
> Jay Hayes: ??

Jay comes out just in time to see me struggling over the fence and lurching onto the snowy ground.

"It's always like this with you, huh," he says, shoulders shaking, offering me a hand up. "Nothing can be simple."

I get up without taking his hand. "Don't make fun of me."

"But how will I feel joy then?"

We go inside, slipping off our shoes and heading into the kitchen.

Gemma runs full force into Jay and hugs him around the middle. "Make me a snack!"

Jay shakes his head. "We're eating soon. Mom made thịt kho."

The way he says it, easily, the sounds from his mouth that I couldn't hold in mine—why does this make me like him even more? Comparing it to the way I plow over the vowels of *adobo*, with my sloppy American *o*'s.

"Ughhh, I'm so hungry! I hate you!" Gemma runs out of the room, feet pattering on the stairs.

Jay sighs and opens the fridge. The outside of the door is a jumble of reminders, coupons, and Gemma's drawings, all stuck on with magnets, held together with clips. There's nothing on our fridge at home.

I peer around Jay's shoulder. "It's definitely haunted in there," he says, closing it again and opening the freezer. "Ghosts of all the expired vegetables I've killed."

"You murderer."

"They're going to come for me one day."

He takes out some bread, already cut lengthwise, removes the plastic it's wrapped in, and pops it in the toaster oven.

My heart is pounding, thinking about how his mom is going to be here any minute.

When the oven dings, Jay puts the bread onto a plate and opens the cabinet over the counter. Bottles of fish sauce catch my eye. He pulls out a smaller bottle with a yellow label, MAGGI printed in a red bubble, and splashes the bread with it.

We go upstairs to Gemma's door, where he knocks twice. "Surprise for you on the counter."

The door opens and Gemma darts past us, a blur heading for the kitchen.

"Whoa!" a woman's voice exclaims as Gemma hurtles by.

Jay's mom is at the foot of the stairs, cheeks rosy from the cold. "Hey, kids, what's cooking? Oh right, nothing yet." She laughs at her own joke and shrugs off her winter coat.

She's different than I expected, based on the last time I saw her. Something about her illuminates the entire room—people must describe her as "the life of the party" all the time. She wears her clothes like she enjoys choosing them: a silk blouse tucked into black skinny jeans, and electric-blue earrings dangling against her new pixie cut.

She gets a big bowl out of the fridge and starts reheating the food on the stove.

Dinner is a stew with caramelized pork and eggs, warm and comforting, broth over rice. Snow is coming down out the window, and Gemma's eating like it's going out of style. Jay is laughing at a story his mom is telling, interjecting like they're friends. *No, but you— Wait, remember that time—*

It's obvious they actually like each other. Things might get bad sometimes, but there's this warmth there, strange to me. So unbearably cozy with them around the table, I want to crawl out of my skin.

"Deedee, I'm so glad you could help Jason get his act together!" his mom says, nudging him in the arm. "He's so smart, he deserves to get into a good school."

I'm smiling, cheeks tight, wanting her to like me.

She turns her water glass around in one hand. "Where I grew up it was pretty rural, not very diverse, you know? When I got to college it was so different. I was in the Southeast Asian Students Association, and we hosted these movie nights— Oh!" She looks for something in her phone and hands it to me. "He wanted me to show you this."

It's a movie poster, in an older style, a drawing so lifelike it could be a photo. A woman's head flying through the night sky, wild black hair and deathly pale skin, fangs brandished and dripping with blood. From the neck down, there's just a cluster of organs and dangling intestines, tomato-red, fleshy, disgusting.

"Oh my God, I'm obsessed." So the strange things in my head aren't alone in the world. Somehow it makes me feel more real to myself, more solid.

"It's a Thai movie, about the krasue." She smiles as I hand her phone back. "Horror movie nights were my favorite."

I find the poster online to text Suzy, and she replies with a string of heart-eye emojis.

Jay's mom nudges his shoulder. "Yeah, he's such a good kid. Handsome like his father, too."

He breathes in sharp and his shoulders go up, but his mom doesn't seem to notice.

"I think he's handsome like himself." The words just pop out of my mouth, and then my face feels like a small furnace.

"Right," his mom says, with a tight smile. "That's what I meant."

Jay's looking down, trying to suppress a laugh. He gets up to do the dishes, and it's too unbearably awkward to stay here, so I follow. "Go sit down," he says, nodding back toward the dining room.

"No, let me help."

He grudgingly hands me a dish towel.

Standing this close, he smells like . . . something woodsy, smoky. Is he wearing . . . *cologne*? Did he put it on because I'd be here?

He glances at me from the corner of his eye, but when he notices me looking back, his eyes dart away.

"So. That history test coming up." He turns off the tap, dries his hands.

"Oh yeah, uh . . . I need to review for it."

"Yeah, we could . . ." He scratches the back of his head. "Do that. Together. If you want."

His mom calls from the table, "Look at you, so studious!"

"Yeah, um, let's go upstairs," Jay mumbles.

We get up to his room and he shuts the door behind us.

My palms are sweating. *I'm in a boy's room! Mom is going to know somehow! She's going to kill me!*

"Your mom is okay with that?" I point at the closed door.

He shrugs. Maybe the fact that he works makes things different.

It's mostly a mess in here—clothes and stacks of manga on the floor, empty energy drink cans clustered on the desk—but his bed is neatly made, blue plaid blanket tucked around the mattress. Three glow-in-the-dark stars are stuck to one corner of the ceiling, between his desk and the window. Maybe they're a reminder of the world outside to tide him over, late at night when he feels like he's going to meld with his screen.

There's a framed photo of him and Alex on the little shelf above his desk. One of his mom and Gemma and—I guess that must be Candace? And there are the Polaroids of us, taped up on the wall by his open laptop.

Apparently, I'm a member of a pretty small club.

The options for places to sit cycle through my head—desk chair, bed, desk chair, bed—and my brain short-circuits, and I sit on the floor.

Jay laughs and sits down next to me. "So you think I'm 'handsome like myself'?" He adds those air quotes with relish.

"Less gloating, more studying." I'm flipping aggressively through my textbook. "Your mom is different than I expected."

"People are complicated. She gets mad sometimes, but—I mean, I think if you added up all the bad things in my life, it wouldn't get close to what she's been through."

"Is that how it works?" I snap my textbook shut. "You said something, a while ago—the first time we went to the pond. About how the past can be useful. Is that what you meant?"

"Oh, uh . . ." Jay picks at the carpet like we're on a field and he wants to rip up some blades of grass. "I guess . . . my mom just tells these stories. About how she was on her own a lot, while her parents were working all the time. She basically raised her siblings? And her dad would get mad a lot—just kind of explode, yelling, throwing things. Really small things set him off."

This isn't a story about me, so why does it feel like he's reaching inside me now, jamming his fingers in my spine?

"But after what he'd been through, I mean—they were refugees. They barely made it here. People they came over with didn't make it." He takes a deep breath and lets it go again. "I guess it's just good to remember my life is easy, compared to hers."

The shame flares up, blooms out in my chest.

All my days, like punishment!

"Okay, well—maybe I don't want to understand my mom better."
I'm whispering, but my heart stops a little, hearing myself say that
out loud. "Because then I'll just have to be okay with feeling like this
forever."

He puts a hand on my arm, and I jerk away from him. "Feeling
like what?"

There's your sad face, ruining it!

Who would want to come home and see that?

"Like I'm *cursed*."

He looks confused, but I can't tell him, I can't explain. I could really
use a diversion.

My eyes land on the manga left open, face down on his bedside
table. I scramble onto the bed and reach for it.

And next to it, on the nightstand—there's the note I wrote him.
I like talking to you. Like he wants it to be the first thing he sees when
he wakes up.

I can't think about that right now, so I roll onto my back, holding
the book open over my head. Some panels of a guy racing his car down
a mountain pass.

Jay climbs up and reaches for it.

He's laughing, and then I am, too, holding the book out over the
side of the bed away from him, so he has to sprawl across me to get it.

"What is going *on* right now?" he says.

"This is the same as—" *That show that made you cry.*

Jay grabs it and tosses it across the room.

And then maybe his arms get tired, because he slumps onto me,
face buried in my shoulder.

"Leave me alone," he says, all muffled.

He's, uh, lying on me. Quite the mixed message.

My heart is beating so forcefully in my chest, it must be shaking the bed.

"I think I know why you cried," I say through gritted teeth, staring at the ceiling. Maybe I want to hurt him a little now. "That time at Alex's house."

"Can we please not talk about the time I cried in public for no reason?" he says into my shoulder. "Thank you for your support."

"You're just going and going all the time, like, *This is fine, this is fine, this is fine.* Then when you see how things could be different, for a second—that's when you fall apart."

Jay props himself up on his forearms, hovering close, eyes flitting around my face. I want so badly for him to kiss me—I wonder if he can see it. There's this twist to his mouth, like I'm making him suffer.

The air between us feels like when a lightning storm is gathering, full of pent-up energy, ready to spark.

I'm not even thinking now. I reach out and touch his cheek, so warm against my palm. He closes his eyes and presses into my hand, like he's soaking it in, and it's not enough.

Then his lips meet mine, and I'm kissing him back, hand behind his head, and our tongues find each other. I've never felt something like this before, that travels through my entire body. To my spine, to my heart. To places I'm ashamed to think about. Every tiny detail of this moment feels so big, it swallows the entire world. The way his hair feels between my fingers. The way he tastes, like mint and salt and Red Bull. The way his lips are just slightly chapped.

A surge of relief washes over me because I've wanted this for so long.

And then his mom calls from downstairs. "Jason? Can you help me with this?"

And he's scrambling off the bed, like he was dreaming and just jolted awake.

"Shit, I'm sorry." His hand goes to his hair. "I'm sorry! Fuck, I'm sorry, I shouldn't—I shouldn't have done that."

He sounds panicked, and I hate it.

"Are you okay? I—I made a mistake, I—" Jay stammers out.

The rawest feeling of my entire life, and he thinks it was a mistake.

"Just pretend it didn't happen!" I snap. There's too much heat and pressure behind my eyes.

I could have lived with it! I could have hidden how I felt! But now he knows, and I feel so impossibly stupid. I'm out the door, down the stairs, before he can see me cry.

"Deedee, wait!" he calls after me.

I grab my coat and shoes. I'm so mad, I don't even care—I'll risk the front door.

As I'm running back across the street, I can still feel the imprint of his lips on mine, like the shapes that linger in your eyes after a light goes out.

TWENTY-THREE

Jay Hayes: deedee
Jay Hayes: can i talk to you
Jay Hayes: meet me tonight?
Jay Hayes: please

Hours later, we're parked in front of the convenience store, its neon sign washing the interior of the car a soft blue. I twist around in my seat, and through the store's plate-glass windows, I can see Jay joking with whoever is working the overnight shift.

The sliding doors part for him, and I turn back around, arms crossed, staring at the empty road. He gets back into the car, plastic bag rustling as he takes out a can of coffee, an energy drink—green-apple flavor—and a big bag of salt-and-vinegar potato chips.

I cross my arms tighter, so he keeps the chips in his lap and settles the coffee in the cup holder.

I can practically feel him studying me, trying to figure out what to do. I hate being a problem for him to solve.

"Look, I'm—" He heaves a sigh. "That was—"

He was able to make small talk just fine a second ago. Why can't he get three words out in front of me?

Jay looks so good right now, it's sickening. Tousled hair, pretty eyes, kissable mouth—*and I know it now, it's not just in theory!* But more than that, I feel *soft* when I look at him. I want to wrap him in a blanket, hug him tight when he's sad. Ask him more weird questions so I can hear his weird answers. Make him laugh every day of his life.

I can't stand it. It makes me feel like a sitting duck.

He lifts his hands and drops them in his lap again. "Do you want to drive?"

"Sure." Maybe it will give me something else to feel right now.

We switch seats, and I adjust the mirrors, push the seat closer to the wheel, drawing out the time I don't have to look at him.

I was wrong about him. He doesn't like me like that. Maybe he got confused, for a second, but he said it himself—*it was a mistake!*

Jay clears his throat.

"Just forget it, okay?" I snap, still fiddling with the mirror. "It was one kiss. It's not that deep."

"I guess, I just thought, you . . ." Jay moistens his lips, and his Adam's apple bobs up and down, skin tinted this melancholy shade of blue. "I thought, you felt . . . and I just— Right now, I don't know if I can be . . ."

"Who says I *want* you to be anything? What makes you think I even *like* you?"

Jesus, why did I say that? It's like Mom's voice popped out of my mouth.

151

Jay looks a bit like he just got punched in the gut.

But I don't have time to think about that, because right then, over his shoulder, through the window, I see Mom's used beige Mercedes passing on the road.

Everything slows. Jay's saying something else, but I can't hear him. Heart pounding in my throat, I start the car and reverse out of the spot.

"Uh—what—" Jay says.

I pull out and follow her, press the gas to catch up.

"Where are you—"

"That's my mom," I snap. "She goes somewhere. Late at night, a couple times a week. I've been—" I sigh. "That's why I wanted you to teach me how to drive."

She's turning onto the highway, too far ahead, taillights disappearing around the bend. I'm going to lose her.

"Hey, easy on the curve!" Jay grips the door handle.

We get onto the empty highway, and I let up on the gas.

"I wanted to do something about my problems," I say, eyes fixed on the red dots of light up ahead. "Because I can't get answers about her just by asking. And . . . you said I should try to understand her, so . . ."

"Uhhhh, I definitely did not say to . . . do whatever this is?"

"Fine, judge me, Mr. Son of the Year!"

"Wow. *Wow.*" He's leaning to the side, gasping for air, like this is so unbearably funny.

Dark forest whizzes by us on either side, lanes empty.

I don't want to think about what he was saying, or how it makes me feel. And if I can't have more of all the things I want, maybe I can at least get some answers. Some sign that there's more to the story than just: I'm bad, I ruin good things, and it's all my fault.

We're trailing her now, a few car lengths back.

"You're being super obvious," Jay says. "She's going to notice."

"What, are you helping me now?"

"When have I *not* been helping you?" He scoffs, waves a hand toward the windshield. "You probably want to fall back a little."

I ease up on the gas, and her car glides off ahead, still visible but not close.

Lampposts flash by us, and the light in the car ebbs and flows, moon half in shadow above. The highway expands, two lanes, then three, then four.

Jay's been staring at the road, not talking. His arms are crossed around his middle, like his stomach hurts.

"Did you even—" He lets out a rough breath. "So this was . . . actually just about *this*, the whole time? About seeing where your mom goes?"

The moment he said *I made a mistake,* and the searing embarrassment I felt—it keeps looping and looping in my head.

"Yeah. It was just about this." My fingers tighten around the wheel. "The whole time."

Then he's quiet, a crushed silence, while we speed through the night together again.

TWENTY-FOUR

Mom's car slows up ahead, turn signal on. We exit, and I stay as far back as I can without losing sight of her.

She turns into a parking lot, and I loop the block and come back around, pulling into the strip mall after she's already gone inside.

There's a neon sign, glowing pink, advertising a 24-hour karaoke place.

So this is where she goes? Does she meet someone here?

I let go of the wheel, flex my sore fingers.

There aren't that many cars here. I guess it's not that popular at this hour, even on a Saturday night.

"Well?" Jay almost sounds amused, in a distant way. "What now?"

"Why do *you* care?"

He shrugs. "Guess I'm along for the ride."

I get out of the car, make my way to the front door, and he follows. There's no sign of Mom through the glass—just a front counter, and a hallway leading to the rooms.

I open the door and freeze when the person at the front desk says hello.

But Jay cuts in for me. "Hey, how's it going? First time here—how long have you guys been in business?" I guess this is where he's in his element, making small talk with strangers.

While they're chatting, I move down the hall, listening to the music coming through the doors, fear inching up like floodwater.

And my throat tightens, hearing Mom's voice on the other side. I crouch down, so she can't see me through the little window, and listen.

It takes me a while to recognize the song, but then I remember, in a flash, when she hits the chorus: She'd sing along to this on the radio, sometimes, when I was a kid, and we were driving around town. Said it reminded her of my dad.

A bone-deep sadness comes over me.

Then Jay's beside me, peeking through the window, for a second, ducking away again. Another thing I was afraid to do.

"Is anyone with her?" I ask.

"She's by herself."

I'm so stupid. There's no mystery. Nothing to find.

Just me and her, and her loneliness. How bad I am, and how broken everything is.

Jay nods toward the window. "So she does this because she can't sleep?"

"I guess."

Of course she's not hiding anything important. She's just . . . sad? Restless? Needs to get away from me?

I'm so disappointed. If there were a mystery to solve, with clues, and an answer at the end—maybe everything could be different.

The music stops, and there's some shuffling on the other side of the door. Jay pops up again, peeking through the little window.

"Oh shit—*run!*"

I take off through the front door, Jay right behind me.

But once we're outside, it's too far to the car, on the other side of the lot. She'll see us. Two kids running, suspicious as hell.

He and I must realize it at the same time, because he presses me into the alcove by the door, right as the bell jingles and Mom comes outside.

Jay's covering me from view with his body, his palms pressed to the wall, the gray concrete tinted salmon pink from the neon sign. His chest moves in and out a fraction of an inch from mine, breathing so carefully. He's straining to keep his head turned away, so I'm staring at his cheek, his neck.

Mom's leaning into her car, fishing around for something, dome light on. There are too many feelings piled up, chaotic in my chest. I'm scared of getting caught, scared of what Jay's thinking right now. He's so close, I can smell him—not just his soap, the ocean breeze, but what he actually smells like, under that. The scent I don't have words to describe, like exhilaration and safety at the same time. I have this overwhelming urge to press my lips into the tensed muscle right under his jaw.

"Is she gone?" he whispers.

"Not yet."

But then Mom must find whatever she was looking for, because she turns the light off, gets in, and starts the engine.

When her car turns onto the street, out of sight, I finally say: "Okay. Coast is clear."

Jay takes a few steps backward and lets a long breath out, clearing his lungs. He plants his hands over his hips, elbows out, like he just ran a mile.

I rub my arm, trying to calm down. "Why did you do that?"

"I don't know, instinct?" He sounds irritated now. "Give me the keys, please." He looks so done with me as I drop them into his out-stretched hand.

"But she's—"

"Look, I'm not going to race her home. We'll get there after her anyway at this point. Better not to arrive right when she does." He stuffs the keys in his pocket, pulls out his wallet, and looks inside. "Since we came all this way, I'm going to do karaoke, at least."

I guess he must register how panicked I look, because he closes his eyes again and sighs. "I'll just do one song. You can wait here or come in, I don't care."

Then he's gone, back inside, chime sounding behind him.

What else am I going to do? I follow him in.

The lights are dim in here, and we're soaked in the faint blue glow of the big screen waiting for us to make a selection.

Jay takes a while, scrolling through the songs, back turned, like he's trying to pretend I'm not here. Then he stops on one and breathes out sharp, the ghost of a laugh. The words *Dancing in the Dark* come onto the screen. The music surrounds us, up-tempo drums and eighties synths.

Words come onto the screen, and he croons into the mic, raspy and tender. It surprises me a little, like he's a different person, all of a sudden. His voice breaks, and he laughs at himself.

And then he really belts it out, eyes squeezed shut and neck straining as he yells into the mic, all this pent-up emotion rising to the surface.

The parts about being tired.

About being sick of his face.

About having a broken heart.

He tosses his shoulders around, like he's trying to shake off everything weighing on him right now.

Somehow, I just know right then—it's truly what he looks like when he doesn't give a fuck about how anyone sees him. That he wouldn't ever let anyone see him like this, during the day.

Jay's voice drops to almost a whisper as the song ends, and there's a little sax riff, absurd and kind of soothing, this late at night.

Then it's over, and he puts the mic down. Takes a minute, staring at the wall.

"Okay," he says, "let's go home."

The silence has me so on edge, the entire ride back.

Jay keeps sighing, over and over. It's grinding on my nerves.

"What do you want to say?" I snap, finally.

He sucks in a sharp breath, lets it go. "I mean, I guess I was wrong, but . . . I thought, for a while, that you actually . . ."

Jay hesitates, swallows again. Moistens his lips in his mouth.

Say it, you coward!

"It was stupid." He shakes his head, jaw clenched. "Maybe it's for the best, anyway."

I hate everything. I don't care, anymore. I almost want Mom to catch me.

But I slip back into the house, and everything is quiet. From her room, I can hear her snoring. She must have gone straight to sleep.

TWENTY-FIVE

Jay Hayes: hey so my grades have improved, i don't need tutoring
   anymore
Jay Hayes: and it seems like you pretty much know how to drive.
   aced the slow speed chase bonus category
Jay Hayes: so i think we're good! see you around

I don't delete the texts right away. I keep rereading them because they look different each time. As the anger burns off, and the days pass, and I keep thinking about him, pressing me into the wall. How crushed he sounded, once my mom was gone and the task at hand was over. How he seemed to deflate completely.

The image of him loops in my head: eyes closed, mouth open, so focused on pushing out the sound. Singing about his broken heart.

"I feel like we haven't hung out in forever," Suzy says, leaning forward over the wheel as she takes the winding road up the hill to Kevin's house. "I missed you. Sorry I've been so . . . caught up in things."

The house comes into view, three stories with a wraparound porch and a turret, pale yellow with white trim.

"If the paint job wasn't so cheerful, I'd think this was the Clue mansion," I say.

"It was Colonel Mustard, that bastard, I just know it." Suzy pulls in behind a Prius on the side of the driveway. "Ugh, shit. Can you google how to park on a hill and tell me what it says?"

Wheels safely angled and parking brake secured, we trudge up the winding drive. I'm freezing, hugging my jacket around me, wearing this glittery green dress made of next to nothing. And Suzy's boots, for strength.

Suzy helped me buy this dress online. I'd been looking at it for a while, the kind of thing I've always wanted to wear but never thought I could pull off. I imagined I'd feel like someone else in it, showing up to this party that Jay will probably be at. But now things are ruined, and I feel too much like myself, awkward and playing dress-up.

Suzy is talking about Alex again. "Everyone keeps saying he's never dated anyone this long. It makes me feel so . . . conspicuous. But also . . . kind of special? Is that bad?"

"Mm . . . I don't think so?"

I should just tell her. Just spit it out. *Jay kissed me, and now we're not speaking!* But there's that fear again, shrinking my brain to the size of a walnut, and I can't get the words out.

Alex meets us in the foyer, wearing a suit like it's normal. He grabs Suzy in a bear hug and lifts her off her feet, and she shrieks and kicks a little.

He offers to take our coats, and I'm embarrassed, sliding mine off, exposing the dress's plunging back. Bold move when standing up straight feels like an impossible assertion of my existence.

Suzy tugs me by the arm into the living room, where Alex's friends are standing around holding plastic cups, trying to talk over the music.

"Hellooo babe alert!" Beth yells when she sees Suzy. She raises her cup over her head, arms spread wide to give Suzy a hug.

And there's Jay, off to the side, where he always seems to be. Wearing a white shirt, dark jacket and slacks, no tie. He digs two fingers under the collar, tugs like it's attacking him.

There's a tightness between my shoulder blades, too much warmth in my chest.

Suzy's already on the other side of the room, talking with Beth and her friends. A wave of laughter washes over to me, and my stomach twinges. Maybe she only brought me along out of guilt.

Jay's staring at me now, and I'm not sure I like it.

My knees are shaky, and my heart aches, but I can't just stand here. So I take out my phone.

Deedee Walters: it's not polite to stare

It's funny, watching him read it. Seeing him laugh a little and bite his lip while he writes back.

Jay Hayes: you make it hard not to

What does this mean now?

I cross the room to him, and he looks a little terrified.

The noise around us kind of falls away, just Jay and me and this gulf between us. Just the uneasy rise and fall of his chest, as he looks down into the red cup he's holding, a little pink in his cheeks.

"You look nice," I say, voice low so only he can hear.

"I borrowed this from Alex." He lifts the jacket by the lapel, frowning at his own chest. "I don't know, it feels unnatural."

"I feel like I'm wearing a costume."

"Suits you, though." He laughs and squeezes the back of his neck with one hand. "Aren't you scared about being seen with me?"

"I'll live dangerously."

Jay swirls the liquid in his cup. I grab it from him and take a sip. It's an energy drink. He really does live on this stuff.

"Look who showed up!" Kevin is suddenly on the other side of me. "Where have you been hiding?"

He rests a hand on my bare back, sending my skin tingling where I don't want it to.

I move away, cheeks burning.

Kevin steps closer, oblivious. "Aw, don't do that thing you do. Getting really quiet, hiding behind your hair."

That sets my teeth on edge, coming here tonight, hoping to be different than I usually am and getting this reflected back at me instead. I hate the idea that people think I'm hiding.

"Man, fuck you," I say, tone light, because I'm nervous about how he'll get if I actually upset him.

I scoop my hair up into a ponytail and tie it high on my head with the elastic that's always around my wrist.

Jay's eyes are on me while I do it. He looks disappointed.

"See," Kevin says, "I can actually see your face now. You're cute. Look at those freckles."

I feel so exposed, and my face is so warm.

"Wow, you're *so* observant," I say.

"Yeah, I know. I'm a sensitive guy. I always notice you." He touches my arm. "What's your ethnicity? You have, like, an exotic look, you know?"

Just when I might forget about it, there's a reminder, like someone snapped my skin with a rubber band.

"Dude," Jay says, holding his chin up, a warning in his tone. "You're making her uncomfortable. Maybe you should back off."

"Or you'll *what*?" Kevin says.

My God, I'm so mortified. I'm looking around the room in a panic to see if Suzy's watching.

"I can speak for myself, okay?" I snap. I don't want Jay to stand up for me. I don't want to need him at all.

Jay looks stunned, mouth half open.

Kevin snorts. "What are you, her big brother?"

My face heats up. I want to shout, *We're not even the same kind of Asian!*

"Nope!" Jay lifts his hands, shakes his head. "Definitely not."

He moves sideways through the crush of people and joins Josh, Ted, and Alex, standing in a cluster a few feet away.

I force a smile. "Great party," I say, pushing past Kevin, fleeing with Jay's drink into the kitchen and tossing it down the sink.

TWENTY-SIX

IT WAS A BAD IDEA TO COME. *WHAT WERE YOU EXPECTING!*

I run up the stairs and down a dimly lit hallway, shaking my hair out of the elastic.

The hall dead-ends at a door, so I open it. A spacious closet, rows of winter coats tucked toward the back. Like where Professor Plum would stash the body.

There are footsteps behind me, and the back of my neck prickles.

"Boo," Jay says.

When I turn around, he's alarmingly close.

"You asshole!" I shove him in the chest. "Are you following me?"

He puts a hand on the spot where I touched him, near his heart. "Oh no, I just . . . have the same taste in deserted hallways." His hand migrates to the back of his head. "Yes, obviously, I'm following you."

"Why?!"

Jay makes a searching, throaty sound that wants to be a word but can't get it to work out, exactly. He closes his eyes, frustrated.

I cross my arms. "You seriously came after me just to stand here and not talk to me again."

"Do you like it when he talks about your freckles?" he fumes, opening his eyes exaggeratedly wide. "Wow, *so unexpected* to see those on a face like yours."

"You don't get to have an opinion about this!" I throw my hands in the air. "What even *am* I to you?"

Jay scoffs and looks at the wood-paneled ceiling, like I've said something outrageous. His tongue makes a bulge on the inside of his cheek.

"You know," he says, carefully. "For a while, I thought you didn't like me like that, you just needed something from me. And this was . . . this is safe, this is fine. You need something from me, I need something from you. I have an excuse. And no one has to know how spending time with you makes me feel."

Jay looks down at the fancy rug running down the middle of the hallway, hands in his pockets. "And then, I guess, I started to feel . . . *too much*, but I was trying to ignore it, because I felt so guilty. I started to think . . . maybe this means something to you, too. And—I got swept up, and—and I couldn't really ignore it anymore." He huffs out a big breath. "But then it was like we circled back around to where we started, and it smacked me in the face. Like, *ohh, okay.* You're just using me to get what you want, after all. And, fine, great. That's—that's probably better, for everyone. But the things you said . . ."

Jay squeezes his eyes shut and shakes his head. "I felt so stupid. Like, did you even care about me at all? As a person, not someone who can do things for you."

The anger I felt is evaporating, and there's this mounting panic, climbing up my throat. *I'm bad I'm unlovable I ruined everything again!*

But I've been thinking about it, for days. How I feel sometimes, when Suzy breezes past something important to me. When Mom tells me I'm wrong for how I feel. What I wish they would say.

I scream silently into my cupped hands, drop them again.

"Jay, those things I said . . . that's not how I feel about you." I take a deep breath and slow down a little, forcing myself to meet his eye. "I can see how . . . that was fucked up. I'm sorry I said those things. I'm sorry I made you feel like that."

He laughs a little, uncomfortable, and half turns away from me, wipes at his eyes. "Wow. Sorry. It's just nice to hear someone say that."

"You . . . mean a lot to me." I take a deep gulp of air, getting ready for what I'm about to say. "I was hurt, and I wanted to cover up how I felt, because . . . you said it was a mistake, and—" I have to stop, I'm so frustrated. My own tears are starting to form, and I have to bite them back down. "It doesn't feel great, how you try to have it both ways. Holding me close and far at the same time."

I'm going to be sick. This has to be the first time since I was a little kid that I've gotten mad at someone, *out loud*, for how they *make me feel*. As though that should even matter to anyone.

Jay lets out a long breath slowly, the way you're supposed to when you're underwater.

"Yeah," he says, nodding. "You're right."

I'm right?!

Jay takes a few steps closer and puts his hands on my arms. My head is swimming in a feeling I can't name.

"I really like you, Deedee." He looks so exhausted now, eyes half open, gazing at me. "Do you know how many times I wanted to kiss you? And held back."

It's going to hurt, it's going to hurt, the way Mom doesn't want to buy flowers because they're just going to die anyway—*what do I think is going to happen?*

In my head, flowers explode into bloom.

I grab the front of his shirt and pull him backward into the closet.

"Wow, okay!" He laughs as the door closes.

"Hi," I say.

For a moment, together in the dark, we're just voices and thoughts without bodies.

And then my face is buried in his neck, breathing in his smell. His hands are on my back, giving me the goose bumps I want.

We're kissing, and he's moving forward, hands on my hips, and I'm moving back, and the coat hangers rattle. He's pressing me against the wall, and the smell of cedar surrounds us, the smooth wood touching my back where my dress is cut low.

All the pent-up nervous energy rushes out of me, crashing into him, like there's a time limit to learn every inch of each other's mouths. When we come up for air, I almost feel like that one time I got drunk last year, when I tagged along with Suzy to a college party in Eastleigh.

He takes a step back and a weak yellow bulb comes on. The cord dances when he lets go. "I missed your face," he says.

Leaning against the wall, I slide to the floor, carefully so I don't flash him.

"Just because you were jealous of Kevin?"

"No." He pushes the coats so they're all bunched up away from us and sits next to me. "I miss your face all the time."

We're quiet for a minute, just breathing next to each other. I roll my head toward him, and he's already looking back at me. The world tilts from that perspective, like we're lying on the ground next to each other again.

"To answer your question: No, I hated it when Kevin talked about my *exotic look*." I gaze up into the thicket of coats and put on a goofy voice. "I'm an exotic animal, you'll have a hard time getting me through customs."

Jay's shoulder bumps mine. "I'm an exotic car, I'm unreliable and high-maintenance."

I laugh, loud and crass, maybe not even at what he said, exactly. "You seem like the least high-maintenance person to me. You don't really ask anything of anyone. Seems like you just ask a lot of yourself."

He groans and leans forward, arms covering his head. But when he peeks out at me, he's smiling.

"Do you ever feel conflicted?" I ask. "About being more than one thing."

He drums his fingers on his thighs. "I feel conflicted about a lot of things, I guess. But I try not to think about it."

I'm a little too warm under my skin, bracing for him to judge me.

"That was important for my mom, though. Knowing where you're from," he says. "She really wanted us to learn some Vietnamese so we can talk to our relatives. She's always cooking something, telling a story about it. Where she learned about it, what it means to her."

A little wave of jealousy washes over me, but it's a gentler kind, soft and cloying, like nostalgia for something I never even knew.

"I don't know, I guess . . . identity, finding yourself . . ." Jay shrugs. "I'm right here, what is there to find?"

The memory of the first time I saw him in daylight comes back to me—standing in the convenience store parking lot, joking about his quarter-life crisis.

"Why did you change your name?" I ask.

"Oh, uh—" He rubs his arm and looks embarrassed again. "Because my name is just . . . literally my dad's name. Front to back. I guess—except for my middle name. It's my mom's name, her family's name. But I feel kind of . . . awkward, using it. Like, who do I think I am, using a name I'm not even sure I'm pronouncing correctly."

So I'm not alone, exactly. My hand feels its way along the floor-boards between us and covers his.

The muffled sounds from the party drift through the closed door, from downstairs—someone whooping, the thumping of a bass beat on the stereo.

Jay flips my hand and laces his fingers between mine. It makes me feel warm all over, like wearing his sweatshirt did.

"So what happens now?" he whispers.

"You're asking me? You're the one who didn't want to."

"I think . . . this much is okay. I'm doing okay with everything I need to do. And you don't want anyone to know anyway, so." Jay pinches his neck absently, and the skin turns red. "We could just . . . keep hanging out like we were. But different. If you still want to keep it a secret."

Each way I flip it over, I feel like I'm trying to memorize all the contours of a strange object, but by the time I get around to one side I forget what was on the other. It's better for things to just stay the way they are. "Is that okay?"

He swallows so his throat bobs, looking at the floor. "You know I'm not big on telling people things."

There are voices in the hall, then, two of them, getting louder and closer. Unhappy, from the way they rise and fall. Jay reaches up, pulls the cord, and we're back in darkness.

"Do you know what she said about me? Do you even care?" *Oh shit, it's Suzy.* She sounds like she's struggling to keep her voice down.

I don't know why, but I never imagined her fighting with Alex. Whenever I thought of their relationship, it was like one of those show bedrooms at Ikea, too perfect because no one really lives there.

"Is it that big a deal?" Alex says.

I want to yell, *Can't you hear how upset she is? It must be a big deal!*

"You're always looking for something to be upset about," he says.

"Are you fucking serious?!" Her footsteps move away from us again.

"Wait, okay? Suzy. Hang on."

I put my ear to the door to make sure they're gone. Jay's fingers graze my arm, but I'm already peeking outside.

"I'm going to see if she's okay," I say, scrambling into the hall.

I'm running through this ridiculous house, opening doors, smoothing my hair down so it doesn't look like I was just in a closet, furtively making out. There's the room where Alex left our coats, and Suzy's still with mine, so I grab them in case she wants to leave.

Finally, I find her, sitting on a bench swing on Kevin's porch, face in her hands.

"Hey. What happened to you?" I nudge her shoulder with the hand that's carrying her jacket.

"Ugh." She sniffs and shakes her head.

"I think it might be time to watch *Gremlins* again." It's her comfort movie.

She nods. "It's time."

We pick our way down the slushy driveway, and when we get into her car with its nubby gray seats and close the doors, the overhead light shrinks the world back down to something familiar, more manageable.

As we're rolling down the hill, I get a text.

Jay Hayes: did you leave?

"I heard Kevin was a dick to you," Suzy says. "Are you okay?"

"Um. It wasn't a big deal."

Deedee Walters: yeah but i'll see you soon

I stare at it before sending. Do I add a heart? Is that too much?

Suzy glances over at my phone glowing in my hands. "Did you . . . get someone's number?"

I laugh and send it with the heart.

TWENTY-SEVEN

WE'VE BEEN DRIFTING APART, BUT HERE SUZY IS, CLOSE AGAIN, ON THE couch next to me. Reacting like she hasn't seen this movie hundreds of times.

Something is definitely happening now, there's something to tell. Jay's fingers on my spine, his breath on my neck. His laugh reverberating in my chest.

Just say it now! *Jay kissed me. It wasn't the first time.*

But if I start, I don't know where it will lead. It's a loose thread on one end, and the other end is tied around my center, slimy and rotten and the color of pitch. And if you pull, it will unravel all the other things I don't want to tell her.

We get ready for bed, and I get comfortable on the cot her dad always sets up for me. And as usual, a few minutes after she turns off the light, she starts to talk.

"Are you asleep?"

"Have I ever said yes?"

"I have to tell you something."

Everything tenses. "What?"

"Alex and I had sex."

"Oh. Um. Congratulations?" I'm so distracted by being the world's worst friend, I can't think of a normal human thing to say.

"It was like a month ago. I don't know why I didn't tell you. I guess I . . . maybe I didn't want you to feel bad."

I hate being that person for her, but I try to cover it up, listening to myself laugh and hoping it sounds relaxed enough. "You don't have to tell me anything you don't want to."

Actually, funny you mentioned it, there's something I didn't tell you, too.
But the words get stuck in my throat.

"Do you feel different?" I choke out instead.

"Maybe. I don't know. Not really."

"Was it . . . good?"

"It was okay."

"Wow, glowing review."

She snorts and turns over in bed. "I don't know. Your mileage may vary!"

I'm laughing, but I feel like an asshole.

"Anyway. I just felt bad that I didn't tell you."

Actually, I kissed Jay.

But I can't stop thinking about what else I might have to say. When she asks why I'm doing this, why I've been keeping it to myself, why things with Mom are this way.

And to explain, I'll have to tell her. What I took from my mom, what I did to my dad. Why my mom can't ever love me the way Suzy's parents love her.

That shame spreads everywhere, locking up my body, turning my knuckles white. I can't get enough air in my lungs suddenly. I try to stay very still, under the blanket, taking shallow breaths.

Suzy sighs, across the room. "What am I even doing with these people?"

"What do you mean?"

"You know what Beth said about me? At the party, I overheard her." She sniffs a little. "I went out on this balcony, and she was talking to someone down below."

"What was she saying?"

"That I'm so fake. That I'm the weirdest choice Alex made so far— like it's her business to rate his girlfriends." She scoffs, hesitates for a second. "That I'm not even that pretty."

"Okay, obviously she's bad at, like, basic facts."

Suzy laughs and draws in a breath like she's about to say something important. But then she swallows it, and the moment passes.

Right when I'm almost drifting off to sleep, she pipes up again. "I miss you."

There's a dull stabbing feeling in my gut. "I'm right here."

"Yeah, but—" She sighs and rolls over. "Yeah. Good night."

What was she going to say? Anxiety pulses through me, but I try to keep my tone light. "Sweet dreams."

The only one who's ever chosen me, really, is Suzy.

When she had just moved to Rosemore, showed up to fourth grade and decided I was her people.

And now maybe Jay, but—did I dream it?

When I close my eyes the memory plays again, his mouth, his smell, his hands on my back, and I forget what I was thinking about.

TWENTY-EIGHT

"How far are we going?" I'm on the highway during the day for the first time, under a thick canopy of flat-bottomed clouds. They're unchanging in a way that makes it feel like we're the ones staying still, even as we hurtle terrifyingly through space.

Jay tells me to take the next exit, and I look over my shoulder, in the mirrors, back again. Wondering when to trust what I perceive. Anxious about not seeing everything I need to.

It's mid-January, and I've been his girlfriend for almost a month. Meeting up late at night, sneaking around after school, texting and talking when he went away to see family in Boston for the holidays. He sent me a photo with some of his cousins, kids of different heights and ages who all look vaguely like him, and I felt that soft ache again.

Mom left last night on a business trip, and now Jay and I have a whole glorious day together.

We're turning into another mall parking lot, a few towns away from ours, no chance we'll run into anyone we know.

As we walk up to the entrance, Jay holds my hand, his palm flush with mine, warm against the cold.

"Are you hungry?" he asks.

We stand in line to buy mini pretzel dogs from a kiosk in the hall, and I hug him around the middle, rest my head against his chest. He pays for the food before I can fight him on it, and we wander around, sharing the pretzel dogs until they're gone.

Passing a reflective window, I stop for a second, surprised at the sight of us, actually here, together.

Jay hugs me from behind, leans his chin on my shoulder, and our eyes meet in the mirror. I kind of can't believe we get to do this.

Jay's mom is out all day with Gemma, so we go back to his house. We're in his room, on his bed, and we're kissing.

I pull back a little and look at him, breathing like I just ran somewhere. "It's wild that feels so good, it's . . . just *mouths*? The things you eat with? Pressing against each other?"

He kisses a spot on my neck just under my jaw, tilting my head. This intense want passes through me, like wind rippling through tall grass.

"So this isn't good?" His lips linger there, warm breath on my skin.

"Don't make fun of me," I mumble.

"I love making fun of you." His nose nuzzles into the hollow behind my ear.

Then my earlobe is in his mouth and the feeling is so overwhelming, I could just slip away from myself, get lost in it forever.

You have so much more to lose than he does.

"Okay. Wow." I put a hand on his chest. "I think I need to stop."

Jay moves back, giving me some space. "Are you okay?"

I'm nodding, not wanting him to worry.

"We won't do anything you don't want to, okay?" His face is so filled with concern, it's hard to look at for too long. "Just tell me what you want."

It's so tense between my shoulder blades, the way it always gets when I'm stressed.

"Would you touch my back?" I whisper.

Jay slides a hand up the back of my shirt. It's so comforting, his warm fingers on this tender spot that's not used to being touched. I lean my head on his shoulder, hug him tight again.

I don't know how to absorb it, this good feeling. It's like a story I saw once on the news, about a flood in the desert. The ground gets so dry and parched, it hardens, and when it rains, people drown.

I'm trying to focus on my breathing, on his smell, his fingers by my spine.

But I can't relax. I miss this moment before it's even over. I'm so scared of it ending, already. Of this going away.

TWENTY-NINE

I'M PROBABLY CALLING HIM TOO MUCH. EVERY TIME MOM AND I FIGHT, every time I lie awake—I basically can't fall asleep without talking to Jay, now. I'll hear the clacking of his keys in the background, like low-quality ASMR. And then I'll remember, like waking from a dream, *Oh shit, he's working.*

"I'm bothering you. I should let you go."

And he'll sigh, a heavy sound, and say, "You're never bothering me," before we hang up.

Jay looks more tired during the day, dark circles under his eyes.

And at night, when I ask if anything is wrong, he always says he's fine.

I try to hold myself back when Jay goes to see his family for Tết, no more than three texts at once without a reply. But I break my self-imposed rule after half a day, dam overflowing with all my want and need. I can feel myself being *kind of intense*, but I don't really know how to stop, as I'm sitting there, spiraling about why he didn't text back right away.

I'm thinking so much about Jay all the time—the next time I'll see him, the next time we'll kiss—it's like I'm sleepwalking through the rest of my life, pretending to pay attention when Suzy's around. She acts like nothing was ever wrong with Alex now, talking about him extra, like she wants to make up for wavering.

"Deedee?" she says. "Are you even listening?"

So I say the last part of her story back to her to cover my tracks.

Jay and I never fight, but he gets really quiet sometimes. We're still avoiding each other at school—and I'm still too scared to change it—but I take different routes between classes, so I can go by his locker, get a glimpse.

And suddenly Beth is there a lot, hovering, talking to him. Touching his arm and laughing. I can't see his face, can't see his reaction—have to keep it moving, or it will be weird. But there's a chill in my bones, a new thought in my head, to circle and circle and keep me awake.

Even though I still hate her for what she said about Suzy, I can see why someone would like her. She seems fun, warm, in control of herself. Not a sinking weight like me.

I'm having trouble sleeping again, and headlights shine through my window. I get up to see Jay's car disappearing into the dark.

Another time, we're out at night together. I keep asking what he's thinking, and he keeps giving me a nonanswer, fewer and fewer syllables each time.

"You sure nothing's wrong? Did I do something?"

"Deedee," Jay snaps. "Not everything is about you."

That cuts straight through me.

"Sorry. Shit, I didn't mean—" He sighs, shakes his head. "I'm just stressed. With the same stuff. It's boring. Oh—"

Jay clicks on the dome light and reaches into his backpack. "Got you this."

It's a key chain with a little plush toy of a ghost attached. "For your car keys someday."

I'm so embarrassed, staring at this cute thing dangling from his hand. I didn't think he was much of a Valentine's Day person. "I didn't get you anything."

"I got it because I wanted to give it to you, not because I wanted something." He presses it into my palm. "That's kind of the point of a present."

And I feel bad after, for at least two things: that he probably went home thinking I didn't like it. And that I left him empty-handed.

I want to fix it, but I can't order things online. My brain overheats, thinking about how to get a ride from Mom or Suzy without explaining what I'm doing. So after school, I take a long walk to the convenience store and get a half dozen eggs.

I can't draw like him. Even though he still won't show me, from the little glimpses I get of his notebook, it's clear he has skills I don't. But I print out a picture of a fish-sauce bottle and trace it.

The next time we meet, I hand him the egg carton with a drawing taped to it, *Add fish sauce* written in bubble letters across the top.

He laughs until he's out of breath. "You're so cute."

"I have limited means to buy things discreetly, okay?"

"I'll cherish them," he says, and hugs the carton to his chest.

THIRTY

Suzy Jang: we're going to lunch! with alex's friends
Suzy Jang: you're coming
Suzy Jang: i'll be there in 15

It's a Saturday, and I'm out of excuses.

Jay's not one of the people sitting around the table when we get to the restaurant, and I try not to let the disappointment peek through. It's a sit-down place, on Main Street—colonial-style building, chairs with spindle backs, nice silverware.

Alex smiles and nods at me and gives Suzy's hand a squeeze on top of the table. Kevin and Josh are arguing about something, and Beth is telling a story while Ted nods along.

"You'll come to the lacrosse game tomorrow, right?" Suzy asks, squeezing my arm.

So I say I will, and try to ride out the conversation, laugh on cue, not wonder too much where Jay is. I order clam chowder and dump in two whole packets of oyster crackers. Suzy insists I share her fries and wrinkles her nose when I dip them in my soup. We finish and pay—it's a process, splitting up the bill, and Suzy directs it.

And right when we're about to leave—there's Jay, across the restaurant, walking in the door. I blink, rub my eyes, like maybe I'm hallucinating.

He's with some people I don't recognize. An Asian woman who's not his mom or his older sister. Who looks somewhere between them, in age. And a man, pale, tall, with curly brown hair.

Oh. *Oh.*

That has to be his dad.

When they're side by side, it does stand out more, how much they share. Jay's face shape. The way his unruly hair curls a little. The way he looks when he smiles from one side of his mouth. Even the features that look like his mom's have some of his dad mixed in—funny, how that works. From the side, his nose looks more like his dad's, from the front, like his mom's.

Jay notices me then and looks a little miserable. They're being seated, across the room, far from us.

Jay's dad must see Alex because he raises a hand and waves.

"Oh hey!" Like something happening in slow motion in a horror movie, unstoppable, Alex gets up, drifts over, and everyone else follows. I hang back, next to Suzy. Jay seems to be making an extra effort not to look at me.

"Mr. Hayes, how've you been?" Alex says, and Jay's dad stands up, claps him on the shoulder.

Beth is so focused on Jay again, laughing, chatting. Jay's dad elbows him, like he's trying to get him to reciprocate, and the muscles around my spine tense.

"Hey, I need to use the bathroom," I whisper to Suzy. There's a wall that sections off the area by the restrooms, and I dart behind it, out of sight. But I can still hear them.

Then the group is leaving, passing my hiding spot without glancing this way, the murmur of their overlapping conversations receding. My phone rumbles.

Suzy Jang: waiting for you outside

"Is there something going on there?" Jay's dad says, on the other side of the wall. "You and the blond."

I press my back against the wall and close my eyes, not even daring to peek.

"It's literally none of your business," Jay says.

Why wouldn't he just say no?

"She's practically throwing herself at you. You can see that, right?" His dad laughs. "You definitely don't take after me! Got no game."

Ugh, what?

Jay coughs, like he choked on his water.

His dad just keeps talking. "That other Asian one's hot. The one standing in the back, with Alex's girl?" My cheeks burn, and my scalp prickles. "If I were you, I'd go for her instead."

There's the sound of a chair scraping, silverware rattling, like Jay hit the table. *"Shut the fuck up!"*

"Whoa, buddy."

"I'm not your buddy!" He sounds winded, like for every word that punches through the surface, there are dozens more he can't get out.

"Listen carefully, okay? We don't need you. We don't need your money. I can take care of them *without you*. I only showed up today because Mom asked me to."

A surge of affection squeezes my heart because it feels like he's standing up for me, too.

But I've never heard him talk like that, and something about it scares me. How different he sounds from the person I know. From the one he lets me see.

He didn't even tell me his dad was coming to visit.

This new fear breezes in, like someone left the window open, and there's suddenly a draft. I thought I was in the inner circle of his life, but I'm actually on the outside, with everyone else.

His dad laughs and says something too quiet for me to hear. And then they're leaving, coming this way. Jay sees me, and we make eye contact, for a second. It's over so fast, but he looks annoyed, embarrassed. Like he feels betrayed that I'm here.

He got so mad when his dad mentioned me.

I thought I understood why, but the meaning shifts, changes shape, the more I turn it over in my head.

Part of me knows what it means. But another part zooms in on the Beth thing. Fixates and fixates, until I can't hear the rest anymore.

It's late that night, and I'm calling him.

The phone rings for a bit, but he doesn't pick up. Across the street, his light is still on.

And then he answers.

"Hey. Hang on."

His mom is screaming in the background. Furious, accusatory. The heft and weight of great resentment.

Then there's Jay's voice, muffled, like he's covering the phone. "Mom. Mom, you have to stop. I'm not *saying* you're crazy. And I'm not Dad, you can't keep saying that. Okay? I'm not arguing with you about this anymore. I'm going upstairs."

I hear him walking, a door closing.

"Hey." His voice is low and a little raspy, different than before. "It's not a great time. I'll call you later."

"Then talk to me about it!" I can hear how desperate and scared I sound, but I don't know how to stop. "What's wrong? You can tell me."

He sighs, and his breathing changes. It sounds like he's moving. Out the window, I can see him going onto his roof.

"*Fine.*" There's something I haven't heard in his voice before, pinched and sneering. "You want to know what's wrong?"

I try to lend my voice some strength. "I do."

He takes a deep, gulping breath. "I'm trying to smile, and act like things are fine, and I can handle everything. I'm playing this part. A good son. Good brother. Good—" He exhales sharp, sounding so disgusted with himself. "But I *hate it*. I wish I could be the kind of person who didn't hate it. But I can't. I fucking *can't.*"

He's talking faster, picking up steam, like he's worried someone is going to walk in on him and he won't be able to get it all out in time.

"I just want to be alone, *all the time!*" His voice breaks, and I imagine him trying to blink the tears back again, out there above the street. "I just want to get in the car and drive and drive and not stop. Just *leave*, just like my fucking dad. *All the time.*"

"Jay," I say into the phone uselessly. I must be letting him down.

"It's not a nice answer, is it?" Suddenly, he's shouting. "Maybe you should think it through before you ask shit like that!"

Then there's dead air. He hung up.

I just stare out the window for a while, in shock, barely breathing. Watch him go back in, turn off his light.

Is this how he always feels, under the surface? When he seems like he's about to get upset, but then he takes a deep breath, makes a joke, and smooths it over. Shoves it under the rug, pats me on the head. Tells me he can handle all of it.

And I believe him, forget to be worried. Because I already think he's stronger and better than me.

I thought I knew so much about him, but now I'm going over everything he's ever said to me. Wondering how many times he's been beside me, feeling like that. And I should have known better, but I told myself he's fine.

THIRTY-ONE

IT'S EXCRUCIATING, GOING TO ALEX'S LACROSSE GAME THE NEXT DAY. But Suzy's practically glowing, sitting on the cold metal bleachers beside me.

"Let's go, let's go!" she whoops. Alex has the ball and he's running with it.

People are clustered near the railing closest to the field, leaning over it and cheering, a row of gray hoodies and green beanies.

And then I see Jay, arriving late, and my phone rumbles again.

> Jay Hayes: can i talk to you
> Jay Hayes: please

He tips his head to show where he's going and heads down the steps.

I squeeze Suzy's shoulder and get up. "Bathroom break."

Jay's waiting for me under the bleachers. Overhead, people are cheering again, stomping their thundering feet.

"Hey." He takes a big breath, once I'm in front of him. "I didn't text earlier because I wanted to say this in person. I'm really sorry for how I acted. I shouldn't have talked to you like that."

"It's okay," I say quietly.

"No, it's not! It's really—" He gulps for air, a little panicked, like he doesn't think he can find the words in time.

Jay gets closer and puts his hands on my shoulders. "No one should ever talk to you like that, okay? Don't let anyone talk to you like that." He sniffs, exhales like it hurts. "Especially not me."

What is he *saying* to me right now? Mom talks to me like that all the time. It's practically the only way she talks to me. There's that surge of heat behind my eyes, everything getting a little wavy. No, fuck, I don't want him to see me cry.

Then Jay lets go and takes a few steps back. And the way he can't look at me, now—a sinking feeling tugs at my chest.

"Deedee. I care about you a lot." He's breathing really carefully, jaw tense, nostrils flared. "But I can't do this anymore."

It's happening, the thing I'm always scared of, it's actually happening. I think about this all the time, but I'm still so unprepared.

"Is it because of Beth?"

"What?" It's like I slapped him, the way his face crumples. "Why would you ask me that? Is that what you think of me? You agree with my mom, I guess. That I'm just like him."

"No, that's not—"

"You're just— You're always unhappy and—I can't fix that!" He takes a shaky breath out, like something has been building up for a while. "I can't fix how you hate yourself."

I'm biting my tongue, wishing I could hold on to something, like we just went around a tight curve.

The way that bursts out of him—does he feel like that all the time?

"I suppose you don't hate yourself," I say, calmly as I can, in the prim phone voice Mom taught me.

Jay looks up at the bleachers, blinking a lot. "I just feel like I'm *failing*, all the time! And I'm hurting you, too, I'm not making you happy—"

I wince, remembering Mom saying, *Not that sad face, either!*

"You make me so happy!" I know I sound desperate. "I can do better! I can stop calling you at night! I can give you more space!"

"Please don't—" Jay clutches his head, squeezing his eyes shut. "It's my fault, okay? It's my fault. It's my fault. I'm sorry. I really am. For everything. I just—I need to be alone for a while."

He looks so exhausted, face puffy, begging me to let him go. I can't stand it.

I take off running, ducking under the metal bar, tearing across the grass toward the school building. This is what I get, letting him in, giving him the chance to see too much. He saw through my bullshit to how rotten I am inside. I was smart with Suzy, but with Jay I made a mistake.

I was in this bubble with him, golden light and his cozy laugh and the nowhere places he takes me. I'm going back where I belong now, to my house full of secrets and things that go bump in the night.

THIRTY-TWO

A FUNNY THING HAPPENED WHEN I WASN'T PAYING ATTENTION. WHEN I'd spot Jay from a distance, when I'd get in his car, when we'd talk late at night—seeing his face made me feel like I was at home. At least, what I imagine home could maybe feel like, someday.

And then I looked again, and his expression was like a house with the door shut, no lights on and no one to recognize me.

Going to school feels unbearable. The sun is too bright, and I feel like everyone can see my insides, all the gross fleshy stuff that's impolite to show.

After school, I put Jay's camera and sweatshirt in an old cardboard box and leave it on his porch, ring the doorbell, and run.

At night, when I can't sleep, I take the secret photo from my night-stand and try to imagine a time when Mom was happy. Then I wake up to a room full of Saturday sun, and Mom is hitting me with my pillow.

"Get up! Do you know what time it is! It's two o'clock in the afternoon!"

I raise my arms to shield my face. "I think I'm depressed."

"You can't be depressed, Deedee, that's for white people who don't know how good they have it!" She sounds like she's at her wit's end. "Get up! How dare you be depressed, with everything you have, honestly! It's selfish to indulge in your emotions like this!"

I remember when Suzy broke up with her first boyfriend, and her mom rubbed her back while Suzy cried, telling her to let it all out.

Mom hits me with the pillow again, a few times in a row. Then she drops it and hits me with her little hands, sloppily, random places on my shoulders and torso. "I can feel your sadness from *downstairs*! Life is hard enough, then I have to come home to you, *draining me of everything I have!*"

I squeeze my eyes shut, and Jay's in front of me, under the bleachers, saying, *Don't let anyone talk to you like that.*

And I kind of hate him now. But maybe he had a point.

I grab the pillow and use it to push her off me. "You could just *close the door and ignore me!*" I shout. "That's an option!"

It's hard to say who is more stunned, Mom or me. We're both gaping at each other.

Then Mom notices the photo, lying there loose on my mattress, and she scowls. "What did I tell you about this?" she asks, low and steady, the most frightening.

It's the last reminder I have of when we were all together, complete. But I'm too exhausted to fight it.

Mom makes a disgusted sound and disappears down the hall with the picture.

All I want to do is sleep, but when I'm awake, envelopes start arriving in the mail. The future reasserting itself, even though it doesn't feel real to me. Rejections from Princeton, Yale—there wasn't enough to make my application stand out, I guess.

Mom shakes her head. "I expected better of you."

I get into Georgetown, but it's also so much money, and when I picture DC in my head, all I see is gray.

"You seem down lately," Suzy says on the way to school. "Did something happen?"

"Just stressed about next year." What's the point of telling her now that it's over?

"You'll get good news, I know it."

My fingers are pressed hard into my palms, trying to hold myself in. "What about you? Are things with Alex . . . good?"

My question hangs in the air between us longer than I expected.

"I just can't shake the feeling like I won the lottery or something," she says after a while, eyes straight ahead. "I keep thinking, he's never dated someone this long. I'm just nervous? Like if I question it, it will evaporate."

"If it evaporates that easily, how good was it?" I blink, hearing myself saying it.

Her brows knit together. "I mean, how would you know, right? You haven't dated anyone."

That lands hard in my gut. "Yeah. I guess." The thing with Jay—who even knows what that was?

All day I want to be asleep and all night I have a hard time not being awake, trying not to look out the window because of the headlights I might see. Really, it was a strategic error, falling tragically in love with my neighbor.

At 2 a.m., I open my notes app. And on a whim, I write:

Upsides to being an aswang:
- She has her own transportation
- Men fear her
- She's not afraid to let other people see her insides
- She's adaptable (shape-shifter)
- She's probably fine with being more than one thing
- She's probably not worried about being Kind Of A Lot

I read the list back and feel a little less lonely, in on my own joke. It's enough to fall asleep.

Weeks pass. I'm sleeping through the night more often. And when I do, I have strange dreams.

In one, I'm wandering in a garden at nighttime, and the headless ghost of a Spanish knight tells me in a wailing voice to *enunciate*.

In another, I stand among the glittering vases in the living room as the sun is setting, pick them up one by one and throw them to the ground so they shatter, and there's only a floor of shards left.

When I wake up, Mom is sitting on the edge of my bed. She smooths down the blanket, looking kind of sad and small.

"Did I ever tell you about the time your Tito Andoy caught an aswang?"

She wants to tell the stories again?

"It was when we were kids. Your Lola Cecilia—his mom, your great-aunt—was ill." She gives me an annoyed look, like my lack of knowledge of our family tree is a personal failing it takes great patience for her to accept.

"He heard something on the roof." She raises her eyebrows, widens her eyes. "So he tried climbing up there, with a ladder and a flashlight. And he found someone—*something*—there. Lurking. Waiting. With its looong, hollow tongue poking through an upper window, searching for your Lola Cecilia."

A faraway look passes across Mom's face. I wonder what this story reminds her of.

"But when he shined his light on it, he recognized its face. It was a girl he knew from school. She swooped down to the ground, rejoined with her lower half, and he chased her into the woods."

"Then what happened?"

She gets up suddenly. "He never saw her again. They said her family moved away. Lola Cecilia recovered soon after."

Mom's stories are like this, sometimes—tearing off, incomplete. She gets up to leave again, and I'm lying in bed, unsettled.

There must be more to our story than this.

I didn't find much out, following her last time. But I did when I went into her office. The letters flash through my mind again, spilling out on the floor.

What else is in there, that she keeps locked away?

When I asked Jay how he learned to do his job, he shrugged and said he looked things up obsessively online. I was annoyed, the way he made it sound simple. But now I open YouTube and search for *how to pick a lock.*

Mom's footsteps come back down the hall, and I close the app. She gives me a skeptical look from the doorway. "I forgot," she says, handing me an envelope. "You got this."

It's from Eastleigh, and my hands shake, opening it. Mom's already gone. I guess she's not interested in what a state school has to say.

We are delighted to inform you that . . .

A full scholarship.

I read and reread it a few times to make sure.

It means I'll live here next year, that I won't get out of this town. But blood rushes to my head, thinking about doing something on my own. Like I brought in some money, finally.

Maybe it's not love, but it sends my heart racing.

I'm going into physics later that week, and there's Jay, leaving late. He's in the AP class, I'm not. And I guess something delayed him, because he's the last one in the room, scrambling to go, trying not to look right at me. So preoccupied, he leaves something in the desk.

I can't help being curious. I sit down and peer inside.

It's his copy of *As I Lay Dying*, open like he was reading it in class. We're not working on this book in English anymore. There's no reason for him to read it now.

Wedged between the pages, there's my drawing of the fish sauce bottle.

I close the book and shove it to the back of the desk. I can't let myself think about it, can't trust him again. All through class, I try to forget about it.

THIRTY-THREE

THE TREES THAT LOST THEIR LEAVES ARE GETTING THEM BACK NOW, vivid green bobbing in the breeze. I stop at the end of the block and take a picture of them rippling in the same direction.

I've been taking more walks, after school sometimes, if Jay's car isn't in his driveway. And before I go to sleep, I'll look at the photos again. I used to force myself not to, just sent them into the void, like something bad would happen if I indulged myself. But I guess the way Jay talked about my photos stuck with me. Like I can make something new, not just furiously cling to what's there. Something between what I feel and what is.

I'm almost home again, thinking about the lockpick set I casually picked up at Jang's that I haven't worked up the nerve to use yet. And as I turn onto our street—there's Jay, in his front yard. Sitting out on his lawn, in a folding chair, next to Gemma. She's wearing a pair of bright pink sunglasses, lounging with her head tilted back, getting some sun.

His car's gone, he's not supposed to be here! *This is a breach of the fucking social contract!*

I pick up the pace, powerwalking for my front door, just as he scrambles up and jogs over to me.

"Deedee! Deedee, wait, I—"

"What do you want, *Jason*?" I snap. He's standing in front of me, now, in the middle of the street. Hands raised, palms facing me. "Why are you here? Your car's not in the driveway."

"It's in the shop." He laughs, tense. "You really are avoiding me."

"Why *wouldn't* I be avoiding you?"

It's hard being face-to-face with him, like this. A lot of things are muscle memory still. The impulse to touch him. The knowledge of how easily our bodies would fit together if I took a couple steps closer. How he would smell, if I did.

From their lawn, Gemma's craning her neck to get a better look. She lifts her sunglasses and lets them sit on top of her head.

"That's what I need to tell you, I . . . was wrong. Before. I just—I completely panicked. I wanted to tell you, but—I didn't see you at night anymore and texting felt wrong, but if I talked to you at school, you wouldn't want—" He sighs, stops himself. "I fucked up, Deedee. I'm sorry."

What?

I can't listen to this right now.

"Great. Now you've told me. Bye!" I run for my front door.

"BYE, DEEDEE!" Gemma hollers behind me.

Who the fuck does he think he is?

Shear line, driver pins, key pins, plug.

I'm crouched in front of Mom's office door, sweating, fumbling with the tools inserted in the lock. She's not supposed to be back from work for a couple hours. The videos made it look so easy, but I guess my muscles don't have the right memories.

Push the pins up, one by one. You should be able to feel the give.

Just when I learn to live without him, Jay pops back up again.

Breaking up with him was like being thrown out of a warm bed into a freezing lake. But looking back on how I felt, near the end—it's not the way I want to be. I don't want to go to sleep again, wrapped in gauze, hiding from the rest of my life. So scared of what I had to lose, like I needed him to breathe.

I get it now. I have a hole in my heart, and a boy can't fix it.

To fix it, I need to break into my mom's office.

I pull the tools out of the lock, let the pins drop and reset. Flex my hand, clench and unclench. It makes me think about all the times Jay's engine stalled, how sweaty and stressed I was then.

But I did it.

The way he said, *You'll get it, keep trying.*

Beside me, my phone rumbles against the hardwood floor.

Jay Hayes: i miss you

This asshole.

I want to call him, since he likes the phone so fucking much, and yell, *Can't you see I'm busy?!*

Maybe I'll push him, scare him off.

Deedee Walters: be more specific

I delete the messages, no screenshot, and take a big breath, inserting the tools again. Emptying my head, barely breathing, going slow. Pushing up on the pins, one by one, and—

It turns. I'm in.

Holy shit.

I feel like I'm opening an ancient tomb, letting my eyes adjust. The air is stale, and dust motes float in the light seeping through the half-closed blinds.

There's a big closet in one wall, a folding door that slides. When I push it open, there's a bunch of bank boxes there, stacked on top of each other.

I take them out, one by one, trying to remember the order they should go back in.

And there's one stuffed with yellow envelopes, from a photo development place that must have folded a long time ago.

A goldmine.

I flip one open, and there's a shot of my mom and dad, standing in front of the Eiffel Tower. Mom wearing these big sunglasses, looking glamorous. I never knew they went to Paris. I don't know why it's so surprising. That she felt joy once, that she did something that wasn't related to strictly *surviving*. The idea that I came in at the middle of the movie, and because I didn't catch the beginning, I might not really understand the end.

One of the envelopes is full of photos from New York.

One of a diner, its flagstone exterior.

One of my dad, sitting in a booth, hiding his face behind a menu.

My heart beats a little faster. I haven't seen these before.

These pieces of when they were happy, of the time before I came along.

There's a brick building, sitting near the green elevated tracks.
My phone buzzes again, several times, beside me.

> **Jay Hayes:** i miss your sense of humor
> **Jay Hayes:** your million questions
> **Jay Hayes:** how you're sweet and prickly at the same time

It's annoying, how my body reacts—the way my stomach lurches, that familiar shimmering feeling in my chest. Ugh, God, why did he have to actually answer?

I delete the messages, put the phone on Mom's desk, and lean deeper into the closet.

In the corner, behind the boxes, there's an old photo album. I take it out, flip it open. It's filled with pages of clear pockets stuffed with photos, a chaotic jumble of sizes and shapes.

Unfamiliar faces gaze back, people who look vaguely like me. Frozen shards of the past that I can't piece together into a story. Children with bowl haircuts against a backdrop of scraggly pines.

There's Mom as a kid, posing before a wooden church door, wearing a white dress. It's a contrast against her skin, browner than she ever lets it get these days.

My phone will *not shut up*, constantly rattling against the desk. What could he possibly be saying?

> **Jay Hayes:** i miss your way of seeing things
> **Jay Hayes:** the way you think
> **Jay Hayes:** your laugh
> **Jay Hayes:** the way you can get really intense about an idea
> **Jay Hayes:** your very specific taste in chips

There's a prickling in the corners of my eyes, but I bite it back and switch my phone off, settle on the floor again, turn the page of the album. And something feels very wrong.

In every photo I see, there's a hole, something missing.

Some of the pictures are jagged on one side, an edge torn off, a person ripped out of the frame.

Others look like something was excised with an X-Acto knife.

A gash in the picture, with its arm around my grandmother.

Old anger reverberates from that jagged wound in the glossy photo paper. The emotion Mom must have felt when she tore and cut, sometimes frantic, sometimes surgeon-precise.

It screams silently from the page, this absence so loud. The negative space where a man used to be.

That blank space is challenging me, taunting me.

A mystery to solve.

There's a pocket in the back cover with some folded papers inside. Thin, flimsy.

I slide them out carefully.

There's a page clipped out of a newspaper, or maybe a magazine. Yellowed, fragile. And there's the woman who looks so sad in the old photos. The one who gave me my cheeks and mouth.

Gone too soon, it says. A tragic accident—a car crash not far from her home.

She was an actress. There are the names of some of her films. She hadn't had that many roles, it says, but she lit up the screen.

Survived by . . . her husband. A name I don't recognize.

Not Lolo Ric. Not Ricardo. Someone else.

I try to google the new name. Nothing at first, but then I try his name and my grandmother's together.

There's a short article. An obituary. For a man who apparently *was* my grandfather, but not the one Mom told me about.

This man died over ten years ago. Right around the time she had me start writing these letters to a grandfather who didn't actually exist. Another ghost.

My hand flies to cover my mouth, biting down on my finger so I don't scream into the stifling room.

I drop the album and start throwing her desk drawers open, looking for something, anything more. Pens, paperclips, files, receipts. Receipts upon receipts. A stack of checks. Old checks with the word *rent* written in.

Made out to her. From an address in New York.

I search the address and look at it on Street View.

A brown-brick building next to a set of elevated tracks.

I shuffle through the photos, find the one I'm thinking of again.

It's the same.

Why does she have these? What does this building have to do with her?

Next to them, there's an envelope, the word *Spares* written on it in ballpoint pen. Inside, there are keys. House keys. It looks like copies of the same one.

I slip one into my pocket and gather up the album and the photos.

My head is spinning with so many questions as I lock the door behind me, head up the stairs, and carefully hide these things in my closet.

Why would she lie to me about him?
Why did she have me write those letters?
What did her dad do to her?
What happened to her mom?

What is this building, what are these keys?

And having a key in my pocket, something to hold on to—I feel like I just have to *go there.*

It feels like a *clue.*

A shred of hope that there's a mystery to solve, with answers at the end.

And I need that to hold on to, right now. Because none of this makes any fucking sense.

All through dinner with Mom, I'm trying to seem normal.

I'm nodding at her story about work, but in my head, I'm adding up the money I've saved from lunch and tutoring.

Liar. Liar. Liar. The word churns in my head after every word she says.

And when I get up to my room, I turn my phone back on to look up bus ticket prices. While Mom is on her next work trip, I could go to New York. Try this key out for myself.

There are a bunch of messages from Jay.

> Jay Hayes: i miss your face
> Jay Hayes: the way you wear your clothes
> Jay Hayes: the way you're kind of wild
> Jay Hayes: the way you scare me a little
> Jay Hayes: because you talk about things i tell myself not to
>   think about

It's like when he was trying to answer my question about what his job feels like. He'll probably keep throwing out answers until he feels like he's landed on the best and most right one. Or until I tell him to stop.

Another one pops up, while I'm staring.

> **Jay Hayes:** and your writing tips, obviously. very helpful.

It makes me laugh.

> **Deedee Walters:** naturally
> **Jay Hayes:** yeah i hear you charge good money for that usually
> **Deedee Walters:** what else?
> **Jay Hayes:** i miss talking to you
> **Jay Hayes:** and i miss sitting next to you in silence
> **Jay Hayes:** i miss all of it

My throat is tight, warmth and pressure threatening behind my eyes.

> **Deedee Walters:** i kind of hate you
> **Jay Hayes:** i understand that
> **Jay Hayes:** i want to make it up to you

I turn my phone off again, don't write back.

THIRTY-FOUR

THE AUDITORIUM AT THE ELEMENTARY SCHOOL IS BUZZING WITH people on the night of the Spring Concert. The Jangs are standing in the aisle, and I catch Suzy's eye and wave to them.

"I'll be over here," Mom says, moving toward a seat near the back.

She insisted on coming tonight for some reason, even though she obviously didn't want to. "You're always at their house!" she said. "I have to be friendly. How would it look?"

There are so many things I want to say. *What is your problem with them? Why would you insist on coming because of how it looks, then not talk to them?*

"You don't want to say hello?" I ask.

She shoots me a look. "Isn't it enough that I'm here?"

So I bite my tongue and make my way down the aisle toward them.

"Hey, there she is!" Suzy's dad pats me on the shoulder. "Can't wait for next year. You'll have to tell me all about the old alma mater."

He's still so excited that Suzy and I will both be going to Eastleigh, like they did.

Suzy's mom wraps me up in a hug. "So proud of you girls."

Over her shoulder, Mom looks miserable, a tense island to herself. I'm a little sad for her, thinking about the hole in her old photos. And I'm mad at her for lying to me, at the same time. The two feelings twine around each other, a rope tugging me in one direction: Maybe if I went to the place where she had been happy, that would help me piece together a story I could accept.

Suzy's mom and dad are laughing together. "You should start the band back up!" She gives him a teasing look. "You were always saying you were just ahead of your time. Well—it's been quite some time!"

"Very funny," he says, bobbing his head, pretending to laugh.

Alex comes down the aisle toward us, and Mrs. Jang gives him a hug, drawing him into her orbit, asking a million questions. He looks nervous when she asks what his favorite book is.

"Well . . . I like a lot of them . . . It's, uh . . . hard to pick just one." I can practically see a giant cartoon drop of sweat forming on his forehead.

"Oh!" Charlie says. "I nearly forgot." He pulls a worn camera bag out from under one of the seats. "It's a late congratulations present. Or an early going-away-to-college present. But we thought you should have one of your own, for all the memories you two are going to make."

The room is blurring around the edges. I'm barely keeping it in check, too scared to look over at Mom. What is she going to think? Her two least favorite things, together at last—Suzy's family and my interest in photography.

"It's actually the one I used when I was your age. Still in good condition, and Suzy's never going to pick it up, so . . ."

"I love it," I manage to get out, half strangled. "Thank you."

He pats me lightly on the back as a teacher announces it's almost time for the concert to start.

I join Mom again, sweat gathering under my shirt.

"What's that?" she asks, mouth pinched.

"A present." I tighten my grip on the strap, worried she's going to take it away.

But she just looks ahead at the stage, jaw tight, and says, "That's nice."

The burgundy curtains part, and the school choir takes the stage. Ben and Jake are wearing matching white shirts and slacks, hair slicked down and combed. And there's Gemma, standing on the other end of the row, wearing a light blue dress and white sandals. So Jay and his mom are somewhere here. My palms sweat against the hard plastic seat.

The choir takes a collective deep breath and starts to sing, arms stiff at everyone's sides, chests out. Through the next two songs, Jake starts to loosen up. Soon he's gesturing so wildly with his arms, he almost smacks the kid next to him.

At the end of a particularly boisterous rendition of "Let It Go," I get up to use the bathroom.

And when I come back out into the lobby, Jay's walking toward me. It's just him and me and this shrinking space between us, the echo of his footsteps on the white linoleum and the muffled sounds of the concert, coming through the heavy wooden doors.

I hate that the sight of him still gives me butterflies.

"Hey. Hi." His hand goes to the back of his head, elbow out at an angle. "Can I talk to you? Outside?"

Jay holds the door open for me, and I pass through, heart thumping.

It's even quieter once the double doors close behind us. Crickets chirp in the dark parking lot, and an old light fixture hums overhead, glowing orange, shadows of dead bugs pooled in the bottom.

It seems like Jay's still working through what he wants to say, staring at the concrete between us.

I can't stand it anymore. I have to talk first.

"Look. I'm not going to lie and say I don't miss you. But I'm still mad at you." I cross my arms, wrestling down the urge to reach out and touch him. "And I've been thinking about what you said, and . . . if things were so bad that you couldn't stand talking to me anymore, what is actually different now?"

He takes a big breath in and lets it out slowly. "You know that time I yelled at you? When you called. I still feel bad about that—and this isn't an excuse, but—" Jay looks me in the eye. "I was asking my mom to go to therapy."

It takes a second for this to sink in.

"You can just *ask* your mom to go to therapy?" Mom says it's a scam, that *only crazy people become therapists.* But it sounds . . . kind of good and important, based on what everyone else says? Not that I have the option right now to do something like that.

Jay opens his mouth, and a shaky laugh comes out. "I mean, it was hard to. Because I still . . . feel like I let her down, I guess, just . . . watching my dad treat her like shit for a long time. And Candace actually tried to get my mom to go, a while ago. And it went badly."

"So what did she say?"

"Um, she wasn't happy at first. She was all, *Are you saying I'm a bad mother?* and *You're just like your father, telling me I'm crazy.*" One of his hands rests against his chest, thumb pressing on his fingers, a few times each in turn. "But, for some reason . . . yeah, she listened to me, this time. She's been going."

"That's great," I say quietly.

"Some things Candace said, before—I thought about them, when the fights with my mom were getting worse, all fall and winter. And, I guess—I don't know, I started to think . . . we can't keep going like this."

You can just *decide*? That you can't keep going like this?

He huffs out a rough breath, head angled down. "When my dad was here—"

"You didn't even tell me he was visiting."

"I didn't want to think about it, until it was literally happening. And—" Jay's fingers drum over his heart, like he's telling it to calm down. "My dad's new girlfriend—he talks to her the same way he used to talk to my mom, like he just copy-and-pasted someone into the space she used to fill. But my mom wanted me to go see him, right? So I spent the day with him, and later we picked Gemma up for dinner." He shakes his head and looks away into the parking lot. "He just . . . slapped his girlfriend on the ass in front of us. I wanted to cover Gemma's eyes, but I didn't react in time. I just— I felt helpless, like I used to. And I felt like I'm going to let them down again, and . . ."

Jay's eyes follow a moth as it flits past his head, flapping its wings around the orange light.

"My dad said this thing that got stuck in my head. *You think you're better than me? You're my blood, we're not that different.* I guess, I thought—" He squeezes his eyes shut. "I can protect you by taking myself out of your life. That's the only way to make sure. That's one thing I can do."

What he said on the bridge at night comes back to me. *It's a thing I can do. It's a thing I understand.* The way it seemed like he was knuckling down on those words, clinging for dear life.

"How fucking condescending, thinking you can figure that out for both of us."

Jay's arms fall to his sides, and he nods.

"You just shut me out," I press on.

"I know. And I want to—" He breathes in deep, holds it for a second before letting it out again. "I want to be better than that. I know I can be."

"You know how you said you felt like you were making me unhappy? Maybe I wasn't happy, but it wasn't because of you. I'm not another job for you to do. I don't need you to fix me."

But I'm embarrassed, because if things had kept going the way that they were—I probably did want him to fix me, back then. And I wouldn't be saying this now.

"I know," he whispers, and meets my eye in this way that makes my chest tight.

There are so many other things I want to say, right then, but the one I land on is: "I don't know, Jay, my mom is here. I should go back inside."

When the concert is over and the lights go up, Mom turns to me, annoyed, and says, "Fine, let's go say hello."

Charlie nods when he sees us approaching. "Gloria. Thanks for coming."

"Of course," she says, *enunciating* maybe even more than usual. "Wonderful concert. The boys are getting so big now."

"More of a handful every day," Mrs. Jang says.

Jay, Gemma, and their mom are moving up the aisle then, on their way to the exit.

"Deedee!" his mom exclaims and leans in to give me a hug. "So wonderful to see you again, how are you doing?"

The way her whole face lights up, the way her voice is so warm—it's like she wants me to date her son, like having me in their lives would be something nice.

"Mom, these are our neighbors across the street," I say, trying to smile. "It's, uh, funny you haven't met them yet!"

Mom barely acknowledges them, looking down her nose in chilly silence.

Jay looks even more uncomfortable than I do, which is an accomplishment. "Mom, we should get going, right?"

His head is turning away, but his eyes follow me.

"Didn't you like that girl?" Jay's mom says, when they're not quite out of earshot.

I can't hear his answer. And I'm so tense as we walk to the car, wondering how much Mom heard.

THIRTY-FIVE

"So," Mom says from the driver's seat as I clutch the camera bag in my lap, "you really like taking photos."

I'm almost touched, the way she says it, like it's neutral. And then I'm annoyed and confused, thinking about all the times we've fought about it. About how stiff she was with Suzy's parents, and the look on her face when she met Jay's mom.

"Is something going on with you and that boy?"

Okay, breathe. She's just on alert for this all the time. You can still get out of it.

"No," I say, watching the lights of the school disappear in the side mirror.

At a stoplight, the red glow lights up the disdainful twist of her mouth. "That boy's mother dresses like a teenager. How old must she have been when she had kids?"

"Mom," I mumble. "You don't even know them."

"What's happening to the neighborhood?"

Usually I don't press on it. Pretend not to hear it. But what I found in her office and what Jay said to me—it's all churning, frothing this urge to be reckless. To break things, like the vases in my dream.

"What do you mean?"

She shakes her head. "It's getting so *ethnic*."

"Mom, that's racist," I say, a little too loud. I've never said something like that to her, never turned the distress outward. Just pushed it down until it blended into the rest of my shame.

She laughs, short and mean. "You kids think everything is racist. What are you going to do, cancel me?"

"What is your problem with them? *Really?*" It's like something else is speaking through me now, stronger than I know how to be.

She sighs like I just asked her to recite the periodic table from memory. "They're just— Those boys? Not well behaved. That girl wears too much makeup. And the mother—acting like she's a friend instead of a parent, it's irresponsible. Where will they learn discipline? And the father . . ." She trails off, like it goes without saying. "So crass. So American."

We're home now, and I grip the strap of the camera bag as I follow her inside.

It feels like I'm betraying all of them by letting this conversation rest.

"Which is it now?" I say, too loud again, and Mom stops ahead of me, so I'm talking to her back. "Is it because they're too ethnic, or too American for you? *Both?*"

If I don't know how to make it better, and I don't know how to live with it staying the same, I guess I just have to make it worse.

"Is it because Suzy's dad has tattoos? Or is it because they don't *hate themselves?*"

She turns to face me, and a bitter little laugh escapes her throat. "What would you know about hating yourself? You don't have the first clue."

She really doesn't see me at all.

"I know I want to associate with *them* more than I want to associate with *you!*"

The distance between us vanishes in an instant, and she slaps me, her open palm a flash of pain across my face.

"*How dare you.* After everything I've done for you." Her eyes are filled with disgust. "You just take and take and *take!* Do you have any idea how much you've *taken from me?*"

A little voice in the back of my head says, *Yes, by now maybe I have some idea.*

But the anger is shrinking, evaporating. The anger that's been propelling me upward, making me brave, it's leaving and I'm curling back in on myself again, that contaminated feeling rising up, hot and sticky, pulling me under, burying me.

She grabs a bit of skin on my chest between two fingers, through my shirt, right above my right breast, and pinches, hard, twists so it will hurt. I yelp.

"*The disrespect!*" she says through gritted teeth. She shakes her head, crosses the room, and sinks down onto the couch. And then she starts to talk, like I'm not even in the room with her.

"My dad was so angry at the Americans. Said they took advantage of us, thought they're better than us. That I shouldn't buy it."

The skin on my arms prickles. I've never heard this story before.

"He came here for a while. Because he was a veteran, he fought for this country. But he said they treated him like dirt."

My mind is scrambling. This is so different from the story she usually tells. It's not a story about Lolo Ric, my imaginary friend who's never done a bad thing in his life. It has to be about the man missing from the photos.

"He was so *stuck in that*." Mom starts up again, like she's talking to herself. "He talked about it constantly! I always thought, *Why don't you let go of that? Why can't you move on?*"

She looks at me then and a chill runs through me. "Your sad face just reminds me of him. His endless self-pity."

All the times she'd yell when I cried come back to me, piled on top of each other.

"He said all that." She looks away from me and leans back into the couch again. "But he told me since I was small that I should come here. My whole life, I was getting ready to come here. We barely spoke Tagalog at home."

So conflicted feelings run in the family.

I follow her line of sight, like if I stare long enough at the same point, the ghosts she's seeing will appear to me, too.

"Then I meet your father's family, and they don't even know what the Philippines is." She laughs unhappily, rolls her head from side to side. "You have to forget about history to live comfortably in this country."

That's all she's ever wanted, isn't it? To live comfortably.

"Your people fought us, killed hundreds of thousands of us. Tried out waterboarding on us. Dominated us. Made us think we should be like you. Propped up a dictator who terrorized us. Now you can't even find us on a map."

That familiar configuration of islands floats into my head, the one I've stared at so many times on the maps app, like it's going to tell me something one day. I'm clinging to it now so I don't have to be part of this "you," but the harder I try to focus on it, the more the map loses its shape.

"I've told you a million times, it's pointless to think about the past. You can't change it now. But somehow you always find a way to drag me back there." She stares at me, chin jutting forward. "You don't listen. You don't know how lucky you are. And my best years were all just—just *wasted* on you!"

She stands up, shoulders tight, clenching her fists. Her vases around the room glimmer in the lamplight.

"You know what? Knowing you taught me that love *dies*. That it goes away. I didn't know that before."

My brain is spinning, unable to grasp anything. Nothing connects.

Somehow all I can think to do is go to the fridge and get out the bagoong and a mango. She watches me scoop some bagoong into a small bowl, get the cutting board and a big knife, separate the fruit from the pit.

"I'm not hungry," she says. "I'm going to bed."

I finish chopping in silence and transfer the slices to a bowl, listening to her moving around upstairs, heavy footsteps, a door closing.

The feeling in my chest is the same as when I'm scared on the highway, gripping the wheel, wondering how long this will last, if I'll make it to the other side.

Clean the knife, wash the cutting board.

I stand there in silence, eating by myself.

Deedee Walters: take me to new york

My phone screen is the only point of light in my dark bedroom. Three dots pop up, disappear, reappear.

Jay Hayes: can you say more?
Deedee Walters: if you miss me so much
Deedee Walters: drive me there
Jay Hayes: like . . . right now?

I snort.

Deedee Walters: would you have?
Jay Hayes: maybe

He can't be serious.

Deedee Walters: in a couple weeks
Deedee Walters: when my mom's on a work trip again

He won't, right? Even he wouldn't.

There's this feeling, tangled and wild, egging me on. Like I have nothing to lose now, and I'm flipping a coin, letting fate decide. Because I don't know what I want more: to push him away, or to go there with him.

Deedee Walters: you could even see candace, while we're there

The dots emerge again, vanish.

Jay Hayes: i'll think about it

Now I really won't be able to sleep.

But somehow, I do, because when I open my eyes again, it's morning. And there's a good smell from downstairs.

Mom is waiting for me in the kitchen, wearing an apron. Ladling something into a bowl, setting it on the counter.

What?

"I made you breakfast," she says. "Go ahead and eat."

Mom hates cooking. And after last night, and what she said to me?

Knowing you taught me that love dies.

I really feel like I'm losing my mind. But I sit down at the counter. Pick up the spoon, take a bite.

It's arroz caldo, a dish I remember from the last time we stayed with her family. Piping-hot rice porridge, soothing like a hug, with ginger, shredded chicken, a hard-boiled egg.

She must have gotten up early, maybe even gone to the store, just for this. All these things I know she hates.

This shows she loves you! Feel loved!

It's a flood in the desert. I don't know how to absorb it.

I'm eating too fast now, almost choking. Tears start to form, and there's that stress around my spine from holding them back. It makes me think of Mom driving over a bridge, St. Christopher watching over her.

She has so many of those medallions. One in the car, one in her purse, spares in a drawer in the hall table where she keeps her keys.

"Is it good?" she asks, and I nod, cheeks full.

What is wrong with you! Feel loved!

I take another bite, try to let it warm me up. But I can't stop thinking about what she said last night. Can't stop wondering which is most true, this food or her words.

Knowing you taught me that love dies.

I squeeze my eyes shut, waiting for it to pass. Trying not to cry in front of her, because that will definitely make things worse.

It's a relief when I finally escape back to my room. And there are some messages waiting on my phone.

> **Jay Hayes:** okay
> **Jay Hayes:** i'll take you
> **Jay Hayes:** send me the dates

The floor tilts beneath me. He has to be kidding.

My hands are shaking, holding the screen close to my face. Oh my God, what have I done?

THIRTY-SIX

"So I booked the one you picked." Jay hands me his phone with the confirmation, and I click through to the listing. *Whole apartment, two beds, two nights.*

It's two weeks later, and we're back in Jay's car, parked behind the bowling alley where Ted is celebrating his birthday, going over last-minute logistics. The sky is starting to blush pink over the flat roof of the building. There are dumpsters to our left, the woods behind them.

Jay has a credit card, so he had to be the one to make the reservation. But when I take the cash I'd saved out of my bag and hand it to him, he separates out half and presses it back into my hand.

"No! What are you— You're already saving me money on the bus. And . . . I feel safer going with you than I would by myself."

It's funny how he makes this plan seem more realistic and more absurd at the same time.

"Good," he says, staring me down, and I drop it just so he'll stop looking at me like that.

We're leaving tomorrow. I feel like I'm about to blast off to the moon—I've barely been able to listen, all day, when Suzy's been talking to me. And I couldn't find a way to weasel out of it when she said, *You're coming to Ted's party! End of discussion.*

But she and Alex have been fighting all night, going off into corners to *have a talk* for long stretches of time. So it wasn't too hard to sneak out here.

"Why are you doing this?" I say too fast.

"Because you asked."

I shake my head. "Maybe this was a bad idea."

His laugh is sharp. "Probably?"

"Are you expecting something to happen when we're there?"

"I have no idea what's going to happen," he says.

"You know we're not going to . . ." *Get back together?* "Maybe it was . . . unfair of me to suggest this. You really don't have to do this. It was just—" I shake my head. "I shouldn't have asked you."

"It's important to me to do what I say I will." He flexes his hand, eyes glued to his screen. "And I kind of like how ridiculous this is. I want to do something impulsive for once."

Jay looks up at me and narrows his eyes. "So your mom is a landlord? What do you plan to do when we get there? There's someone living there, right? Do you think they would even—"

"I just feel like it will tell me something! To go there. Just being there, I think it will . . . help me understand her better. Somehow. If I go." Sweat pools under my shirt. "I know she's been lying to me. About my grandfather."

"And you don't want to ask her . . ."

"We can't all just *ask our moms to go to therapy*, okay?" I snap.

"Look, I'm not here to judge you," he says, hands raised. "Sorry she's lying to you. That must feel bad."

Your sad face just reminds me of him. His endless self-pity.

The gash in the photo paper floats in my mind.

"I guess," I say, "sometimes I get this feeling . . . like my mom is fighting someone who isn't there. If it could make more sense, maybe I could . . ." I don't even know how to finish that sentence. My nails dig into my inner arm. "I feel like . . . I just don't know what to be. She says these things about other immigrants. It makes me really ashamed? And confused."

My heart is beating so fast because I never talk about this. Barely even to myself, when it's not actively happening, let alone to other people. There's this guilt pressing down on me, making my brain over-heat. Not wanting to be associated with what she's saying. Not wanting to embarrass her, at the same time.

"I know I'm not really making sense." I let the air out of my lungs slowly, sinking into the passenger seat. "I guess I've just been stuck in the same place for so long, with her. I need to try something different. Even if it's the wrong thing."

Jay looks out the window to his left, at the pastel sky over the dark silhouettes of the trees. "Candace would have said something about *internalized racism* probably. If you told her that. She had all these big opinions, about . . ." He looks back at me. "I don't know, she had smarter things to say."

"Have you been thinking about going to see her?"

"You know, after you said—what was it? *Are you considering it from her perspective?*" He sighs and runs a hand over his face. "I actually kind of thought about it, more. And I guess . . . I don't know, I thought about how our dad was harder on her than on me. And . . . she felt like our mom never had her back about it, maybe."

I feel so chaotic right now, guilt on one side, this restless feeling tugging from the other. Maybe part of me wanted Candace to be awful, because that would mean the restless feeling is wrong, and I can stop feeling torn. Even if it would mean giving up on myself.

"I guess I just always tell myself . . . I should be able to deal with everything," Jay goes on. "So she should, too? Like if I try to understand why she did that, I'll have to . . ." He tilts his head back and stares at the ceiling, like he's appealing for divine intervention. "I do miss her. A lot, still. But she didn't show up for, like—the divorce, the move, any of it. She didn't come see us at the new house all summer. I don't really know how to get past that."

I want to reach for him, but I'm scared to fall into how I was before. Needing him so much, thinking he can fix me. And when I try to picture how I want to be, there's just a murky gray, no clear shapes.

So instead I take the St. Christopher medallion out of my backpack and hand it to him.

"What's that?"

"Patron saint of travelers."

"Like for luck?"

"To watch out for you."

Jay laughs and clips it to the sun visor.

The wind rocks the car from side to side, and I shiver. Maybe a little part of me wanted him to back out, scared again about what I'll find.

And who I'll be going to find it with.

And how he still makes me feel.

I go back inside first, so it won't seem like we were together. People are clustered around the bowling machines, shouting over the bad music, novelty lights swirling. There's Beth, perched on Ted's lap, head thrown back laughing at something he said. He looks startled, like he didn't even think it was that funny.

"Have you seen Suzy?" Alex asks, appearing beside me, looking stressed.

"Um, I thought she was with you?"

He shakes his head, exasperated, looking around the room.

And then those famous green eyes turn on me, and he takes a step closer, lowers his voice.

"Hey, so—I don't know exactly what's going on with you and Jay, but—"

All my nerve endings jump to attention. "What?"

Did Jay tell Alex? How could he tell him?

"He might not show it much—he keeps himself to himself. But he's . . . more sensitive than he looks. And he's had a rough year. Go easy on him, okay?"

"There you are!" Suzy says, emerging from the crowd, looking confused that we're talking.

What the fuck, Jay! I'm boiling, but I can't be mad at him right now, not when we're leaving so soon.

I bite my thumbnail and watch Alex and Suzy go off again. She's angled away from him, arms crossed, like she wants to run.

Is Alex going to tell her?

My fingers go numb.

He's more sensitive than he looks. He's had a rough year.

And a wave of shame washes over me, thinking about how lonely Jay seems and how I gave him something else he has to keep from everyone.

Kevin is nearby, talking to a guy I don't recognize. Every question begins with, "Who do you think is . . ." His voice is loud, like he wants people to hear.

"Who do you think is, like, a secret slut?" the guy asks.

Kevin looks right at me. "That quiet girl, definitely."

He knows I can hear him. The way his eyes are taunting. His self-satisfied grin.

All the stress I've been carrying, combustible in my spine—it's like someone just tossed a match.

That raw feeling travels upward, pressure bursting, too much heat and noise inside my head. It propels me forward, across the floor, where I shove Kevin with both hands.

He laughs, like I'm a joke, and I slap him clean across the face. Hand to cheek, Kevin stumbles back, drink spilling on his shirt.

There's some awkward laughter, a chorus of *"Ohhhhh shit."*

My hand flies to my mouth. Some pins crash, a ball someone threw before it happened reaching its destination.

"Jesus!" Kevin says, arms out like a question, holding his dripping, empty cup. "What the fuck is wrong with you?"

My God, I am my mother, I'm becoming something I don't understand!

"Yeah, Kevin, you shouldn't have said that!" Beth interjects. "Everyone knows she's a virgin anyway."

There's a smattering of laughs.

I see Alex then, standing in the circle of people gathered around. Not laughing along with them but looking kind of amused.

And there's Suzy, shoving his shoulder. "Are you fucking kidding me?"

"What?" He holds his hands up. "This is my fault?"

I'm ruining everything. I can't be here anymore.

I take off running, shoving past people, out the front doors. Past Jay, where he's standing with a group of people outside.

"Deedee!" he calls out as I head behind the building, little monster on the run.

I hide behind the dumpster, sinking into a squat. I'm crying now, oh fuck, oh shit.

"Deedee. Hey." Jay's crouching down next to me, touching my face.
You're missing something everyone else has.
Knowing you taught me that love dies.
Holding on to this will just make you miserable. Fixating on what you can't have.

I push his hands away and cover my face.

"Hey. Hey." He sounds like when he's comforting Gemma, and I don't want that, that's not what I want! "Talk to me. What happened?"

"You *told him*? You told Alex about—whatever we were doing?"

"What? No, I didn't." His voice hardens, a defensive edge to it. "What did he say to you?"

Stress prickles between my shoulder blades.

"I didn't tell anyone." His voice gets gentler. "But maybe . . . people just figure things out, eventually."

I bite the inside of my cheek. Maybe if I don't say anything, he'll get tired and leave.

Jay puts a hand on my back. "What happened in there?"

"I slapped Kevin!"

Jay laughs.

"It's not funny!"

"Look, I'm not saying violence is the answer, but—" He can barely keep the laugh out of his voice. "I think he'll live. He probably deserved it."

I can just barely hear him through all the noise in my head. Mom saying I ruined her life. The ambulance disappearing behind the trees, because of me, and what I did.

If I could destroy a mother's love, what else could I ruin? Jay's whole life, probably.

He reaches for me, and I twist out of his grasp.

"Jay, just *stop it*!" My voice sounds so wounded, high-pitched, strange to me. "You should just—you should just *get away from me while you can!*"

His brows knit closer together. "What are you talking about?"

I stand up suddenly, and he loses his balance, tips backward onto his palms.

He scrambles to his feet, and I glare at him the way the aswang looks at me in my dreams—eyes blazing, soul-penetrating, ready to take flight. Guts about to burst all over the place. Like I'm the monster in this story, not the one who has to be afraid.

"Because I ruin people's lives," I say, enunciating every word.

Then I rush past him, checking his shoulder, back to the front door where Suzy is waiting for me, and I run right into her arms.

"Hey. Ugh. Those losers." She gives me a squeeze. "Come on, we're getting out of here."

THIRTY-SEVEN

There's no way he's going to want to go with me now.

I ruined it. He's seen what I'm like.

The bag that's hidden under my bed is useless. I should just unpack it, but I can't bring myself to get up.

The sky is lightening outside, deep blue turning pale.

We won't be able to get a refund this late. I'll have to pay him back. All that money wasted.

Mom is up, moving around in the hall.

I swing my legs out of bed, bare feet on the cold floor. Get dressed slowly. Go downstairs.

She's standing there, rolling suitcase ready, handle raised. "Will you be okay?"

I don't know why she's asking that. She's left me home alone lots of times before.

Then she gives me another tight smile, and she and her rolling suitcase are gone. The house is quiet.

I sit at the kitchen table, staring at the vases on top of the cabinet. The curves I've traced in my mind more times than I can count, the light shifting on them as it gets brighter outside.

And there's a honk from the driveway.

Jay's car is there. He's leaning on it, hands in his pockets. Waiting for me.

What.

I stuff my feet in my shoes and hurry outside.

"You're not ready yet?" he calls out to me, like everything is fine.

"I thought—maybe you wouldn't want to go. After last night."

He scoffs and looks at his feet. "Come on, get your stuff. We don't have all day."

When my bag is in his trunk and the house is locked and I'm in the passenger seat next to him, we sit there in silence, wondering who's going to talk first.

"Hey." Jay reaches over and puts his hand on top of my head. "What's going on in there?"

I'm not sure if I want to slap his hand away or soak up the feeling, like a house cat in a puddle of sun.

I cross my arms and try to ignore the tingling under my skin. "I didn't scare you away."

"Sorry to disappoint you. But you're not that scary."

"You're not worried I'll ruin your life?"

He shakes his head and smiles like I'm ridiculous.

I feel stressed again, trying to bite back the urge to cry. It's too much. I can't absorb it. I'm going to drown.

"I'm not worried," he says, and starts the car.

I can't believe he actually wants to do this.

But Jay's next to me, in the driver's seat. Humming along to the music he put on, strangely carefree.

It's almost relaxing, barreling through space with him, suspended between the past and future.

Then Suzy texts me, and my heart jumps into my throat.

> **Suzy Jang:** hey, are you okay?
> **Suzy Jang:** do you want to come over?

Shit. Shit, shit.

> **Deedee Walters:** hey, i can't this weekend. i'm grounded

It's believable enough. It happens all the time.

> **Suzy Jang:** oh nooo
> **Suzy Jang:** well i'm sorry about last night
> **Deedee Walters:** don't be sorry! i'm sorry i was a mess
> **Suzy Jang:** you're the best mess
> **Suzy Jang:** you'll be ungrounded for prom, right?

It's been impossible to forget that prom is next weekend. The committee was late getting it together this year, so it's happening right before finals. Lockers are decorated, signs posted. The other day, I got trapped by a promposal that monopolized the entire hallway, blocking me from getting to French.

Oh God. Just do what Mom does. Compartmentalize. Press on.

Deedee Walters: yeah definitely

I take a long, slow breath out and turn off my phone.

Jay glances sideways at me. "You okay?"

"What did you tell your mom? About what you're doing this weekend."

"That I have to go to New York for work."

"Oh. She knows you're going to New York?"

"Yeah, I figure that's easier. She didn't really question it." He shrugs, eyes on the road, one hand on the wheel. "Their office is there actually. They're still open on Memorial Day. I could drop by, say hello."

"Casually blackmail Phil."

He grimaces. "Try to get a real job there."

We pull into a rest stop after a while and get some sandwiches from the gas station. I go to the bathroom while he settles in at a picnic table under a cluster of trees.

And when I come back, there's some Tupperware arranged on the table.

One normal sized one, with mango slices inside. Three small ones, filled with dips.

"That one has shrimp paste. This one's made with fish sauce. And . . ." He picks it up and tilts it toward me. "Chili salt. You can branch out."

I'm biting the nail of my index finger, pressing my trembling hand into my face, and he looks at me kind of uncertain. "You said you liked—"

"No, I do!" Oh my God, I'm crying and it's not even dark out, I can't pretend he doesn't see.

"Are you, uh—are you okay?"

"Um, it's just—" I wipe my face. "Really nice. Too nice."

Jay's hand goes behind his head. "It's not a big deal."

He dips a mango in the chili salt and takes a bite.

I slip the camera out of my backpack and take a picture of the spread on the table.

It's the first time I've felt brave enough to use it. It's just been hiding in my closet since I got it, because I was hoping if Mom didn't see it, she would forget to be mad.

Jay looks really happy, leaning on one elbow, watching me eat most of the rest.

He likes taking care of people, I can see that. And that makes me worried about him, remembering that time he yelled on the phone. He likes it until he gets burnt out and realizes there's nothing left for himself.

"Why did you actually agree to this?" I ask.

"I guess . . . I just want a break from everything. I want to live in the moment, for a weekend. I don't even care what we do there, honestly." Jay squints into the middle distance, sun in his eyes as it dips behind the trees. "My life feels kind of heavy. And going around with you, being all these places we're not supposed to be, I don't know—it feels light, for a minute." His eyebrows scrunch down and his nose wrinkles. "The way you're impulsive. The specific way your plans are kind of ridiculous. It really cheers me up for some reason?"

"Wow, thanks." I'm bouncing with laughter, shaking in my core. "Glad I could help. By being ridiculous."

I have too much pent-up energy then, so I reach over and tickle his sides.

And wow, he's really ticklish. His voice gets so high, giggling, and his arms curl in. Why didn't I figure this out sooner?

He grabs my wrists to stop me and looks me in the eye, all soft, earnest brown. I have to close my eyes, take some deep breaths, because I'm scared of too many things. Of needing him too much. Of myself, and what I'm made of. How I could be bad for him. How he could hurt me again.

"Yeah," he says, so close. "I'm strangely glad I'm here."

He lets me go, and I open my eyes and pick up the camera again. The lens barrel feels reassuring in my hand.

"To commemorate the moment," I say.

And instead of covering his face like he used to, he tries to smile. Barely flinches. Lets me.

THIRTY-EIGHT

WE GET THERE AFTER DARK, GLITTERING LIGHTS AND TALL BUILDINGS rising around us.

I'm gaping out the window at all the people, the life unfolding.

We pass a wall of trash bags piled on the sidewalk, and I think I see a rat scurrying past while we're stopped at a light.

Suzy pops into my head, belting out "City Baby Attacked by Rats," and I try not to think of what she might say about what I'm doing right now.

The maps app announces we've arrived at our destination, and Jay is leaning forward, peering at the street signs. It takes forever to find a place to park. It might be the first time I've actually seen him stressed about driving.

My chest feels tight, thinking of the intense thing we're about to do. Staying overnight together. In an apartment. Just the two of us. In a strange city.

I really didn't think this through.

In the elevator, Jay seems completely spent. He slumps against the wall, holding his backpack on one shoulder.

It's awfully close in here. The beige paint on the doors is chipped, and a rusty brown color peeks out underneath.

I can't help but notice every little movement he makes—the rising and falling of his chest, the way he flexes his fingers. One of his knuckles cracks.

The elevator comes to a stop with a bounce, shuddering as it tries to find the floor.

The hallway is narrow and dark. An ambulance goes by outside, siren distorting as it gets closer then farther away.

Mom would definitely say this is a mistake.

Jay puts the key in the lock and struggles for a second, jiggling the knob.

"It's stubborn." He forces a quick smile, like it's his apartment and he wanted to impress me.

The door opens, and—there's not much to this apartment.

"Are you kidding me?" Jay says.

My back tenses. I should have thought of this. I should have suggested staying at a hotel instead.

Jay's pulling up the confirmation email, frowning at it. "Look, I swear I didn't—" He hands me the phone so I can check it again.

I shake my head and hand it back to him. "Yeah. I believe you."

He takes off his sneakers and steps onto the bed in the middle of the small room, bouncing a little. Barely stretching his arms out all the way, he can touch both walls. "There is . . . definitely not another bed here. Or a couch. Or . . . anything, really."

Jay searches on his phone and lifts it to his ear. "I'll figure it out. I'll get them to . . . switch us to a different place, or something."

"Just leave it!" I sigh and put my backpack down. I'm so overwhelmed with the absurdity of being here. I want so badly to sleep. "It's fine."

He stares at me, still bouncing a little. "Are you sure?"

"It's just— We're not here for that long. It's not so bad."

He ends the call and hops down from the bed. "Um, okay. I can sleep in the tub."

We crowd into the doorway of the bathroom together and turn on the light. As we watch, a giant cockroach crawls out of the tub drain, and I jump back with a full-body shudder.

Jay grabs some toilet paper and squashes it. One quick motion and it's gone down the toilet.

"You can't sleep there," I say.

He looks at me, waiting for me to say where he should sleep instead. My stomach gets wavy, limbs tingling, picturing him lying next to me.

This is fine, this is fine. It's going to be fine, don't make a big thing of it. We'll just go to sleep.

"I'm so tired, I won't even know you're there," I say.

We take turns changing our clothes and brushing our teeth.

When I come out of the bathroom in a loose T-shirt and little cotton shorts, his eyes linger on me for a few seconds before he looks away at the floor.

Then we get into the bed, and, in fact, I do know he's there. I'm painfully aware of every tiny movement of Jay's body. I can practically feel the tension in his shoulders, the way the mattress shifts as he breathes. He flips over several times, lying on his stomach, his side, his back. Every way but facing me.

"I'm going to leave a strongly worded bad review," he mumbles, eyes closed, hand on his chest. His knees make triangles under the blanket.

My eyes follow the lights of passing cars sliding over the popcorn ceiling. I'm holding myself so carefully, trying to breathe as lightly as possible.

Eventually, he says to the wall, "Are you asleep?"

"No, are you?"

"Yeah, this isn't really working."

Jay sighs and rolls over to face me, so I face him, too.

His head rests on his folded hands. For a second it feels like this is a slumber party, and we're about to start telling scary stories.

The corner of his mouth quirks upward. "Do you still kind of hate me?"

"Hard to say." I can barely control the smile that stretches my face, and he laughs.

My heart aches, seeing him this close.

"Thanks for coming with me," I whisper, even though no one else is around.

Jay's eyes travel across my face. "What do you want right now?" he whispers back.

It feels like there's a rock in my throat. It takes forever to swallow.

"Can we hug?" I say so quietly, maybe he won't hear.

"Come here." Jay eases me closer, so my head rests against his chest.

It's such a relief and it's so stressful at the same time, pressing into him, surrounded by his smell. That overwhelming want washes over me, wind through the grass all over again. Why did I think we could do this? Maybe if I stay very still, breathe in and out, it will pass.

I'm going to ruin his life, this nice boy who's hurting and deserves better.

"Maybe I shouldn't have gotten you involved in my mess again," I say.

"I don't know," he whispers into my hair. "I'm having a pretty good time."

My head bobs up and down with his breathing, a boat on a gentle sea.

"You're nothing like him," I say, eyes closed, his heart beating by my ear. "You know that, right?"

His chest shakes as he laughs. "Thanks." He doesn't sound convinced.

Jay's hand slips up under the back of my shirt, resting flat on the tender spot between my shoulder blades. "Is this okay?"

"Yeah," I say, choked up, because he remembered.

It makes me feel secure, somehow, his hand not doing anything. Just reminding me he's there.

I fall asleep quickly after that.

Jay is already dressed when I wake up, leaning against the doorframe, sipping from an energy drink.

"Eggs?" He runs a hand through his messy hair and yawns. "I went to the bodega."

I get up and hover next to him in the kitchen. On the counter, there's a can of black coffee waiting for me.

Next to it, there's an egg carton, an open takeout box from the Chinese place downstairs filled with white rice, and a little bottle of fish sauce.

I point to it. "Did you bring that from home?"

"Um." The color rises in his cheeks a little as he looks in the cabinets for a bowl. "Yeah, I wanted to have this for breakfast."

I get the camera from my bag and take some pictures of him while he beats the eggs with chopsticks that also look like his own. He planned ahead.

Jay laughs while he pours the eggs into the pan. "Okay, that's enough of that!"

There's a hollow feeling in my gut, remembering the full reports I used to give Suzy about the slightest word or glance from a boy I liked.

Now the boy I like is making me eggs in this shitty kitchen that can barely hold two people.

And I slept in the same bed next to him.

Which we're going to do again. Tonight.

He puts two plates down on the counter, eggs steaming over the rice, and I start to eat. They're fluffy, buttery, soothing.

"So what's the plan?" he says, in between bites.

"You don't have to come if you don't want to."

"I'm a little worried about you out there, honestly. I'd rather stick together. For my peace of mind."

We both finish eating quickly, and I take his plate, start washing the dishes. My restless feeling has grown so big now that Jay and I have moved into it together, and we're playing house inside.

"Maybe after, we can go see Candace," I say.

"Maybe." There's a little edge to his voice. "We'll see."

THIRTY-NINE

I'VE NEVER BEEN ON A TRAIN LIKE THIS BEFORE, AND MY PALMS SWEAT as it shudders and screeches. Jay nods off next to me, head leaned back against the scratched-up glass, eyes closed and mouth slightly open. He looks so innocent like this, no tension in his face.

The train climbs aboveground and we pass over a cemetery, the tops of houses going by, the green of trees.

I nudge Jay and he jolts awake.

We get down from the train, and there it is: a duplex in brown brick, looking out onto a square with a tiny park in the middle. I pull the yellow envelope of photos out of my bag for reference, and spin around, taking in the scenery.

There's the same church spire in the window, in this one of my dad in the living room. They must have lived in that building before I was born.

"So what do you think?" Jay says.

"I think this is the last place my mom was happy."

"Oh." He chews on that for a second. "Are you . . . going to try out that key?"

But before I can answer, the door of the building opens, and someone is coming out. Someone familiar. All the nerves in my body jump to attention.

I grab Jay's hand and run across the street, ducking into the bodega on the corner.

"What? What happened?" He moves with me as I crouch down by the window, not dropping my hand. "You look like you saw a ghost."

"It's my mom!" I hiss, watching her take a seat on a bench in the little park.

He blinks, dazed, and peers through the window. "Did you know she was—"

"I thought she was on a work trip!"

Mom's just sitting there. Reminiscing maybe. I always think of her as looming so large, but from here she looks small, lost, uncomfortable.

Jay runs his thumb over my knuckles, sending sparks up my arm. "I'm surprised you didn't bring binoculars."

I tear my eyes away from Mom for a second, and Jay's face is so close, the way he's squatting next to me. It would be easy to lean in and press my lips to his.

His brows push closer together. "What?"

A cat jumps down from a stack of newspapers next to me and rubs its face against my leg.

"That's a real compliment!" a guy from the counter calls. "Mimi doesn't usually like strangers."

Jay stands and stretches out his back. "Maybe I'll get a scratcher."

"Seems like a waste of money," I mutter, absently petting the cat as I watch Mom staring at this building.

How often does she come here, reliving the past she never wants to talk about?

Somewhere behind me, Jay orders a slice of pizza instead.

Mom must sit there for at least half an hour. And then she's moving again, walking back toward the elevated tracks.

I rush over to Jay, and it sounds like the guy at the counter is giving him relationship advice now. "I'm telling you, it's all about communication, right? If you and your girlfriend—"

"Hey! Sorry to interrupt, but—" I make a frantic movement with my hands.

"Okay, boss," the guy says, and fist-bumps Jay. "Good chatting with you."

"Take care, man."

It's funny how Jay keeps so much from the people closest to him, but it's so easy for him to talk to people he doesn't know.

"So I'm your girlfriend now?" I grab his hand again and we race back to the tracks, staying far enough behind Mom that we can dart into a doorway if she turns around. "That's news to me."

"I was—uh—simplifying," Jay says between breaths as we run. "He assumed—and I just—rolled with it."

We rush up the stairs, onto the platform, and into the train she's boarding. My eyes are glued to the sliver of her red windbreaker I can see through the window between the cars.

She only goes a couple stops, and then she's out onto the platform again.

"Oh shit!" I grab Jay's hand and tug him outside before the doors can close on us. Peering from behind a newsstand, I watch her choose an exit, head up the steps.

"Your tradecraft is hilarious here," he says, and I give him a look. "What? I've watched spy shows."

When we get aboveground, Mom is going into a diner across the street.

It's the one from her photos. Same flagstone exterior, neon sign unchanged from years ago.

It's selfish to indulge your feelings.

It's pointless to think about the past, but somehow you always drag me back there.

I'm boiling inside. The heat in my face could run a small power plant.

"You hungry?" Jay says.

"Wh-wh-what? Wait—" But he's already crossing, and all I can do is run after him and try not to get hit by a car.

My nerves seize up, seeing Mom sitting by herself in the corner.

"Don't worry," he says as the hostess leads us to a booth. "I'll sit facing her. I doubt she'll remember me."

He settles in across from me and studies the menu. "Want to share the chicken basket?"

I glare at him, scared to turn around and check on Mom, but also scared to not look.

When the food comes, Jay asks for the check. "You know, so we can leave at a *moment's notice.*"

"You're enjoying this."

"Nice change of pace, thinking about problems I didn't cause."

We eat largely in silence, but it's actually delicious. Better than I expected, looking at this place.

Jay glances in my mom's direction at regular intervals, taking the lid off the pot before my discomfort boils over.

"Target on the move," he says, and we're up and out the door a few minutes after her.

We walk behind her for a long stretch, under the elevated tracks. Finally, she turns into the cemetery. The skin prickles on the back of my neck.

I knew Mom buried Dad somewhere out here, that she brought him back after the funeral. But she never wanted to bring me to visit. *No use dwelling on the past.*

We follow her inside, peeking around a bush. She's crouching down in front of a gravestone, talking to it. Placing something there—a note.

Finally, she leaves, and I don't care about following her anymore. I watch her disappear, a red dot that vanishes through the gates.

I need to read this note. I don't care if it's wrong.

"Deedee," Jay says, voice full of concern. "Hey!"

His fingers brush my arm, but I rush forward anyway and grab the envelope sitting on the grave.

"Are you sure you want to—"

But I'm already tearing it open, hands trembling, holding it close to my face. Jay turns away, like he wants to give me some privacy.

There are three letters inside, neatly folded.

The first is addressed to my dad.

I'm selling the apartment finally. The last tenants moved out months ago. I knew I had to let go of it, but I couldn't bring myself to do it yet. I spent a lot of time there, just remembering. Standing in the empty rooms. Looking at them from different angles, trying to focus on the good times we had.

Usually I try not to think about it, because I'll regret too much. How much time I wasted, being a way I don't want with you. I still feel ashamed about some of the things I said to you. How angry I was with you, sometimes.

I told myself I'm holding on to the apartment because it's a good investment in Deedee's future, but really, it's because it's the last piece of you that I have.

And Deedee is so hard to talk to. When I would read her letters, it was like seeing someone else. I got a glimpse of her life.

I have to laugh, and Jay glances at me.

Those letters!

In a sick way, we are the same. I'm spying on her, and she's spying on me. Violating each other's privacy, trying to understand each other.

A sadness moves in then, penetrates my bones like humidity in cold weather, because half of what I wrote in those letters was bullshit I thought some distant, lofty man would like.

But she doesn't want to write them anymore.

I'm so lonely. I can't get close to anyone, I get too scared. It's a struggle not to indulge. In the grief, in the sadness. But I can't afford to feel sorry for myself. It could threaten everything, if I let those feelings in. My ability to do my job. To survive.

I thought I have to just do my best to push it down and keep going, not let it in. I'm weak but this is the best I can do.

But maybe I've made a mess of things this way.

I'm always thinking about what could go wrong, all the bad things that could happen to Deedee. I can barely stand to spend time with her, because every memory we make, it will just hurt more if something happens to her.

But then, seeing how she is with that other girl's parents.

I feel so confused and alone. I wish you were here for me to talk to.

I think I understand something about her now, a lightning bolt to the heart, fresh and searing and all at once. She couldn't stop grieving because she didn't let herself really start. So scared of her emotions, she can't move through it, lingering in the lobby of grief forever.

I can't bear to get rid of the letter you wrote me, but it hurts to hold on to it. I'm trying to move on now, so I'm returning it to you.

I unfold the next one.

Something about the handwriting looks familiar, the same as the cramped scrawl on the back of the photo in my nightstand. And the name at the bottom. My dad's.

It's the kind of letter you write when something has become so impossible to talk about, there's no way but to get your thoughts down on paper.

YOU NEED TO GET HELP FOR YOUR ANGER ISSUES. I KNOW YOU'VE BEEN THROUGH A LOT, BUT I CAN'T KEEP DOING THIS.

Jay's words from before echo through my head: *We can't keep going like this.*

The way Mom talks, I used to think most of her troubles began after I came along. And even though it's getting harder to believe that now, it's still stunning to see it in writing.

She had anger issues.

Before he died.

And someone else noticed.

I unfold the third letter, in my mom's handwriting again. It looks like one she'll never send—just talking into the void, like the ones she has me write.

To my family, it says.

> *I know he still blames me for Nanay's death, and he made all of you believe it was my fault, too.*

A vague memory comes back to me, from years ago. When we were parked by the beach, and she was talking about her mom, she used that word. Nanay, mother.

They blamed her?

The yellowed magazine clipping floats in my mind. Mom would have been my age when her mother died. Why would they think her death was Mom's fault? How could it be her fault if it was a car accident? I remember the way Mom talked about her, like her mother was her entire world.

I'm shaking, and the tears are coming. My knees can't hold anymore, so I sink down into a crouch.

Jay's hand is on my back. "Hey. Breathe. You're okay."

So she knows exactly what it's like. We really must be cursed.

"Maybe that's enough now," Jay says, pushing the letter gently down so I can see him. "Why don't we . . . do something else?"

I feel so grateful for him right then, his comforting smile, the way he touches my back. So I tuck the letter into my bag and hold his hand as we walk to the subway.

FORTY

MY HEAD IS SPINNING FOR THE ENTIRE HOUR WE'RE ON THE TRAIN. MY hand rests on Jay's leg, fingers entwined, while I stare at our reflection in the dark window across from us.

You need to get help for your anger issues.

I know he still blames me for Nanay's death.

I feel so confused and alone. I wish you were here for me to talk to.

The sadness of those words creeps into my bones. And I feel panicked, the way empathy for her starts to feel like I'm choking. Because if she's not so bad, it means I am, and everything she said about me must be true.

We transfer at Fourteenth Street, surface again at Lexington and Eighty-Sixth, Jay leading me by the hand like he's lived here for years.

Inside the Met, the ceilings are high, and there are so many people, voices echoing off the shining floors as we head up the big staircase.

Jay guides me through the halls until we find the photography exhibition, in a series of quiet rooms with beige carpets. The photographs are slices of crystallized emotion, stilled in time. So much unsaid, reverberating out of the frame.

My face is puffy even though I didn't let myself cry. It's such a relief to be surrounded by art right now. He knew the exact right place to take me.

He's looking at each image seriously, considering it.

"You like this stuff." I poke him in the chest. "You like art. And drawing. Admit it."

Jay laughs. "Okay, Inspector Deedee." He takes my hand again, tugging me forward. I guess this is a thing we're doing now. "Let's go to the roof, I think it's open."

We get into an elevator, and the doors open onto a rooftop garden, with the trees of Central Park spread out around us, and the buildings of Manhattan rising on all sides.

"This is— Wow. This is incredible."

We're quiet for a while, standing by the railing, looking out at the city. I could stay here for hours saying nothing at all.

"So do you think you found what you came here for?" he asks.

A gust of wind sends the leaves in the park fluttering, a ripple through the sea of green.

I don't know what to say, so I give his hand a few quick squeezes.

Jay presses my hand to his chest and looks off into the distance. It rises and falls with him as he breathes, a few times before he lets go.

When we get back to the room after eating dinner, it looks even smaller than before. Suddenly, the question of what is going to happen next is very loud.

We take turns again, changing clothes, brushing teeth. When I come out, Jay is sitting on the bed, drawing in his notebook.

He snaps it shut when he sees me and slides it back in his bag. I sit about a foot away.

"It's bright," I say, and he leaps up and turns off the light.

I really don't deserve him.

Jay settles back down, closer to me than before. His face looks soft in the light from the street lamps outside. It's funny how it's never all the way dark out here.

"Deedee, I wanted to ask you . . ."

My heart beats a little faster. Is he going to ask about having sex? I've been thinking about it, in the back of my mind, all day. And I know now that I'll be disappointed if we don't, but still kind of terrified if it turns out he wants to.

"About what you said at Ted's party. Outside."

Oh.

"That you ruin people's lives."

Oh, *that*. I sit up, instantly tense.

"Why did you say that?" His voice gets quieter. "I kept wondering . . . if that's something you actually think about yourself."

I draw in a shaky breath and bounce a little on the mattress. "You really want to know?" I laugh through gritted teeth. "It's not a nice answer. Maybe you want to think it through."

"Yeah," he says, gently. "I want to know."

I've been dreading this for so long, but I was going to have to tell him sometime. A warm numbness comes over me, a distant ringing in my ears.

Maybe this will push him away, finally, and I don't have to be scared of it anymore. Maybe it's for the best. Might as well rip the Band-Aid off.

"When I—" My voice comes out as a croak, and I clear my throat, swallow. "When I was a kid—when I was four—my dad got sick. We had to be really careful around him. His face changed. His body changed. I went to school and came home with a cold and . . ."

I'm shaking a little, because I can still see him in the hospital bed, right after. How *not-him* he looked, lying there, shirt cut open. How obvious it was that he wasn't there anymore.

And then, days later, after the funeral—I'm in our living room again, filled with people, and Mom is in the corner, hiding by the table crammed with casserole dishes. I can see the flowers painted on one of them, the pattern of the wood grain at eye level. The veins in Mom's hands as she clutches the edge for support.

Jay's looking at me, worried, and I have to come back here, be in this room with him again. So I try to hold the words lightly, at a distance, like they can't hurt me.

"He got sicker. It got worse. I killed him, basically." I tell myself that all the time, but I forgot how brutal it sounds when you say it out loud.

Jay puts his hands on my shoulders. "Deedee—"

"That's what my mom said. After his funeral. That it's my fault. That I ruined her life."

"That's not—"

"The life she worked so hard to make for herself, you know?" I'm rambling, and it's tumbling out, all the sticky mess I try to keep hidden. "And now she just has to live with me. Every day. This reminder, this *punishment*. It would be better for everyone if I just . . . if I just never existed."

"Hey. Don't say that." His voice is firm, worried in a way that's different than before, and he's gripping my arms like he needs to keep me from disappearing. "That's— Wow. That's not true."

I'm trembling now, everything just getting so on top of me. Suddenly, I'm sobbing. It feels so violent, this shit that tears up my insides, finally coming out. I'm afraid of what else it can destroy. I want to put it back in, protect him from it.

His hands are around my face, turning the mess of it toward him. "Don't ever believe that. Don't, okay? Look at me. That's not true."

I'm covering my face in my hands, just bawling now. God, this is it. This is going to chase him away. I'll lose him. There he goes.

Jay presses me close, his hand on the back of my head, my face against his neck, and it feels like hours pass. So much time, and he's still holding on to me.

"You can't blame yourself for that," he whispers into my hair. "I'm so sorry that you—" He sniffs, like he's crying, too. "It breaks my heart that you actually think that's your fault."

I feel a strange calm now, like I really cried myself out and something else can move in where the sadness used to be.

"I think I need to lie down," I whisper.

He doesn't let go of me, just leans over so we flop onto our sides, tangled together, my damp face pressed into his chest, my leg slotted between his.

Maybe we'll just go to sleep like this. He really was going to make it through this whole weekend without making me feel a moment of pressure to do a single thing. He's always so concerned about making me comfortable, on top of everything he's carrying. And I worry about that, but . . .

A surge of affection fills up my chest, overflows. I need to be as close to him as possible. My hand in his hair, I find his mouth with

253

mine in the dark, and he kisses me back, warming up the center of me.

Jay leans back and studies me, in the half light from the street. Like I'm something so precious to him, he just had to take another look.

"I'm obviously glad you exist," he says.

I shift so I'm on top of him, and something moves, through his shorts, and— Oh.

"Hey," I whisper into his ear.

His chest jolts a little under me as he laughs. "Hey."

"I want to, but—do you have—"

He leans over for his bag and comes back with a condom, because of course he has one. He doesn't seem like the type to be unprepared.

He leaves it on the bed and puts his hands on the waistband of my shorts, tugs them down just a little and kisses me there. A shiver runs between my hips.

"Is this okay?"

When I say yes, he slides off my shorts, down to my ankles, and I kick them off onto the floor. He inches my underwear down, kisses the skin he uncovered. Slides them down some more, looks up for my reaction, kisses me again. He moves so slowly, I'm halfway out of my mind when he gets to the spot I've been longing for him to reach. And when he does, the feeling is so consuming, for a second, I forget my body's lines and edges, all its limitations. There's just this joy I didn't know about, elastic, growing to fit all of me inside.

He's back to kissing my mouth again, and my shirt is off, his clothes are off, my hands slide over his back, so much of his skin pressing against so much of mine. It's a strange relief, finally being this close when I've told myself not to think about it for so long.

He rolls on the condom and seems kind of nervous, and then he's on top of me and we're moving against each other, and there's this pressure, this new sensation overwhelming me, taking me somewhere

I haven't been. I'm staring at the ceiling, my fingers digging into his warm shoulders, his jagged breath on my ear. *I can't believe it's really happening*, that I can't be closer to him than this. We're so close, and I still want him closer, and closer, and closer, and closer, and closer.

Then it's over, and Jay lies on top of me for a while before he kisses my shoulder and gets out of bed.

And I feel a little empty, watching the lights pass over the wall while I hear him kill another cockroach in the bathroom. I miss him already when he climbs back into bed and hugs me from behind, and the change in his breathing tells me he's finally asleep.

FORTY-ONE

JAY'S STILL HOLDING ME WHEN I WAKE UP IN THE MORNING, HIS ARM around my waist, his breath on the back of my neck.

I told him and he's still here.

He's still here. He's still here.

The words in my head match my heartbeat as I watch the light coming up golden along the wall, catching the lines of the fire escape.

I slip out of bed to get my camera and take a picture of him, face half buried in his pillow.

He wakes up and smiles at me, rubs his eyes. Looks at his phone.

And then he sits straight up. Eyes wide, neck tense. His hand goes to his hair, closes around a clump.

My stomach clenches. "What's wrong?"

A weak laugh squeezes out of his lungs. "You're fucking kidding me."

Jay stares at the phone for a while, hand over his mouth. He's shaking his head, color draining from his face. "I'm going to kill him."

He throws himself on the bed and punches the mattress. "Fuck!" he yells into it. Such a wild, pained sound. It hurts my heart.

"Jay, you're scaring me!"

"Can you just be quiet while I think!" He's clutching his head, hair sticking up between his fingers.

All I can feel is white-hot panic. In my head, I'm with Mom again, and something has gone wrong, and there's nothing I can do for her.

"My fucking job—" He punches the pillow a few more times. "Doesn't exist anymore! Fucking Phil got *found out* and *shitcanned*. And he's saying—"

He throws the pillow across the room, and it bounces off the wall, lands with a soft sound on the floor.

"He can't even make my last payment! And—and—" Jay's gasping, like he can't get enough air. "And *now what the fuck am I going to do*?"

I'm letting him down, I'm letting him down, I'm a useless dead weight.

He's sitting up again, head in his hands. "I need to figure out what to do. I need to think. I need to—to—" Jay scrambles off the bed and almost trips, kicking off his shorts, pulling on fresh clothes and shoes. "I need to go. I'll come back. Just stay here."

"Where are you going?"

"I have to do something. I'll come back, just—just sit tight, okay?" Then he's gone.

It's almost 9 a.m. now, and we have to be out by one. Mom is driving back today, and my stomach lurches, imagining her getting back before me.

The panic is growing in my chest, squeezing my lungs as I sit on the bed, hugging my knees.

The way he looked at me in the kitchen yesterday.

The way he looked at me last night.

How was that just hours ago? How was that the same lifetime?

The hours tick by. I shower, get dressed, pack as much as I can. Sit on the bed, rocking back and forth, panic spiraling upward.

What am I going to do?

I want to call Suzy, but oh God I can't, I can never explain this, what the fuck have I done?

I feel so confused and alone. I wish you were here for me to talk to.

I'm so scared right now.

How must Mom have felt, being alone, a child depending on her, having to decide everything on her own?

At 12:30, I'm beside myself. He hasn't replied to any of my texts.

His car is still parked outside, but he has the keys.

I wish I could talk to someone, someone who would know what to do.

What would Mom do in this situation? She always says to never depend on a man. She would take things into her own hands.

Jay's backpack is there, at the foot of the bed.

I want to stop being this person who goes through people's things, but . . . maybe some other day. I slide out the notebook and try to page through as quickly as possible.

There are drawings of me. Some unfinished.

But that's not what I'm here for. I flip past them, trying not to let my eyes rest on anything for too long.

There's nothing I can use. I don't know what I was expecting.

But then a postcard falls out—dated a couple years ago, with a New York return address. From *Candace Đình Hayes*. My patron saint of not talking to your mom.

On impulse, I pull up Instagram and do a search.

I recognize her from the photo on Jay's desk. Her skin is a shade deeper than his, but they have the same nose, same eyes. Her dark hair is tied back in a high ponytail, bangs cut short in a way that makes her look like she should be in a band.

I scroll through her profile, kind of fascinated that there can still be a life out there for you, if you don't talk to your mom.

There's a picture of her in a park, in autumn, sitting on a blanket with friends, smiling for the camera. Another of her on a beach with a girl in a wetsuit, laughing and kissing her on her cheek, captioned *One year together*.

In another, she's sitting at a table, in a small apartment with art on the walls, gentle clutter on every surface. It feels like people *live* there, a feeling our house doesn't really have.

She's surrounded by people, gathered at the table. Her friends, her girlfriend, handing each other food. The atmosphere of a family dinner. Like you don't get just one chance at family.

I'm out of ideas, and maybe she would know what to do. So I hit "follow" and send her a message.

> Hi! You don't know me but I'm friends with your brother, and we came to New York together, and he's having a rough time right now. He lost his job. He's kind of panicking. He ran off somewhere. He's not answering my texts. I don't know what to do, but I thought maybe you would know, or maybe we could figure it out. I'm sorry this message is so weird. I don't know who else to ask.

As soon as I send it, a wave of guilt hits me, like a blast of hot air from the subway. Jay would definitely not want me to be doing this right now.

I bite my nails, scroll through more of her photos, stare out the window.

A notification pops up. She wrote back.

You came to New York with Jay?
Are you okay? Where are you? I'll come meet you.

But then there are footsteps outside the door, the key turning in the lock. So I close the app.

Jay looks *off*. The way he's moving, unsteady. The way his face is flushed, kind of red.

"Okay, change of plans. We're going to have to take the bus. But I can pay for your ticket."

"*What?*"

His breath, when he talks—what is that *smell*?

"I got paid, I can pay for your ticket." The way he repeats that, clinging to it. *It's a thing I can do. It's a thing I understand.*

"Did you . . . are you *drunk?*"

He rubs his eyes with his fingers. "I needed to get my last paycheck. I was pounding on Phil's door, yelling, bothering the neighbors. And he was already drinking—"

"Who is even drinking this early?!"

"An alcoholic who was skating by having me do all his work for him? Yeah, it turns out that's what he meant about work-life balance." His laugh is grim. "I was at his door, screaming so much the neighbors were looking into the hall, and he said, *Whoa, dude, you're so wound up, you have to calm down first. Have a drink with me. Then we can talk about that paycheck.* And everything is ruined anyway, so I thought, *fine.*"

"You *what?* How much did you have to drink?" Oh my God, he's actually drunk. The way his breath smells, there's no way it was just one or two.

"I had one, whiskey or something, and—everything is so fucked already, it just—" He gulps, shaking his head faster and faster, this jerky, repetitive motion. His words are tumbling out, like he needs to purge them all from his system. "It felt like it didn't matter anymore. I couldn't calm down. I felt like, like—the sun is never going to come out again, I'm never going to feel okay again. Like you're not going to—"

He breaks off with a jagged breath. "I already feel like I'm *failing* all the time, like it's not enough, no matter how hard I work, and now—" Jay looks at the floor, unable to meet my eye. "But after one, I felt a little better. So I had another. And then I guess, I—I grabbed the bottle, drank straight from that."

"Jay, what the fuck, we have to be home, like—*now.* My mom is going to—"

"You can take the bus, I can buy your bus ticket."

"Stop saying that! That's not going to work, we won't get there in time!" I'm so frustrated, tears are springing out. "Why were you— You were just—just drinking with your asshole boss who *screwed you over*, and you wouldn't even answer my texts?"

He squeezes his eyes shut. "I didn't want to have to *talk* about it and answer your *questions* and—" Jay presses the heels of his hands into his eyes. "And why do I have to be *responsible for everything? Why am I always the one who has to fix it?*"

The way his voice is scratchy and raw and kind of hoarse, it hurts my heart.

"You have to call Candace." I try to sound as stern as possible. "You have to ask for help."

"Would you stop!" Jay's face twists. "She's the last person I want to—" He huffs out a panicked breath. "I was being like you for once, okay? Impulsive! Thinking about myself, instead of about you for two seconds!"

There's that thing in his voice again, like when he yelled on the phone. That curdled resentment, from everything he shoves down.

I'm so angry at him, but I'm still scared of what he'll think, if I tell him I messaged her.

"Fine, then," I say, my voice all hard edges. "Then I'll fix it. I'll drive."

There's a prickling in my gut, pins and needles everywhere, remembering how it felt, the last time I was on the highway. Hands gripping the wheel, thinking, *Okay, okay, you're almost there. You can make it to the other side.*

He looks at me, taken off-balance. "Maybe that's not—"

"We'll never make it home before my mom if I don't!" For once I'm glad to channel the terrifying weight of my mother's voice.

He covers his face with his hands. "Okay. Okay. You're right. Okay."

"So *get your shit* and let's go!"

Jay drops his hands and looks at me for a long moment, damp brown eyes that warm up in the light. Digs in his pocket. Tosses me his keys.

FORTY-TWO

I DIDN'T WANT CANDACE TO WORRY, SO WHILE JAY WAS IN THE bathroom, I wrote a second message.

> He came back. I think it's okay now. We're driving home.
> Sorry to bother you.

Now I'm sitting in the driver's seat, palms sweating, mirrors adjusted.

I pull up the maps app. *Is there any possible way I can do this all on surface streets?*

There's no way we'd make it back before Mom.

"Are you trying to memorize the entire drive?" Jay reaches for my phone. "I can navigate at least."

"Just sleep it off," I snap. "Stop trying to do me any favors."

He blinks, stung, and looks out the window as I put on the navigation with the volume up, start the car, and turn very nervously into traffic.

It's slow getting out of the city, but then, *oh shit, the highway!* The merge is nerve-racking, but it's too congested, nothing is moving fast.

And then traffic starts to clear and we're moving and oh my lord there are *so many cars*! Why are these lanes so narrow, how does literally anyone do this? Checking my mirrors, side, back, front—am I in the lane?—so many lanes, so many cars! How fast am I going? What gear should I be in? What if I forget the clutch and stall out here?

"Hey, breathe," Jay says.

"Please never speak to me again!" I yell, trying so hard not to rage-cry, because crying and driving sounds fucking dangerous.

But okay. Okay, he has a point.

Breathe. Focus. Breathe.

How the hell am I going to do this for four hours?!

Jay puts on some music, and the anxious background noise of my brain gets cancelled out a little.

"You're doing good," he says quietly.

A truck honks its horn and passes me on the right.

I'm going to cry, I'm going to cry.

Why did I think this was a good idea, why did I think I could do this? I should have told Candace what was happening, even though I don't know her. Maybe she would have come get us, helped us figure out another plan. We're going to get pulled over, and what is going to happen to him then?

"Can you put something else on!" I shout.

"Yes! Anything! What!"

He laughs when I tell him, but he finds "City Baby Attacked by Rats" and turns the volume up when I ask.

I scream along to it while he winces, like his head hurts.

"Feel better?"

I give him an exasperated scream-groan in reply.

He's quiet for a few minutes, looking away from me, out the window.

"At least I don't have to be so scared about letting you down anymore," he mumbles.

"You do *not* get to say that to me right now!" I readjust my grip on the wheel and press the gas a little harder. "You do not get to say something that tragic! And pitiful! To me! Right now! Because! I AM TRYING TO DRIVE!"

He laughs like I shook him out of himself.

When I glance over, he's looking at me with something like admiration, maybe. And I guess he listens to me, finally, about not speaking anymore, because he stays quiet most of the way through Connecticut.

The driving gets easier. My heart rate slows, and I realize how much my back hurts from clenching everything.

It seems like Jay is actually asleep.

Then, out of the corner of my eye, I see it. Mom's car. Unmistakable.

That familiar used beige Mercedes, her exact license plate, her short, dark hair in the driver's-side window. She's in the far right lane and I'm in the left, and she probably can't see me, but I speed up anyway, try to create some distance.

Jay wakes up. "Hey, I know you have a need for speed, but—maybe slow down?"

But I can't listen to him now.

If she gets home first, and I'm not there—

She'll say I'm ruining my life, on top of hers.

She'll lock me up forever. She'll slap me stupid.

She'll never want to make me arroz caldo again.

We pass her and I lose sight of her in the mirror after a while, even though I keep checking.

Jay lets out a big puff of air and loosens his grip on the door handle. "Are you actually going to go the rest of the way without talking to me?"

"Are you actually drunk?"

"I think I've been sober since you almost rear-ended that guy near New Haven."

"Then I'll drop you here and you can walk home."

The road signs fly past, counting down the miles to Eastleigh. Once we get there, we'll be in the home stretch.

"Hey," he says, "can we pull over? I'm not—I'm not feeling so good."

When I get off at the next exit and pull into a gas station, he tumbles out and throws up in a trash can.

St. Christopher stares at me from the sun visor.

"What are you looking at?" I whisper.

Jay goes inside to clean up, and when he gets back into the car, he hands me a sandwich.

"You should eat," he says.

I'm screaming inside, but right then I also realize I'm starving. So I choke it down as fast as possible, tears springing to my eyes.

Then we're on the road again, and it gets narrower, more winding, a sign that we're almost home.

And then we're taking those last turns, pulling into his driveway.

I slump forward over the wheel. We made it! We're here!

Jay laughs and rubs my back. "Great job."

I can hardly believe it. I could kiss St. Christopher right now.

I twist around and look behind us, at my house, and see Mom's car already parked in the drive.

Sweat breaks out over my entire body. Oh no, oh no, we shouldn't have stopped!

That sandwich! This is all his fault!

"Deedee—" Jay says as I haul my backpack out of the back seat.

"Stay the fuck away from me!" I hiss as I slam the door and dart across the street.

FORTY-THREE

Mom is on top of me the instant I let myself in.

"Where were you?!" she yells. Her hands are gripping my arms, shaking me.

"I was— I— Oh, you're home!" I spend so much time watching myself, trying to act casual. I should be able to do it now. "I was at the library! Studying! For finals! I lost track of time."

Don't cry, don't cry.

"Why didn't you pick up the phone when I called?!"

"My—my phone was on silent! To be polite. At the library."

If she wasn't shaking me, I'd be shaking on my own, so I guess that's convenient.

Her nails are digging into my arm. "Mom, you're hurting me!"

"If something happens to you it will be my fault, and I can't live with that!"

I'm always thinking about what could go wrong, all the bad things that could happen to Deedee.

Her nails dig in harder, and it almost feels like she's going to pierce the skin.

"Mom, you're hurting me. You're *hurting me*!"

You want to protect me so bad, you don't realize you're hurting me!

She lets me go, and I take a step back, rubbing my arms.

"Just go to your room!" she cries. "I don't want to look at you."

I run up the stairs, something reckless and wild in my blood, like I just cheated death.

I understand her a bit more now, maybe. I can see the lonely person in there. The hurt person I might relate to.

But where does that leave me?

She'll still be set off by small things. I'll still be on edge all the time. Hiding how I feel, deleting my photos, barely breathing. Trying not to look too sad.

The zip pocket of my backpack is open, and when I drop the bag on my bed, Jay's ghost key chain tumbles out.

Suddenly, I'm so tired, all that adrenaline gone. I just want to sleep.

My nails withdraw from the soft flesh of my palms. On my phone there are more texts from Suzy I don't know how to answer.

> Suzy Jang: hey, are you around?
> Suzy Jang: are you ungrounded yet?

It's a relief that she still wants to talk to me. But I can't think of words that sound normal right now. I'll have to wait to write back.

I try to sleep, but when I close my eyes, my head is spinning with everything I've learned.

They blamed her.

Mom would know how much that hurts, and she did it anyway. Didn't try to take it back later. Didn't try to reverse it.

And when my head stops spinning, I keep running into Jay.

Face red and puffy, half spitting, *Why am I always the one who has to fix it?*

Holding my hand, running across the platform.

Beside me when we stepped out of the elevator, and Central Park was spread out below us.

How I felt when I told him everything I'd been so scared to say.

FORTY-FOUR

"So Alex and I broke up," Suzy says when I get into her car the next morning.

"What!" That snaps me out of my fog. "Why wouldn't you—"

"Text you? I did."

Shit, I never answered her!

"It was a long time coming, I guess." She winces, but keeps her eyes on the road. "The way it made me feel, hanging out with them sometimes. Like I snuck in somewhere, and I should be grateful I'm not getting kicked out by security. And he would never stand up for me." Suzy glances at me while we're stopped at a light. "That shit they said to you? And he didn't say a single thing."

"I'm sorry," I mumble through my haze of surprise and guilt. "*Gremlins* and ice cream later?"

When I get to my locker, there's a plastic bag tied to the handle. I unknot it and look inside—three mini bags of chips and a can of coffee. With a note.

My behavior was unacceptable. You told me to stay away from you, so I will. I'm so sorry.

I blink back tears and shove the bag into my locker before Suzy comes by.

All day, I can barely focus. I'm half listening while Suzy talks about her dad's band at lunch.

"He's actually reaching out to the guys about getting together," she says. "Maybe playing a show at Eastleigh for old times' sake. And he keeps talking about . . ."

My eyes wander over to Alex's table, to Jay, slumped down in his seat. He looks up, and our eyes meet.

All I can think about is Jay making me eggs in the kitchen.

Sitting next to me on the bed. Whispering, *It breaks my heart you actually think that was your fault.*

I look away, too fast, eyes landing on the prom countdown poster above the door. *Five days.*

"We should go, right?" Suzy leans her head on my arm. "I was really looking forward to it. We can just have fun, no dates, no pressure. Please?"

From somewhere in the forgotten depths of me, I haul out the ability to smile and tell her, yes, we can do that. We'll go and have a good time.

The poster says THREE DAYS TO PROM.

English is the worst, the class where I can't stop myself from looking at Jay, where our eyes tend to meet across the room.

When class ends, I run out into the stairwell, the first exit I see.

Someone grabs my arm from behind. I spin around, ready to yell at Jay, and—green eyes look back at me.

"Hey, I need to talk to you about something," Alex says.

"If you want to get back together with Suzy, you should probably ask her yourself."

Alex laughs, a little sadly. "Um, tried that, actually. But no, this is about something else." He rakes a hand through his hair. "I'm worried about Jay. He's, like, not himself. Something's going on. He's barely talking to me."

"Why do you think I would know anything about that?"

The look he gives me is so unimpressed, he must have learned a thing or two from Suzy.

"I talked to his sister," he says.

"Candace?!"

He looks even more confused. "No, Gemma."

"Okay, well, we're not really—we're not exactly talking right now." I try to walk past him. Alex steps to the side to block me and puts his hands on my shoulders.

"Hey. I'm serious. I would mind my own business, normally, but—" He sighs, exasperated. "I just think someone else should try to talk to him. I mean, you went to New York together, you must . . ."

Gemma, you snitch!

Suzy appears at the top of the stairs, and I can see the exact moment she notices Alex's hands on my shoulders.

He takes a step back, which certainly doesn't look suspicious.

Suzy's brow wrinkles, like she's trying to make sense of what's in front of her. Then she shakes her head and moves down the stairs past us to her next class like nothing is happening.

I find her at her locker.

"Anything you want to tell me?" she says as she switches out her books.

"No," I say, maybe too quickly.

I don't know how to even begin telling her about anything that's happened. Just a little bit and it will be like a ball of yarn unraveling, and I'm terrified to find out what of me will be left.

"Okay, well." Her locker slams shut. "You know I trust you. I'm here if you change your mind."

Suzy's working after school, and I usually take the bus, but I feel so restless. I want to walk, even though it will take . . . an hour, maybe? I can't remember the last time I did.

I pull my camera out of my bag, the reassuring weight of it in my hands. Headphones in, music on. One foot in front of the other, the scenery changing so much slower than in a car.

Along the way, I take pictures. Not frantically trying to keep things, but making something new instead. My perspective in the center, like it's normal. The in-between spaces in focus. My constant rootless floating feeling, captured like it's a place.

Cutting through the park by the library, I stop short by the playground, and my breath catches in my throat.

Jay's sitting alone on the swings, facing away from me.

I'm still mad at him, but . . . his whole world just came crashing down around him. His job meant so much to him, like it was the one thing that made sense.

Are they going to lose their house?

What is going to happen to him?

Jay looks startled to see me. Wood chips crunch under his sneakers as he twists in his swing.

There is something different about him now, crumpled in on himself. I can see why Alex was worried.

It makes me think about how he usually is—holding everything at arm's length with his sense of humor, pretending to carry things lightly. How much work that must be for him all the time.

"Hey," I say. "You look sad."

He laughs. "So observant."

My foot nudges his. "Are you hungry?"

"I'm always hungry." With some effort, his mouth arranges itself back into a smile.

"Okay," I say, "you're driving."

So we go to the parking lot and get into his car again. The St. Christopher medallion is still clipped to the visor.

FORTY-FIVE

"I DON'T KNOW WHAT TO SAY. I REALLY LET YOU DOWN. I KIND OF HATE myself for it." Jay sighs shakily, across the diner booth from me. His eyes are fixed on the shiny plastic-covered table between us, dark lashes hitting his cheeks.

"Yeah, that was a shitty thing to do. And I'm glad you know that. But—" I turn my mug of black coffee around in my hands and sigh. "I can also see how . . . your job was everything to you."

Jay's face is splotchy, and his lower lip looks torn from biting it, a crushed flower petal.

"Not everything," he says, voice hoarse. "I should have thought about you."

I reach across the table and squeeze his hand.

"I have a theory," I say. "I think you go too far in both directions—

you give too much, you panic. Looking back, over the whole time I've known you . . . you really go out of your way, for me. Rearranging your nights, letting me kidnap you to spy on my mom. Taking me on a road trip at the drop of a hat."

He sniffs and looks out the window, lines of his neck tight. Outside, a gust of wind sends the leaves fluttering, showing their pale undersides.

"I think beating yourself up forever probably doesn't help with the give-too-much-and-panic thing," I say. "So . . . maybe don't do that? And . . . I forgive you."

He draws his hand back, crosses his arms. "That makes one of us."

"*Jay.*"

He runs a hand over his face and sighs again. "You know, I was so scared that my mom was going to . . . give up on me, finally. I really thought that. The whole way back, I was bracing myself. But when I told her, she just hugged me and said: *You've done enough, it's my job to figure this out now.*"

Jay leans his head back against the pink booth, folds his lips into his mouth and lets them go again. "She used to talk a lot about how no one cared how she felt, when she was younger. And I thought that meant it was really important for me to care extra, you know? That I owed it to her, to balance it out. But she said she'd been thinking about that . . ."

He clenches and unclenches his fingers, staring so intently at the trees outside, like they're going to hold the answers to his problems. "She said she talked about it in therapy, and she realized it wasn't fair. That she was putting too much pressure on me. And maybe she'll pause school for a bit, get a second job." He breathes out sharp through his nose, blinking faster, mouth twisted in an annoyed line. "But I—I don't want her to have to work another job. Maybe I should be relieved, but

I just feel . . . like a total piece of shit. Like I don't know what my purpose is anymore."

I reach for his hand again, where it's sitting limp on the table. "Do you have to have a purpose?"

Jay laughs, unhappily, and gives my hand a squeeze. "I need to tell you something," he says, voice thick. "There's something I left out."

Then the door to the restaurant opens, with a jingle of the bell, letting in a draft. And—

It's Candace, standing there.

I must seem like I've seen a ghost, because Jay turns around and freezes, body tense. Candace looks startled for a second, but she recovers quickly. She takes a deep breath and walks over.

"What the fuck?" Jay says.

"Wow, I missed you, too."

"How did you know I was here?"

"I didn't!" she says with a strained laugh. "It was a long drive, and I was hungry."

"Maybe I should go," I say, but Jay holds on to my hand.

"Please don't leave," he whispers through gritted teeth.

So I scoot over, and Candace sits down in the booth next to me. She takes a deep breath. "Jay, I know you're angry at me—"

"Do you? Okay. Why are you here, exactly?" His voice is chilly, detached.

"I heard you were having a rough time," she says carefully. "And that you lost your job."

"Where did you hear that?"

Candace opens her mouth, closes it again.

"I told her," I blurt out, tired of having so many secrets to keep. "I messaged her. When I couldn't reach you. In New York."

"*What?*" He pulls his hand away.

"And . . . Gemma's been writing to me, too," Candace says. "She was worried about you. We've been writing back and forth. I'd been thinking about coming out here already."

"I— Wow." He looks like this news gave him a minor concussion. "You just abandon me for over a year and it turns out you've been *writing to Gemma*?"

"Jay, I know you don't understand, but . . ." Candace blinks faster, looking at the ceiling. "I did what I needed to do. Putting some space between me and Mom. I tried to come back, after the divorce. I tried showing up, at the old house. Mom told me to leave, before you got home from school. She told me to stop calling. And, I mean—you said you didn't want to talk to me."

A joyless laugh bursts out of him. "You didn't try that hard! You called me, like, what, one time? And I told you to leave me alone and *you listened to me*?"

"I called you more times than that. I'm pretty sure you blocked me."

"No I didn't!"

"Give me your phone," she says, palm out. He looks annoyed, but he hands it to her, and she finds herself in his contacts, holds it up for him to see. "Did Mom borrow it? She did that to me once. Went through blocking people she didn't want me to talk to."

Jay's staring at the table now, staying very still, trying to take deep breaths.

"It seemed like you blocked me pretty much everywhere," Candace goes on. "And I didn't—I mean, what was I supposed to do, leave you a GitHub comment?"

Jay laughs a little at that.

She leans back and crosses her arms. "I tried writing you all those letters, too."

He squeezes his eyes shut, opens them again. "What letters?"

279

Candace takes a sharp breath in. "Ohhh, okay. Maybe that's another thing you want to ask Mom about."

Jay sighs, exhausted, and slumps forward so his head rests on his folded arms.

"Hey." She reaches across the table and puts a hand on his head. "Whatever is going on, I'm here. I can help. We can figure it out."

He stands up, forcing her hand off, and throws some bills on the table.

"I have to take Deedee home," he says, and Candace looks from her brother to me and back again before she gets up to let me out.

The silence is tense, on the drive home. We don't talk again until we're parked in his driveway.

"Wasn't really your place to message her," Jay says finally, staring at the steering wheel.

"What did you want me to do?"

He sighs and stares at his house through the windshield. "I guess I can't talk."

Jay's quiet again, but it seems like he's not done talking yet, so I don't move.

"I'm trying not to . . . do that thing where I panic and shut you out," he says, haltingly. "So I'm going to say this out loud, instead of just in my head. This is . . . a lot." He looks at me, eyes golden brown from the sun slanting into the car. "I might need a few days to get my head on straight. But I'm not gone. I'll come back."

FORTY-SIX

At dinner that night, my face must look too sour.

"What's wrong with you?" Mom says. "Why are you upset?"

I cross my arms. "I'm not, I'm fine."

"You're never satisfied, are you? What's wrong now, I already said you could go to the dance!"

"I said I'm fine!"

"You're going to have a bad life if you can never be happy, you know that?" Does she think she's helping me, giving me useful advice? "It's very unattractive. It's unlovable."

I want to cry and laugh at the same time. And for some reason my mind goes back to that first night with Jay, when he said, *Maybe you could try asking her different questions.*

What she said hurts, but I feel so alone in the world. I want to be closer to her, somehow. And maybe I can't barrel straight into the past, but I can slip through sideways.

"How did you learn to drive?"

Mom looks startled. "Are you going to nag me about driving my car again? It's not happening."

I sit down at the table across from her and try to unclench what I can. "I'm just curious."

It looks like she's deciding whether to be annoyed.

"I had to, for work. I got a job where I needed to drive, right after I married your father."

I've heard bits and pieces of the story of how they met, usually in the context of a lecture. She came here for school on a scholarship with one suitcase worth of things. They were in the same program.

"Was it hard?"

She frowns. "The driving instructor had some kind of problem with me. My accent was thicker then. And he kept repeating things I said, making fun of it. I was flustered, I kept making mistakes. He kept laughing in this nasty way. Nasty man."

She never really talks about this kind of thing.

"That's awful."

Mom's nose wrinkles. "You know what he said to me? *Just go home, this country doesn't want you.*" She laughs and shakes her head. "What country does? This uncaring place. It probably doesn't want him, either."

What country does? The melancholy of that rings in my ears, the way she's probably never found a place that wants her.

Have I?

Suzy's house, around the dinner table.

With Jay, inside his car.

I need Mom to keep talking. "So, what did you do?"

"Well," she says, "he left me in a field. In the middle of nowhere."

"What?" Maybe I didn't hear her correctly. She's talking so calmly, she could be describing a normal day.

She sighs like I asked her to run an errand. "He told me to get out, and he drove away."

"And what happened?"

"What do you think happened? I didn't know where I was. And we didn't have phones then like you do. I had to walk back." She points at me. "That's why you have to be careful. You can't just trust things are going to work out."

"How did you feel? Were you scared?"

"I felt like I needed to find a phone!" she snaps. "What kind of question is that?"

"So what did you do?"

"What can you do? You think this was the only thing like this that happened?" She sighs again, exhausted by the difference between us, maybe. "Your father wanted to sue, but with what lawyer, with what money? Anyway, he was like that. I just wanted to keep a low profile. Blend in. He got them to refund the lesson at least."

It feels like my skin is on too tight, thinking about Mom trying to hide her accent, and why she might believe that has something to do with survival.

I hate it, but this isn't a story about me now. I didn't live it, and maybe I have to try to understand.

"Then what happened?"

"We didn't have our own car, so I took the test with just the one lesson. I barely passed. Terrible at parallel parking." Her laugh is kind of jarring. "But I needed the job, so I did it. When I made that trip for work, I stayed in the right lane the entire time."

She stands up, stretches out her back, and starts moving toward her office. "At home, I'd always ask your dad to drive."

Maybe she doesn't want to talk about the past because it's painful. But it seems like it's with her all the time, caught on loop, like the ghost stories she tells.

It's not like that pain stays contained in the past. It comes out sideways, shapes how we live.

In the way she doesn't like Suzy.

In the way she blames me, maybe. Tells me I'm unlovable.

The way her face changes when she sees that I'm sad.

Like she has an allergic reaction to it, in her body.

Like it reminds her of something specific.

Like she stops seeing me at all.

FORTY-SEVEN

OVER THE NEXT FEW DAYS, I GET GLIMPSES OF WHAT HAPPENS NEXT.

Jay running outside, storming off around the side of his house. Candace following him.

Candace leaving, another time, getting in her car and driving off somewhere. Coming back again.

Early the next morning, Jay's mom is sitting out on their stoop, and Candace sits next to her and hands her a cup of coffee.

While I'm doing homework in my room, a door slams outside. And there's Jay, in his driveway. Candace comes out behind him. It looks like they've been fighting, the way he's standing, arms crossed, shoulders hunched in.

She reaches out for him, and they hug for a long time.

And I feel sad somehow, wishing someone would hug me like

that. Remembering when someone did, recently. But now he feels so far away.

I can't focus while Suzy's talking on the way to school, can't pay attention in class. Searching my memory for other moments of softness like that.

It's hard to find them.

Mom's love is pushing through and doing what she can to give me a better life than she had. White-knuckling it the whole time, tense and angry. Resenting me for how good I have it, even though that was her goal.

And she gets it done.

Like when she taught me how to ride a bike, so upset and stressed by the end, telling me she's sick of me. I remember how badly I wanted it to be over, but finally she pushed me off and let go. And I did it, kept pedaling, stayed upright.

She got it done, in the end. Even though she took the bike away, if I try to ride again one day, I'll probably still know how.

She's given me a good life, and I'm grateful. And the way she treats me hurts, too.

Both things are true.

After dinner, I look outside again, and Jay is on his roof. Candace is sitting next to him, both of them hugging their knees. Talking more easily now, it looks like, staring out into the distance together.

Jay's voice pops into my head, laughing at me, saying, *I'm surprised you didn't bring binoculars.*

So I close the blinds.

Then it's time to go to Suzy's to get ready for prom, and I'm lying in bed. Getting up feels impossible, but I'm ashamed, remembering Mom's story.

Feelings don't slow her down. A bottomless will to push forward seeps out of her pores. Do I have any of that grit? Am I just a soft, worthless mess?

I get up and try to dress like a person. My green dress is hidden in my backpack, ready to change into.

When I step outside, Candace is there, loading up her car parked at the opposite curb. She waves and squints into the glare.

"Where are you heading?" she asks, closing her trunk. "Need a ride?"

I hesitate for a second, wondering if this is somehow a betrayal.

But the image of her and Jay on the roof together puts my mind at ease. So I climb in and tell her how to get to Suzy's house.

"Are you going back home?" I ask, hugging my backpack in my lap as she starts to drive.

"Yeah, that was . . . a lot! But I think it was good for all of us. And I felt like . . . I was ready for it, you know?" She leans forward to look around the corner. "I can see that my mom is trying. She apologized. Which was nice."

"What . . . was it like? When you stopped talking to your mom."

I've been wanting to ask that for so long, now. Wondered if it's a door that's open for me, maybe. If not to walk through, then to let in some fresh air.

"I don't regret it," she says, choosing her words carefully. "Because our dynamic was really hurting me." She sighs. "The thing is, she wants to change now, right? But you can't make anyone change. And she didn't want to back then, so—all I could do was protect myself. And there was a time when I really needed to."

"What was your dynamic like?"

Candace taps the steering wheel, trying to home in on what she wants to say. "My mom kind of had no boundaries when I was growing up. Her feelings were my feelings, her grudges had to be my grudges. And . . . she blamed me for a lot of things. For being the reason she stayed with our dad, because she married him after she got pregnant with me. Every time I talked to her, that blame would creep back in, you know? Things with my dad got really bad, but . . . she would always make excuses for him. I guess it was easier to blame me instead."

The sun peeks out between the trees we pass, expanding, contracting, ducking away before it dazzles my eyes again. I feel so agitated, like relief might be on the other side of what she's telling me, but also like I'm being turned inside out.

"I asked her to leave him, so many times. I tried telling her how I feel, begging her to get some help. I left home, and I told her to at least stop blaming me. We were talking on the phone every day then, still.

"It just . . . hurt too much, after a while, and I felt like: *Maybe I don't deserve to hurt this much every day*. And I'd been in therapy for a minute then, so I tried setting a boundary. I told her I couldn't keep talking to her if it was going to be like that every time, and she kind of lost it."

We're getting ready to make a left, and the clicking of her turn signal matches my heartbeat.

"But, I mean, I didn't hate her. She makes sense—she's carrying a lot of pain. And for a long time she'd kind of hold herself away from dealing with it, like she didn't think she deserved to. But she also desperately needed us to make her feel better, all the time. And she really makes you feel it if you let her down."

The way Jay is so scared of letting anyone down. The way he took my sadness on his shoulders. I guess he makes sense, too.

"You know how they say, your trauma isn't your fault, but it's your responsibility?" Candace adds. "I think that's the thing, with my mom. Thinking it's too indulgent to deal with how much you're hurting, like you can just walk it off. Keeping all these things inside, and they repeat. Maybe not exactly the same way—"

"But it rhymes."

Candace laughs. "Yeah. I think when you grow up in a dysfunctional situation, sometimes . . . you don't think you deserve to feel better, so you put off dealing with it. But it can eat you up so much, you can't see outside yourself anymore."

We're stopped at a red light, sun high in the sky, a bird cawing in the distance. Candace smiles at me sideways. "So you're not going to the dance with my brother?"

"Are you going to convince me I should be?"

She snorts. "God, no."

A laugh shakes my stomach. Maybe this is what it would be like if I had an older sister.

"He talks about you—I mean, I'm not going to lie, he's totally head over heels for you." The sound of her laugh fills the car, high and bright. "He . . . told me about the stuff with your mom, a little bit. I get why you're asking these questions." She points at Suzy's house. "Over here?"

I nod and she parks at the curb.

"The other thing, though—Jay would kill me for saying this. And I can't tell you what to do, but—" Candace takes a deep breath and lets it out again. "I think when you're younger, and you're hurting from other things, being in a relationship can feel like . . . a solution. But it can open up a whole new world of problems, you know?"

Maybe I do know, in a distant way. Even though part of me wishes I didn't.

She drums her fingers on the steering wheel and gives me a sad smile. "But it's important to remember—this isn't your last chance at anything, being in a relationship right this second. There can be so much more love ahead of you, you know? That can look completely different from what you got used to, growing up."

There's a prickling behind my eyes now. I need to get out of this car before I cry again.

"Anyway," she says. "Just be careful with each other, okay?"

"I think I get what you mean!" I say, opening the door and popping out. "Thanks for the ride. Drive safely."

Outside Suzy's door, I turn to look back one more time, and Candace waves.

FORTY-EIGHT

"THIS WILL BE FUN," SUZY MUTTERS UNDER HER BREATH. "TOTALLY normal to be at an event that Alex is also at. *Totally* fine. It's going to be great." She links arms with me as we head up the stone walkway to the hotel where prom is happening, thumping bass beat already audible from outside.

We join the crush of people milling around the ballroom. Beth passes by on Ted's arm and gives Suzy a poisonous look.

"What was that?" I ask.

Suzy cringes. "I guess she thought, when Alex and I broke up, it would be her chance with him. And then . . . it wasn't?" She laughs, more nervous than mean. "Apparently, she's been trying to make him jealous for months. She was flirting with Jay all the time, but he clearly wasn't into it."

My heart lurches, like an old elevator trying to find the right floor.

"And now . . ." She shakes her head. "I don't know, it's not my problem."

The dance floor is full, and this is quite honestly the last place I want to be. I sit down at one of the tables, but Suzy hauls me up by the arm. "Don't be a wallflower!"

So I try to move my body some way that vaguely resembles dancing. It actually feels kind of okay, for a minute.

Until I see Jay, watching my half-hearted attempt from across the room.

We're both wearing the same outfits we did to Kevin's winter party. Me in my green dress, him in his borrowed suit, no tie.

My heart aches, thinking about how I felt that night.

"Are you okay?" Suzy follows my line of sight and nods in Jay's direction. "You know it's fine? If you're worried about me because he's Alex's friend, it's—"

"No, that's not—" The heat rushes to my face. "I need to sit down, my . . . feet hurt."

"Okay, good effort." Suzy pats my shoulder. "Let's take a breather."

We sit at a table, and Alex comes over and crouches down next to Suzy, bouncing on his heels. The song changes to something upbeat, and he moves his shoulders. "Want to dance?"

"I'm good," Suzy says with a tight smile, not looking at him. "Have fun."

She waits for him to leave, then stands and tries to pull me up again. My eyes stray to where Jay was, and he's still looking at me. I really need some air.

"I, um, have to use the bathroom!"

Suzy pouts and dances over to a cluster of people we've been sitting with at lunch.

I rush out of the ballroom, through the doors and down the path winding across the rolling lawn, breaking away from it to sit on the grass.

It's warm out, and the sky overhead is deep blue, the kind I love so much on the other end of the night.

"Hey," Jay says from behind me. When I twist around, he's walking down the lawn, and suddenly I feel too warm, itchy in this dress.

He grimaces as he sits down, like his pants are too tight.

"I wanted to say—that thing I was trying to tell you before, I . . . I just—" He takes a frustrated breath out, like he's losing his nerve.

There's a long pause, so I fill it.

"I'm sorry I messaged Candace. It probably wasn't—"

"No, it was— It's okay." He drags a hand through his hair. "I mean, yeah, it could have gone very wrong. You should probably check with people before you do that kind of thing in the future, but . . . I should have asked for her help a long time ago." Jay gives me a weak smile. "It was good for me, in the end. So, thank you."

"Did you . . . get to read her letters?"

"Yeah, when I asked my mom about it, she just handed me this whole stack." Jay looks at me, eyes shining, something liquid catching in the walkway lights. "There's something else I need to talk to you about. What I was trying to tell you, before. I was thinking—if you actually meant it, that you can forgive me—"

He lets out a big breath and takes my hand in his. "I love you, Deedee. I want to be better, for you. And we can actually be together next year, because . . . I'm not going to college."

Jay's words float in the warm night air. It takes a second for it to sink in.

"You're not?"

"That's why I panicked so much when I found out about my job.

I was just planning to work after graduation. I didn't even apply to schools."

If my mom didn't like him before . . .

Don't think about that, that's not what matters right now!

"But Candace is helping me figure something out, and—" He clears his throat. "The point is. I could just be here next year. See you in Eastleigh whenever you want."

I dig my fingers into the grass, rip up some blades.

I don't know what my purpose is anymore.

Is he just going to go from worrying about his mom full-time to worrying about me? I hate it. I can't stand it.

"We wouldn't have to sneak around anymore," he says. "I could be your actual boyfriend. Not the secret kind."

Jay doesn't say what he wants very much.

And he has the softest, most aching place in my heart, but *oh God I can't be another person for him to take care of!*

Somehow, lost in the woods of this thought, the only words I can force out are: "Why was I tutoring you?"

"My mom thought I was applying."

Wow, maybe this is why he was so ready to help me sneak around.

"Wait, but you— I definitely thought—"

"I didn't lie exactly," he says carefully.

Shit, we really are the same.

He lets go of my hand. "I mean, I didn't want to tell you because— look at you, the way you've grown up, all sheltered, overachieving. Your mom . . . seems to think *highly* of herself. The way she acted when she met my mom? I guess I thought—" Another sharp breath. "You would judge me. I wouldn't be good enough for you."

"What!"

"And then when I lost my job, I thought . . . you'd see what a loser I am."

"I don't care about that! I wouldn't think that about you." My head is spinning. I hate the way he must see me.

And I feel ashamed then, because I was so wrapped up in my own shit, after he said he messed up and wanted to fix things, I didn't even ask once where he was going to college.

"Jay. This is just . . . all fucked up."

The hurt on his face is instant. Oh no, oh no, that is not what I wanted to say!

The words in my head from a moment ago—*I care too much about you to get it wrong, I love you too but I can't, I think we both deserve*—are all floating away, out of reach.

"Why?" That sneering thing in his voice is back. "Because I'm not going to college?"

"No, I just meant—"

And then Alex's voice wafts down the lawn.

"Jay? You out here?"

We both scramble to stand, and Alex comes into view, hands in his pockets, laughing a little.

"Bruh, are you going to ask her out yet or what?" To me, he stage-whispers. "He's shy!"

Jay is seething, but I guess Alex is much less perceptive than I thought.

"I'm thinking of checking out a graduation party in Ashebrooke," Alex says. "Want to come?"

"Great, let's go," Jay says, voice clipped.

Alex looks at me. "You should come, too."

Jay's arms are crossed, and he's turned away, so I can't see his expression.

I don't want to leave it like that, I want a chance for tonight to end differently.

So I say, "Sure," and follow them to Alex's car.

FORTY-NINE

IN ALEX'S BACK SEAT, THE GLOW OF MY PHONE TURNS MY HANDS A sickly blue.

> **Deedee Walters:** hey i'm really tired but you guys were having fun. i didn't want to break up the party. jay was leaving so i got a ride back with him
>
> **Suzy Jang:** oh my god i knew it!!! get it girl

I feel sick to my stomach, staring at the kiss-face emoji she added at the end. I don't deserve her.

I must sigh too loud, because my eyes meet Jay's for a second in the rearview mirror before he blinks away again.

Alex keeps trying to strike up a conversation, but he can probably tell something's wrong. Eventually he gives up and puts on the radio.

This was a bad idea. The farther we get from home, the more the sinking feeling in the pit of my stomach grows.

As soon as we arrive at the house where the party is, Alex gets swept up with some people he knows, headed for the kitchen.

And now it's just me and Jay and the agonizing silence between us. He's kneading the back of his head with one hand, looking around like he's searching for an exit.

"Jay. Listen—"

"It was my mistake! I won't bother you anymore. Take care, okay?"

If that isn't the chilliest "take care," my God. All his walls are back up, and I'm on the outside, a stranger.

"Wait, listen—"

But he's already pushing through the people crowded on the stairs, disappearing to the second floor.

Should I run after him?

I like him so much, but we just keep hurting each other. Everything is ruined so easily. That old familiar weight is pulling me down again, down and down and I just want to sleep.

I need to sit, so I float into the living room, crowded with people holding bottles of beer. Someone must have just left, because there's an open spot on the couch for me to sink into.

"Weed brownie?" the girl to my right asks, holding out a Tupperware. "Martha Stewart's recipe."

Maybe I shouldn't, because I've never done it before. But right then, the things I want most are: 1) to be somewhere else, and 2) to not be myself, and maybe this will be about as good. So I take one with a smile and a thank-you, keep trying to follow the conversation around me as I eat it, and before I realize it, I've finished the whole thing.

The night stretches out, bends. The voices around me are louder than I remember, melding together like the rushing of the ocean, or cars on the highway. If I get up now, I'll be lost forever in this strange house. So I stay there, glued to my seat.

There's a familiar face, across the room—one of Beth's friends, a girl I recognize from some thing at Alex's or Kevin's, I don't remember. I'm suddenly so excited to see anyone I know, so I wave to her. She gives me a cutting look back, and I blink, surprised.

I close my eyes, and when I open them, someone is talking to me. There's this guy there, where the Martha Stewart Brownie Girl was before, and it seems like he's been talking for a while.

His hand is on my leg.

What *is* that?

It's like I've never seen a hand before.

Why is it *there*?

"What's your nationality?" he's asking.

"Um," I say, mind skittering around, a rat looking for crumbs. "I forget?"

And then I can't stop laughing. I'm nearly crying. This thing that people ask me about, that always weighs on me—*where are you from, what are you actually?*

I forgot! Hahahahaha.

I pick up his hand and move it, plopping it back down on his own leg.

"You're funny," he says.

"Not really," I say.

He laughs, and then his hand is resting on my knee again.

How did it get— It was just—

Panic climbs up my throat, and then I'm yelling, "Just leave me alone, please!"

The guy raises his hands, palms out. "Whoa, whoa, I think you need to relax."

Oh no, oh no, he's putting an arm around my shoulders, he's touching me, what—

"Get the fuck off me!" I shout.

People turn to look at us.

Alex sits down on the armrest to my left and puts a hand on my shoulder. "Sorry, babe," he says, "I got distracted talking to some guys from the team." He hands me the drink he's holding, like he was just getting it for me.

Handsy Dude is staring, confused, so Alex glares at him and says, "Can I help you?"

The guy mumbles something and walks away.

I make room for Alex on the couch, and he slides off the armrest to sit next to me.

"Are you okay?" he asks, angling himself to look at my pupils. "What did you have?"

I slump against him. "God, I thought he'd never leave."

He sighs, arm resting behind me on the back of the couch, and pats my shoulder.

"You're nice," I say. My head lolls sleepily against his chest, and he laughs.

"Make sure you tell Suzy that, okay?"

I whisper like it's a big secret: "I want to go home, but I forgot how."

"Okay, come on, here we go." Alex moves me back upright, and we're getting up then, his arm steadying me. Walking feels jarring, so I close my eyes. The air is cold. Maybe we're outside.

"What happened? Is Deedee okay?" A voice I know, from some-where close—from above us.

"I'm taking her home, she had . . . too much fun, I think," Alex says.

"Wait—wait a second, okay? Wait there." I open my eyes in time to see Jay, on the roof in his borrowed suit, scrambling back through the open window.

I'm so tired, my eyes close again, standing there.

Then arms gather me up, a softness I remember, Jay's smell as he presses me into him again. A warmth I want to curl up and go to sleep inside, but I can't, I can't just go to sleep, I have to wake up. I have to stand on my own, right? Wasn't that—

"I'm sorry, I'm sorry," Jay whispers into my hair.

Then we're separating, a different set of hands on my shoulders, and we're walking again.

"Come on," Alex's voice says, "let's get you home."

FIFTY

When I wake up, my head feels like it's wrapped in packing foam. My tongue does, too.

And on my phone, there are a dozen texts from Suzy and a handful of missed calls.

I shoot upright in bed, staring at the photos someone took from across the living room at the party.

And they look . . . bad.

Alex with his arm around me. Me, leaning my head against his chest, eyes closed. Alex looking into my eyes, close to my face. And there we are, leaving together.

Oh shit, oh fuck.

Suzy Jang: WHAT is happening in these photos??

Timestamped 2:32 a.m.

> Suzy Jang: why would you lie to me?? you said you were going
> home?????
> Suzy Jang: please tell me how you ended up at some random party
> with my ex-boyfriend instead of at home???

And she sent a screenshot of a DM from Beth's friend who was there last night.

> Thought you should know! I heard him call her "babe"!

Oh no oh no oh no oh no!

> Suzy Jang: im so upset i cant sleep
> Suzy Jang: DEEDEE.

The timestamp on that one says 6:12 a.m.

> Suzy Jang: HELLO what the fuck deedee ANSWER ME

That's the last one. Sent 8:56 a.m.

It's past 10 now.

I want to scream. Or throw up. Maybe both.

I scramble out of bed and Mom appears, blocking the doorway.

"What on earth is going on here? I thought you were staying over at Suzy's? What happened to you?! Look at your face!" Mom grabs me by the arms and shakes me. "I knew it was a mistake to let you go to that dance! What did you do? Did you drink? How late were you out?"

It's too bright in here, and my head is too hot, I can't, I can't, I can't— "I have to go!" I exclaim and push past her.

"Deedee!" she screams. "Where do you think you're going? Come back here right now!"

I shove my feet into my shoes and run outside. I don't slow down until I get to Suzy's house, still in the big T-shirt and shorts I wore to sleep.

"You look like shit," Suzy says when she opens the door, giving me a once-over.

My hair is tangled and my eyelashes are sticking together with day-old mascara and sleep.

"Come on up," she says quietly.

Her brothers' voices float up from the kitchen, along with the sound of her mom laughing and her dad scolding them.

We get up to Suzy's room and she shuts the door behind her.

"So you have something you want to tell me?"

I sit on the edge of her bed and look at my hands. "It's not what it looks like—"

She sighs and sits in her desk chair. "Really? Because it sure looks like you lied to me."

"I—I—"

The furrow between Suzy's eyebrows gets a little deeper.

"Did Alex tell you—" I ask.

"Tell me what?" she snaps. "I'd rather hear it from you. Why didn't you tell me you were going to that party?"

"I wasn't doing anything with Alex. I was—I was—" There's the cord I've been so scared to tug on, the rotten stuff tied to the other end. But if I don't do it now, I'll lose her. *I was trying to break up with Jay!*

Suzy looks completely taken off-balance. Her mouth is open, and she's squinting at me, putting together what I just said.

"*What?* You were trying to *break up* with him? So you were dating?"

"Not exactly."

"Then *what*, exactly?"

"We were kind of— We had a thing, on and off. And I was in the middle of saying we should stop, but I didn't get to say everything I wanted to, and then Alex showed up and they were going to this party, and I didn't want to leave it like that. So I went with them."

"OF ALL THE POINTLESS, TWISTED, OBVIOUS THINGS TO LIE TO ME ABOUT!" She widens her eyes, brings her fingers to her temples. "God, it's like you were gaslighting me all year. Why wouldn't you tell me about that? I was rooting for you! I would have been *relieved*!"

She laughs again, a little hysterical. "You could have been *normal* about it! Instead, you just—just let me feel so *stressed* this whole time, worrying about you because—"

"I told you I was over Alex, and I was!"

"That's not the point!" Suzy takes a labored breath out. "So how long has this *thing* been going on?"

"Um. Well." I can't lie to her anymore. "Since . . ." Whew.

"Deedee!"

"We kissed for the first time in . . . December?"

She stands up, eyes wide. "DECEMBER?!"

"And we started hanging out . . . a couple months before that."

She sits back down in her desk chair and spins a little, shaking her head. "That's why you've been acting so weird this whole time. *Ten years of friendship*, and you ditched me for this guy and didn't even tell me."

All my reasons unravel, and there's just this soft, sticky thing at the heart of them.

"Things with my mom were—" I gulp for air. "Kind of crushing me. Sometimes. And things with his family aren't great, and I felt like I could talk to him about it. It kept me going a little. And keeping it a secret—I was scared my mom was going to find out, and you—" I wince. "You might let it slip, you know?"

Her eyes flash. "So you're BLAMING this on me now?"

"I'm sorry," I say in a small voice. "I really fucked up. I don't have an excuse."

Suzy looks so tired, like something has drained the life out of her.

"I think you should leave now," she says.

When I get to the back door, Mom opens it before I can.

"You're grounded for a century. Forget graduation. Forget anything this summer."

Fine. Great. Who do I have to see?

"This is the thanks I get for letting you go to the dance? Are you losing your mind?" She's shaking me, fingers digging into skin. "I was trying to go easier on you, but I see you're not ready for that! If I'm not hard on you, how are you ever going to make it out there?!"

She lets go of me, and I wince, bracing for impact. But she just clicks her tongue. "Go to your room and think about what you did."

I'm relieved to run up the stairs and tumble back into bed.

You don't think you deserve to feel better, but it eats you up so much, you can't see outside yourself anymore.

The way I feel ashamed, the way I hate myself. The way Mom's voice is always in my head, telling me I'm defective, pulling me down.

It doesn't make me a better person or friend. It overwhelms me, takes over everything, feeds my bad decisions.

And there's that restless feeling in my gut again, reaching out for the person I want to be.

On impulse, I get up, take one of the sheets of paper on my desk that used to be for writing to Lolo Ric. And I start writing myself a letter.

It's awkward. I'm cringing the whole time, sweating, pencil hovering over paper. It feels like something bad is going to happen.

But I close my eyes and try to think about the way Jay would talk to me. Try to copy that softness, for myself. And eventually I ease into it.

You're not so bad, Deedee.

It's pathetic, but I'm actually shaking. I feel so blocked from talking to myself like that—like the sky will actually fall, if I do, like I'll be punished.

But learning to give that to myself, instead of leaning on someone else for it—it seems like a good first step to standing on my own. A start on the road to not making all the same mistakes.

You did a bad thing and you can learn from it. You can know why you did it. You can work on it.

You can be different. You can change, because you want to change.

It's not fair to tell yourself you were bad from the start.

Problems have solutions, sometimes. Some of your problems probably do, too.

You're not cursed.

You are lovable. Even if it doesn't last, or it changes, people have loved you, already. You know that. You were there.

When I'm done, I rip it up, because no else needs to see it.

And then I write Suzy a letter and fill it with the things I love about her, the things I already miss. With all these moments from the whole time I've known her. When we both fell at recess, running around the playground, and Suzy asked the nurse to give us matching Band-Aids. When we stayed up telling scary stories and got so scared, we had to build a stuffed-animal fort to protect us before we'd go to sleep. The time after Mom pulled me out of debate, when I felt a sadness so deep and sticky, I could barely talk about it. But when I started crying out of nowhere, Suzy just held me tight and said I'm okay and she's here.

I write about the ways I know this hurt her, and the ways I want to be different. And at the end, I write:

> I'm so sorry.
> I love you.

Even though I fucked everything up, at least I know, deep in my heart, that I mean it.

Then I crawl back into bed, and fall into a numb, empty sleep.

FIFTY-ONE

THERE'S A TAPPING ON MY WINDOW, INSISTENT, STEADY. MY EYES FLY open, and I startle. I don't know how long I've been asleep, but it's dark out. And there's a face at the window.

A ghost?

Then it comes into focus, and Jay waves through the glass, points inside. Somehow, he made it onto our roof, the mirror image of his.

I hop out of bed and close the door to my room. There are bigger rules I'm about to break.

Oh God, how must I look right now?

I rush to open the window. "What the fuck?" I hiss. "You could fall and break your neck."

"Better let me in, then."

I step aside and he hoists himself through, slides across my desk.

Jay's in my room.

I'm so tired suddenly. I sink down to the floor and lean my head against the wall.

"You can't be here," I whisper, but my heart's not in it. "What do you think you're doing?"

He settles next to me. "You weren't answering. And I wanted to make sure you're okay."

"Jay, I—" It comes out choked. I'm scared I won't be able to find the right words this time, either. "I didn't do a good job of saying what I wanted to, before. You need to know—" My eyes get warm, and my nose feels too full again. "You're the furthest thing from a loser to me. In a lot of ways, I think you're better than me. I want to be more like you."

Jay pulls his lips into his mouth and looks very fascinated with his shoes all of a sudden.

"You mean so much to me," I press on. "And I—"

I love you, too.

Maybe it will hurt him more, to hear it now, when I know I have to say goodbye to him. But maybe he deserves to know.

"I love you, and that's why I don't want to do this—why I can't do this, right now," I say. "I don't think you should stay here because of me. I don't want to be another reason for you to put off thinking about where you actually want to be."

Jay looks like he's barely breathing, eyes fixed on the floor. I feel like my heart is going to stop, but I have to keep going, in case I don't get another chance. "Suzy found out that I was keeping this a secret from her all year, and—what was I even thinking? Why did I ask you to do that? I'm sure that wasn't amazing for you either."

He shakes his head, and one of the tears he usually blinks away makes a break for it, out into the open, glistening on his cheek. "I

309

told myself I got it," he says. "Because I know what it's like to keep secrets. I guess I didn't love *being* one, though? I felt like . . . you were ashamed of me." He leans his head back against the wall, and his mouth stretches into the most endearing, self-deprecating grin. "But I could have . . . told you that. Said something about it. Like an adult."

I think about Jay's mom keeping him and his sister apart, when he's so alone in the world, you can see it rising off him like heat off pavement. About my mom, so afraid of me getting hurt, but saying things that hurt me in the most deep-down way.

Who I could become if I don't pay attention. If I don't face the things I inherited.

"I think we're both kind of in the thick of it," I say, trying to make my voice as gentle as possible. "And it can be dangerous to think another person is a way out. And I could see myself doing that, with you. I think I need to spend some time alone."

He laughs unhappily. "So you're doing the same thing I did. Back in March."

"No. It's not the same. Because I'm telling you why. And we don't have to stop talking completely, unless you want to. And because it's not that . . . I'm bad, or you're bad. I know that's part of my problem, thinking I'm bad, in this toxic way."

Jay is staying very still, staring at the ceiling, not making a sound.

"It's different," I say, "because if you want me in your life, I'll be in it, okay? It's up to you. I'll be there." I sniff, wipe my face, too. "If we tried right now, we'd just make each other miserable and break up for real. And then maybe we really wouldn't be able to talk to each other, after that. And I think we deserve better. I want to talk to you for a long time."

His eyebrows go up, and he takes a long breath in, winding up to say something.

"Well, shit, what do I say to that?" He laughs, at a loss, and something about his timing cracks me up.

And then my door swings open, and my stomach drops.

Mom is standing in the doorway.

"Who the fuck is this?!" she yells.

It's so different from how she usually talks, and that makes me laugh harder.

"You think this is funny?" She gestures wildly in Jay's direction. "Get out!"

He scrambles to his feet and looks for a minute like he's thinking of going back out the window.

Mom crosses the room and grabs the back of his shirt, and he yelps in surprise.

"Mrs. Walters! Hi! I—"

She marches him out the door, and their footsteps disappear down the stairs. A door slams. And then, with growing dread, I listen to Mom's footsteps return.

"That's it," she says when she appears in the doorway. "You're out of control. You can't stay here. I'm sending you to the Philippines."

"Great!" Maybe then I'll finally get some answers.

That's clearly not the response she was hoping for. She fumes silently, hands on her hips.

Then she crosses the room, flings open my closet, and—oh no, oh shit.

"Where's your suitcase?" She stops rummaging then and makes a strangled sound. When she straightens again, she's holding the photo album.

"*What* is this doing here?" All the air goes out of the room. "I can't believe you. This is *private*. This isn't *yours*."

Her disappointment cuts me, and she turns her back, moving to leave. For a second it feels like that's it, and we'll just settle into one of the suffocating silences we're used to.

The part of my brain that tells me what not to say out loud is screaming. But I think about Mom gripping the wheel, muttering to herself, scared to death but pressing ahead, going over the bridge.

"I know Lolo Ric isn't real!"

She faces me, looking like I might as well have slapped her.

"I know my real grandfather is dead, and he's not even named Ric, and everything you told me about him is made up! I know that Dad asked you to get help for your anger issues before I was born. I know you think your mom's death was your fault. I know—I know—" I've run out of steam now, and my voice dies to a whisper. "I know a lot more than you think."

She braces herself against the wall. "How do you know all that?"

"Because I went through your things."

She gives me the most scalding look. "I don't know who you are," she says, slow and terrible, "but you're not my daughter."

"Oh, I'm definitely your daughter!" I'm laughing now because this is so absurd. "I'm so much like you! I violated your privacy, just like you always violate mine! Because you act like—like I'm just an *extension* of you, without my own feelings! We're so alike it makes me sick."

Jesus, I really do have her talent for saying the most vicious shit. And I don't want to be like that, but I need to hear her explain. "Why did you have me write those letters?"

Mom scowls. "Because you're so *sad* all the time! I wanted to hear you say something positive!"

"Maybe it's not unreasonable to be sad when you blamed me for *killing my own father!*" I shout, and her jaw goes slack.

"I—I said that but—I didn't mean—" She shakes the hair out of her face. "I must have said that in—in the heat of the moment. A long time ago."

"You always talk about how much I've taken from you! Isn't that what you meant?"

Mom's arms are crossed tight over her chest, and she leans against the wall for support.

"You always say you're the only one who sees what I'm like," I say. "But you're in so much pain, you don't see me at all."

And the way her face crumples, I think, *Oh no, oh God, I've broken everything.* It's like the dream where all the vases lay in pieces on the floor.

She turns and starts to leave.

"Should I— Don't you want to—punish me?" I say in a small voice.

"Do whatever you want," Mom says, and disappears down the hall.

FIFTY-TWO

I WAKE UP IN THE MIDDLE OF THE NIGHT—MY SCREEN SAYS IT'S 12:53 a.m.—and foggily realize a phone is ringing and has been for a while.

A heavy ache settles between my ribs, remembering how things are ruined now with everyone I care about.

The phone is still ringing.

I get up and move down the hall in my slippers. Mom's door is open, bed empty. Phone plugged in beside it, ringing.

My reflection in the dark window stares back at me, ghostly. Pressing my face closer to the glass, I can still see her car in the driveway outside. But the house is so quiet.

I pinch my cheek and turn a light switch on and off to make sure

I'm not dreaming. Her phone is still ringing. It says ANDOY on the screen.

So I pick it up.

"Glor? I called back as soon as I got your message. It must be late there. Is everything all right?"

"Tito Andoy?" He shows up in so many of Mom's stories. I wasn't sure if he was real.

"Deeds!" he exclaims. "My gosh, it's been so long. Is everything okay? I got your mom's message."

"Do . . . Do you know me? You're just . . . you sound like you know me, but I don't think I know you?"

He's laughing.

"Sorry, is that rude?" I add.

"I know your mom, so I feel like I know you."

What a thing to say.

"And we did meet before. You were a rambunctious baby."

His accent washes over me, musical and warm. Something I missed without knowing it.

The way he's talking, like no time has passed since he last saw me—it's making a lump form in my throat.

"Did something happen?" he says. "Is your mom okay?"

"I think she just . . . stepped outside?" My American accent sounds sterile and grating side by side with his.

"I just listened to her message. I was in class when she called—I'm teaching at U.P. these days."

University of the Philippines, a memory buried somewhere in the back of my mind tells me.

"Your mom kind of . . . drifted away from all of us, after your dad died. But we were best friends growing up." There's a smile in his voice.

"Aren't you her cousin?"

"Cousins and best friends."

Voices echo behind him. Maybe he's in his office at the university, door open to the hallway.

"Did you . . . Did you actually catch an aswang?" I ask.

His laugh comes through the line again, astonished, energetic, round and full.

"On your roof?" I add, like it's going to help.

"Your mom is quite a storyteller." He takes a minute to catch his breath. "Tita Gabby—your grandmother—she was, too. Runs in the family."

Outside the wind picks up and the tree branches rattle against the window.

"It's sad, what happened to her," he says. "She was so young."

"What happened to her?" My throat is dry.

"Oh, I—I don't know if it's my place to tell you. You should ask your mom."

We're quiet for a second, listening to the dead air across so much distance.

Tito Andoy sighs. "You know . . . some say that the aswang doesn't deserve its reputation," he says, putting on a voice like he's telling a kid a ghost story. The world shrinks down until there's nothing else but the sounds coming through the phone from halfway around the world. "When the Spanish colonized the Philippines, they demonized it. Used it in their campaign to scare people into embracing Catholicism."

"So it's just misunderstood." My voice is jarring, the way it's sarcastic and flat.

But he just laughs again, like I'm hilarious.

In the generosity of that sound, I can almost feel what could have been. Another life where I grew up with Titas and Titos and Ates and Kuyas, like the people in Mom's stories. Where it wasn't as lonely, maybe. The warmth of a distant, unfamiliar sun.

What else did she lose, coming here?

What did it take from her, growing up always being told that she needs to leave?

He sighs. "And the CIA used aswang stories to suppress the communists, after World War Two. They punctured holes in the necks of people they'd killed, to make it look like an aswang came for them."

"Shit," I say, and then, when he laughs again, "Oh sorry! For my language."

"But these stories are old, old." It sounds like he's in full professor mode now. "They tap into old fears. Anxieties about life being out of control. About losing our children, about sickness and death. Or about women exerting their independence, maybe, not acting the way society expects them to."

I readjust my grip on the phone, trying to soak up what he's saying, a strange lifeline.

"I always loved the image, though. Those bat wings," he says dryly. "These legs aren't doing it for me, let's lose them and go flying instead."

"The audacity," I say, setting off his laugh again.

It's nice, being together on the line like this. The way he feels far away but close.

"Anyway," he goes on. "What might seem monstrous isn't always so straightforward. It can be more than one thing. It can be a lot of things at once."

He's quiet for a moment, pensive. Then he says, in a softer voice, "You know, your mom tried to hide on my roof once."

I stop breathing for a second.

"Her dad forbid her from going anywhere, but she wanted to visit my mother when she was sick. So she snuck out of her house to see us. Her father was . . . scary. Mean. He could get . . . violent. He would kick her out of the house a lot of nights and make her sleep in the backyard."

The pieces I had are shifting into place.

All the stories that take place in the garden in the middle of the night.

The White Ladies getting vengeance on bad men.

The monstrous women taking flight.

The threads running through her stories.

"He was much older than Tita Gabby—by twenty years, something like that. He served in the war. The Japanese tortured him. Lots of people wouldn't be the same after that."

He sighs again, like with each intake of breath he's weighing how much more to tell me. "He was furious when he showed up, looking for her, and she was so scared. I told him she left already, and Glor went out onto the roof to hide. But her dad saw her and pulled her back in through the window—I was so afraid she would fall, the way he was being rough with her, and he didn't seem to care."

My palms are sweating. For a long moment there's nothing but the air hissing between us on the phone.

"What happened then?"

"He dragged her out of the house by the back of her shirt, kicking and screaming. She wasn't allowed to come see us after that. We lost touch for a while." He takes a deep breath, lets it go. "It's funny how stories start."

I think I understand more now, how everything is layered.

How Mom couldn't stand to let herself grieve what she's lost, even while my dad was alive—the things her father took from her, the things she lost coming to this place. How her anger was already there, and then, when my dad died, it must have shifted, changed shape.

How her anger at me must be easier for her than all the other feelings she's keeping at bay.

There's a noise downstairs, and I jump a little.

Phone to my ear, I go investigate. And there's Mom, locking the door behind her.

"Where were you?"

She startles, too, blinking like the sight of me is a lot right now. "I took a walk."

Her eyes look swollen. Maybe she was crying.

I hold the phone out to her. "Tito Andoy."

She takes it cautiously and holds it to her ear.

Sometimes it's hard to find softness in my memories of her. But there was something when she told those stories. Eyebrows raised, letting herself laugh, accent peeking out.

Those old stories that survived the years, floated through when they could have been forgotten, erased. Passed through the filter of her imagination, her memories, and her pain.

It's funny what lasts.

It's funny what stays.

On the phone with Tito Andoy, Mom is laughing. She looks much younger, suddenly.

I don't usually think we look very much alike, but right then, I can see it.

The next few days are agony. It's finals week, and Suzy's still not responding to my messages. I see her across the room in our physics final, and when it's over, she's gone again, out the door quickly.

At home, Mom asks: "Why don't you go study with Suzy?"

It's strange because it doesn't seem like I'm grounded. But every time I try to start a conversation, she just says: "Get through your finals first, then we'll talk."

On the last day of finals, I walk over to Suzy's house after school. Her dad is in the driveway, hood of his van popped open.

He straightens when he sees me and gives me an awkward smile. He must know we've been fighting. "Suzy's just picking up the boys. She'll be home soon. Do you want to wait?"

"Can you give this to her?" I hold a cassette out to him, with a letter taped to it.

It's a mix of songs that remind me of Suzy. Mom never throws anything away, and there were some old blank tapes in a cabinet in the kitchen. They must have been there since before I was born, but they still worked.

I wrote out the exact memory each song brings up for me. The first time I went to H-Mart with Suzy's family and her dad played this song on the stereo. The time we spent hours listening to music in her room and dissecting what it meant that Matt Gilbert texted me separately, instead of in the group chat. The first time she picked me up for school by herself, and we screamed our lungs out to her dad's old tapes.

Sitting on my desk at home right now, there's another letter. For Mom, but I'm not sure when I'll have the courage to give it to her.

Suzy's dad wipes his hands on a rag and turns the tape over in his hands. "The more things change."

I stand there awkwardly while the wind rustles through the trees. "Okay! Well. Thanks."

"You know—" He clears his throat. "My dad was tough on me. Growing up."

What did Suzy say to him?

"And adults would tell me I'd understand him better, when I got older."

He's just going to give me a lecture about how I should be handling this better. He's going to judge me, I can feel it.

"And I hated when they said that," he says.

What?

"I thought they meant I would outgrow my personality and turn into him." He runs a hand over the stubble on his head. "It just sounded like they didn't care about how I felt. Then I grew up, and I still didn't think he was right about everything. And I didn't stop being myself, either."

He smiles, and the laugh lines deepen around his eyes. "The thing that surprised me was: It's not actually an either-or choice. Sympathizing with your parents or with yourself. I think that's what can get easier. Learning to do both. But it kind of falls apart if you don't start with yourself first."

The way he's looking at me now, with such fatherly concern—a little part of me says, *Hey, turns out you're not impossible to love, actually.*

"Thanks," I say, trying to keep the lump in my throat contained.

"You know, we have that apartment above the store in Eastleigh," he says, hastily, like he's expecting me to run away any minute. "Suzy was going to move in anyway, next year. I'm sure she'd love to have a roommate."

"If she ever speaks to me again," I say with a nervous laugh.

He smiles again. "I know she will."

FIFTY-THREE

WHEN I OPEN THE FRONT DOOR, THERE'S SOMETHING ON THE FLOOR, waiting for me.

A letter, dropped through the mail slot.

With my name on it.

Deedee Walters

And in the place where the return address goes:

Jay Dinh Hayes
From across the street

I lean out the door and look around, like Jay might still be there.

OSONGCO

And when he's not, I close it and sink to the floor, so at least I'll be sitting down for this.

Dear Deedee,

There's a fluttering in my chest. I'm so used to flinging letters into the void. Receiving one is a little surreal.

I'm kind of new to this letter writing thing. But Candace is a big fan, apparently. And it felt like a good way to put my thoughts together.

It's written in black pen, and there are things scratched out with careful crosshatching, every few sentences. I can feel him thinking and rethinking. Wanting to be good, feeling so much, struggling against himself. Hunched over his desk, surrounded by empty energy drink cans and books about a boy and his dad and his car.

First, I wanted to write this letter to thank you.

Topic sentences. I'm going to cry.

Really, truly. Spending time with you made me feel more like myself than I have in a long time. Thank you for

There are things blotted out here, rethought and said again.

listening and understanding. Thank you for making me feel like I could talk about things I always tell myself not to. For helping me make more sense to myself.
I guess for a long time, with my mom, I could only see how

323

I let her down and how badly I didn't want to do that again. And how mad I was at Candace.

But I think, talking to you about it, I could see different angles of it. Like I wasn't holding it so tight in my hand anymore because I had to loosen my grip to show you. And I could see why Candace needed some distance, even if I was still mad about it. And I could see the part where

More crosshatching here, more things shaded out.

I could be less mad at myself, or start to be. And I could see how the pressure of everything was getting to me, and maybe it wasn't the only way it had to be.

There's a thing I realized I do, keeping people at arm's length because I'm terrified of saying no to anyone I care about. Maybe because I have a hard time thinking I owe myself anything, or that I deserve anything. And it's easy to just get eaten up with guilt.

Obviously, I was hoping for a different answer when you turned me down. But part of me felt like maybe I could learn something. In a way it's kind of inspiring, how you were able to say no to me.

Second, I wanted to write to tell you: I had this long talk with my mom about what happened and how things need to change. And I thought about what you said, about where I actually want to be.

And we decided Gemma and I are going to go stay with Candace for the summer. We're leaving after graduation.

Shit, that's in a few days. This is a goodbye letter.

We agreed it's a good idea, to make up for lost time.
And then I'll probably stay there, for a while. I'm not
sure how long yet, but I'll take the summer, figure out a
new plan. Maybe find a job there and apply to schools for
the year after.

My eyes are welling up, and I'm biting the inside of my cheek, trying to keep it contained.

So I thought about the other thing you said.
About how it's up to me, what I want to do now. If I want
you to be in my life, or if it's too hard.
I still feel the way I feel. And it hurts, but

Some things are scratched out here. He tried a few times to get it right.

I want to keep talking, if that's okay. Like you mentioned.
For a long time, if possible. I think we deserve it.
Maybe we could write to each other.
So if you want to, here's where I'll be:

A Woodside address is written there—Candace's, in New York. And there are more clouds of crosshatching where he second-guessed how he wanted to end it.

Maybe he wondered how I'd feel, if I would be uncomfortable, if it would make me mad. But in the end, he settled on:

Love,
Jay

I lean back against the wall, filled with this aching sadness shot through with joy, like a dark sky with a dusting of stars.

I read it another time, and another. Hold it to my chest and stare into space. Read it again.

Out front, a car honks, and I jump a little.

And a feeling of relief catches me, seeing it's the Civic.

FIFTY-FOUR

"So I got your note," Suzy says as I climb in next to her.

The volume on the stereo is turned down, and I'm straining to recognize the song that's playing.

She whacks my arm with the envelope. "Why does this sound like a goodbye letter?"

The song changes, and I can tell it's the tape I made her.

"Because guess what, you're stuck with me."

I exhale and slump down in my seat. "The best news, honestly."

"I'm still mad at you, though!" She looks out the windshield and starts to drive. The humidity presses in, even with the faint stream of air coming through the vents.

"You know Alex came to talk to me, like, two minutes after you left?" she says, turning the corner. "To explain everything. I know he was just helping you get home. Beth's friend sent her those pictures, and Beth told her to start some shit, I guess."

Locust trees sway in the breeze on the side of the road, straining against the power lines.

"And the day after that, your boy came to see me."

"What?"

"He was trying to say it's his fault, that he wanted to keep it a secret, and I shouldn't be mad at you. He's kind of a bad liar."

I'm not sure if I want to laugh or cry.

"And my mom and dad both talked to me about you." She laughs. "You have, like, an entire village vouching for you."

Oh my God?

You're not unlovable after all, actually.

"Still, it really hurt, you know? But I thought about some things my dad said. Maybe there's a reason you felt like you couldn't tell me." She pulls into the parking lot of the 24/7 convenience store and looks over at me. "So, explain it to me. What did you mean, about your mom?"

"It's kind of a long story."

"We've got time."

So we get slushies and sit on her hood, looking out at the passing cars while I tell her everything—about the letters, and sneaking around, and the fights with my mom. When she hears what Mom said I did to my dad, she hugs me tight. And as I describe all the ups and downs with Jay, she's alternately swooning and looking like she's going to kick his ass.

"OKAY, WELL, TELL ME NEXT TIME!" she says when I finish, and punches me lightly on the arm.

I guess that doesn't quite do it for her, though, because she grabs my shoulders and shakes me.

"I love you, you asshole!" she practically yells. "It's my business to know shit like this."

I hug her as tightly as I can. "I love you, too."

I was always so scared to say it to her. Trying to protect myself, even though never saying it would definitely not have made losing her hurt any less.

"I'm pissed that you kept the stuff with your mom to yourself," she says. "But I guess . . . I was pretty wrapped up in my shit, too. I'm sorry it took me so long to get what was going on with you. To even ask."

Suzy sighs. "And I'm really sorry about the debate team thing. I wasn't thinking. I realized that, after, but . . . we never really talked about it again. Of course I would have helped you keep Jay a secret, if you asked."

"I should have told you. I was scared it would mean . . . telling you all this other stuff. That I didn't really know how to talk about yet. I needed to figure some things out."

Suzy stabs at the bottom of her cup with her straw. "I guess I kept things from you, too. I didn't want to tell you about stuff with Alex. About how I was struggling, because I thought, I shouldn't complain, I have this thing you wanted that you don't."

"That's awful." My face scrunches up. "I hate that."

"He came to your rescue after prom, though." She smiles a little. "So I can't hate him."

"He was just respecting your wishes, you know?" I lean back against the hot hood. "He was your poor stand-in. Imitation Suzy."

She snorts. "Like imitation crab meat?"

We laugh so much, the car shakes.

"Well, I mean, you drove yourself home from New York?" Suzy says, catching her breath. "Seems like you came to your own rescue."

I roll my sweaty plastic cup between my hands. "So what's going on now with you and Alex?"

"He wanted to get back together. But I think I realized . . . I mean, he's fine. But I felt like he's someone I was supposed to like. Like a place everyone's so excited to go, there's a line out the door, and then I get there and—this is it?" She laughs at herself. "Wow, that sounds so mean!"

She tosses her empty cup into the trash can, and it lands even though it's pretty far away. "What I mean is: A lot of what I imagined, when I dreamed about him, was a way I wanted permission to see myself, I think?" she says. "But actually, up close—I kind of disagreed with the way he saw me. I liked my version better."

"I would trust your version over his any day."

"I think we're going to be friends, though. Like, actual, straight-forward, boring friends. Not whatever you two have been doing." She waves her hands in my direction.

"Okay, wait," she adds, sitting up suddenly. "That car he drives. Did you learn to drive stick?"

"Yeah." I laugh.

"That's hilarious. You're taking the test in this, though, right?" She raps the car with her knuckles. "You're driving on the way home."

An idea tugs at me, one that's been taking shape while I've been lying awake at night, thinking about Mom's vases and the softness I want.

"Okay." I grin at her as she hands me her keys. "But I want to stop somewhere first."

FIFTY-FIVE

MOM GETS HOME FROM WORK AFTER DARK THAT NIGHT. WHEN SHE turns the light on, all the vases are filled with flowers. Pink peonies, white carnations, orange tulips, yellow roses, bright little spheres of craspedia. Suzy and I had to go to multiple supermarkets to find them all.

"What is this!" Mom's hand flies to her mouth, and she sinks down into a chair at the kitchen table.

I cross the room and try to hug her, awkwardly, from the side. We never hug, and she tenses.

I shift around, crouch so I'm really holding on to her, give her a squeeze.

"Okay, fine, enough," she says, wriggling away, clearly uncomfortable. She fixes her hair. "My mom loved flowers."

"Mom," I say, sitting next to her, worrying this is all wrong, "I wanted to ask you some things. I have some questions for you."

She swipes her fingers under her eyes. "And I owe you some answers."

That surprises me, the world tilting slightly. But where do I start?

"I know about the apartment. Were you actually just going to New York all the time, when you said you were traveling for business?"

She laughs and gives me a confused look. "No. No, I really have been wearing myself out, flying all over the country. I wish I was making that part up." She presses the heels of her hands into her closed eyes. "That was the first time I'd been back in years. I couldn't bring myself to get rid of that apartment, where we used to live." She sucks in a breath and lets it out through her gritted teeth. "But I didn't like going back. I got someone else to take care of it."

She gets up and goes to the cabinet, leans in to smell the flowers. "But after you stopped writing the letters . . . after that concert, when I saw you with Suzy's parents, I—I knew something needed to change, I just wasn't sure—" She swallows hard. "Maybe I don't know how to change. I do love you. Maybe I just don't know how."

That guilt is reaching out for me, and there's heat and pressure gathering behind my eyes. But I still have so many unanswered questions.

"Why did you have me write those letters?"

"Because you seemed sad, and . . . I thought, maybe it's because you didn't fit in here. You didn't have a sense of who we are, of your family."

My back tightens up, trying to keep the anger in, thinking about the gap between what she wanted and what she did.

I'm nervous, stepping out onto this thin ice, but I have to ask. "What . . . happened with your mom?"

I put a hand over hers, and she lets it sit there.

"He said I provoked him." She shakes her head, and her jaw trembles. "They were fighting, he was—he was in a rage. And I wouldn't let it go, I wouldn't back down. Everyone said I was just aggravating him, *asking for it.* And my mom just—she couldn't stand it anymore, had to get away, took the car in a panic. I don't think she meant to—I don't think she wanted—"

She sounds like she's struggling to breathe.

"You can't blame yourself for that." My voice is a surprise, strange to me. "You didn't make him like that."

Leaning her elbows on the table, Mom covers her face with her hands.

"Is that why you fought with your brothers? The last time we visited."

"I don't think they believed that anymore, when we got older—that I was responsible. But they had a hard time with it when I didn't want to speak to him. It caused a lot of misunderstandings. Especially when he was near the end.

"I still feel so much regret—" Her voice sounds so tired and small. "My anger at him cast a shadow over the time I had with your dad. I cut my father off, but I felt so ashamed. I didn't want you to know about all of that. I thought—well, I can make something up for you. Give you a better version. A gift I didn't get to have."

She huffs out a big breath, like she's running uphill. "I thought, if kids write to Santa Claus—if that's supposed to be a nice thing for them—why not this?"

I want to scream, *That makes no sense!* But instead, I hold on to the edge of the table.

She sniffs. "You don't know how good you have it. He would hit me in the face, tell me I was ugly. Grab my head and slam it into the wall." Her expression is different, now, defenses up. "You don't know what suffering is."

"What he did to you is terrible," I say quietly. "It doesn't mean I don't feel pain, too."

She narrows her eyes at me. "I had you write those letters because I wanted you to be *proud*. Proud of our family."

"But not proud of where you're from?"

She makes a dismissive sound.

"That . . . matters to me," I say. "I've spent so much time feeling out of place here, feeling . . . wrong, ugly. But I don't really have the context to feel proud. To make sense of it."

There's a look of genuine shock on her face, mouth open, like this would never in a million years have occurred to her. "Where I grew up, everyone couldn't stop talking about how pretty mestizas are. People would kill to look like you. *Typical of you.*" She almost spits. "Ungrateful for what you have."

"Okay, well, I didn't grow up there." I'm trying to keep my voice level. "And that sounds fucked up."

"Language!" Mom cries. "I was just doing my best, all right! I don't know why you have so much anger. Maybe that's some of him, coming out in you."

I fold my lips into my mouth and take a good long look at her.

"You're pretty angry," I say.

"What did you say?!" she yells, and stands so her chair scrapes back. Then she pauses, remorseful, like she's hearing herself for the first time.

She tilts her head back, looking at the ceiling. "If you didn't already know she was dead, I would have had you write to my mom."

It feels like we're sliding now, arms pinwheeling, back into the land of the ghosts.

"Mom," I say softly. "Did you think about how this would make me feel?"

"What do you want me to do?" She's still yelling. "I can't change the past!"

But I know that's not how it works. That the past doesn't stay where it is, separate, unchanging.

"It's not like my feelings ever mattered!" she exclaims, face red. "Growing up! Coming here! At work!"

"And you tell yourself a story about that," I say, pressing my fingers into my palms. Knuckles white, hoping I'll make it to the other side. "The way you think about the past is shaping your decisions all the time, in the present. Like about how it's okay to treat me."

Mom folds her arms tight across her chest.

"Maybe if you change the way you think about the past," I say, voice hard-edged, "you'll be able to make some different decisions. Today, tomorrow, the day after. Maybe if you could tell yourself you didn't deserve it, you would see I don't deserve this, either."

She's staring at me, mouth in a hard line. Not moving.

I take a deep breath in, trying to draw on the calmest part of me. The part that feels like blue-tinged nights and conversations in the dark with someone you trust.

And I take the letter I wrote to her out of my back pocket and slide it across the table.

The letter where I say this isn't working and I need her to go to therapy.

"Some of the things you do make more sense to me now." I swallow hard as she picks up the letter and slowly opens it with trembling hands. "But some of the things you do aren't okay."

It's agony, waiting for her to read it. Watching her facial expression change, her scowl deepen.

"So you're saying I'm crazy," she says, looking at me over the unfolded pages. "This is offensive. You're saying I'm a bad mother."

"Mom," I say, trying to ignore the feeling this is all going sideways. "You said something needs to change. And you didn't know how. It's so we can do things differently, together. For the survival of our relationship."

She heaves a sigh and looks so tired now, maybe more than I've ever seen before.

"I'm sorry I say things I don't mean," she says. "In the heat of the moment."

"There's never a not-heated moment." I'm trembling, gripping the table, trying not to shout. "And those things stick. You know? I have no way of knowing you don't mean them. It's not okay."

Mom seems like she's about to say something, but she catches herself and takes a deep breath instead.

Then she gets up and leaves, vanishing down the hall.

So that's it.

I lost her.

There she goes.

"Are you going to come help me with this?" Mom shouts from her office.

I come to the door, and she's on her computer, peering at the screen.

"Since you're insisting I try this." She looks over at me, waves me closer. "Help me find someone who takes my insurance."

I pull up a chair next to her.

"I'm sorry," she says quietly, eyes straight ahead, like that's safer. "I'm sorry I hurt you. I should never have blamed you for that."

"Thank you," I whisper.

She leans back in her desk chair and runs a hand over her face. "I bought a ticket."

"Okay." Fear and excitement tangle together, a knot in my throat. I guess I'm going to the Philippines. "When am I leaving?"

"You're not. I need to go back by myself." She looks at me again and puts on her storytelling voice. *"Lay some ghosts to rest."*

"So I'm not going? I . . . kind of wanted to actually."

"You will. We'll go again. But this is something I need to do alone first. I'm going to stay with Andoy. We have a lot of catching up to do."

I show her how to filter her search results, and she clicks around, frowning at the screen.

"In the meantime," she says, writing some names on a Post-it note, "I talked to Charlie."

"You talked to him?" My throat feels thick.

"He said you can stay with them while I'm gone. Maybe it would be fun for you. And you can work with them in the store."

She looks at me sideways, like she just remembered something. "What's going on with that boy?"

I almost choke on my spit. "What boy?"

She rolls her eyes at me, and I feel like I can see a flash of myself in her expression.

"I know something is going on." She's shifting into gossip mode, leaning forward, eyebrows raised. "Because you made him cry."

I should probably be terrified, but I can barely keep my smile tamped down.

"Nothing is going on."

"Sure." Mom sighs, turning back to the screen. "You're not cursed, you know. We're not cursed. Whatever I might have said."

FIFTY-SIX

I SEE JAY FROM A DISTANCE AT FIRST, GREEN GRADUATION GOWN BIL-lowing in the wind, dark pants beneath it. He's got one hand over the cap so it doesn't fly off his head.

I run up to him, then stop short, because I didn't think through what I wanted to do when I got there.

"Um. I got your letter."

"Oh. Good." He squints into the sun. "I was worried I had the wrong address."

I glance back over my shoulder at Mom, sitting next to the Jangs. It looks like she's actually laughing at something Suzy's dad said.

Jay's mom walks up the grass toward us and gives him a big hug, rocking him back and forth. He pats her back with the hand that's not holding his diploma.

"Oh, Jay, I'm so proud of you!" she says. This might be the first time I've heard her call him that.

Gemma comes running after her, Candace and her girlfriend trailing behind. They drove in from New York, made a long weekend of it.

When everyone starts drifting toward the parking lot, Jay hangs back a little, looking over at me.

I have no idea what else to do, so I punch him lightly in the arm.

He laughs, but it's more air than sound. "I miss you already."

"Well. You'll get over it."

"I don't think so," he says. "But that's okay."

A few days later I see him from my window, packing up his car in the driveway. Jay and Gemma hug their mom goodbye before she gets in her own car and drives off somewhere. I come outside and walk across the street, hugging myself like it's cold out, even though it's not.

He closes the trunk and stares at his car, arms crossed. "I'll probably sell it. When I get there. I won't need it anymore."

"Wow. End of an era." I'm choked up, remembering how I felt sitting beside him, all those moments suspended from the rest of my life. Even the terror of driving back from New York feels softer, gold-tinted now.

Jay pulls me in for a hug. It's still the best. Undisputed.

We stay there like that for so long, Gemma honks the horn. "Are you going to do that all day?!"

I laugh and pull away from him. "Drive safely, okay?"

He narrows his eyes at me and pulls me close one more time, real quick, a tight squeeze. Then he jogs around to the driver's seat before Gemma can honk again.

She waves frantically while he reverses out, and I stand there watching until they're out of sight, behind the trees.

FIFTY-SEVEN

I DON'T WRITE BACK TO JAY RIGHT AWAY.

I want to give him space, and a lot is going on. Working at the store. Easing into staying with Suzy's family. Taking the driving test and passing.

Suzy's dad gets me access to Eastleigh's darkroom early, because he knows a guy.

And when I finally develop the film from New York, there's Jay, staring back at me, dark eyes sad and tender. Someone who feels like family to me.

I reread his letter when I get home, and I just can't not write back.

> Dear Jay,
> Sorry it took me a while to answer. I needed to clear my head.

I tell him about getting my license, and the weird people who come into the store. How Mom and I have been talking more since she's been in the Philippines than we have in the past six months combined.

> Tito Andoy will be in the background when she calls, saying, "Let me talk to her!" like it's a treat. He tells me stories about engkantos and duwendes and the tikbalang (look it up, it's wild). It's been nice.
>
> I'm trying to learn as much about photography as I can in my free time before classes start in the fall. I'm going to do a graphic design major, photography minor. I'm making a Powerpoint about the kinds of jobs I can get with that, to show my mom when she gets back.
>
> How is New York? What is it like there?
>
> Love,
>
> Deedee

His answer arrives a week later.

> Dear Deedee,
> Well shit, it's good to hear from you. I can't say I wasn't worried.
> New York is good. It smells like hot garbage a lot of the time, but I like it anyway.

He tells me about family dinners with Candace's friends, and about late nights sitting on the couch in her living room, catching up with his sister.

Gemma and I hang out during the day, while everyone is at work. We went to the Queens Museum and stared at the big diorama of the city, trying to find Candace's block. We saw the mummies at the Met (she thought they were creepy). We go to Flushing a lot. Gemma has her boba order down to a science now.

It's kind of surreal, just getting time to exist. I actually took up a hobby that I'm not trying to monetize. Candace has been teaching me to surf, on the weekends, when her friends go out to Rockaway.

I'm drawing more, too. I used to be so embarrassed of it, even when I was by myself, and no one was watching. But I'm trying harder to tell myself it's fine.

Here are some sketches of our neighborhood. Since you asked what it's like here, I can kind of show you.
Love,
Jay

After that, we exchange letters every week. His arrive like clock-work, a pile growing in the corner of Suzy's desk that she set aside for me.

I can't text him anymore. It feels too close to how we used to be.

Whenever he messages me, I say, *I'll tell you in the next letter*, and eventually he stops trying.

It's like our friendship exists in another dimension. Another century, pen and paper only. An in-between place where the rules of the rest of our lives don't quite apply.

At the end of the summer, Jay gets his job back.

Apparently, the day he lost his job, he went to the company headquarters first, looking for Phil.

> I talked to this guy in the elevator when I was there. I was half delirious, trying to explain the situation. He seemed like he was about to call security on me.
>
> It turns out he was really impressed with me? He's been trying to get me hired for real ever since. It took them forever to process it! And I had to do fourteen panel interviews and a test. Kind of funny since I was working for them for four years.
>
> I kept thinking I can't wait to tell you. They have a tuition reimbursement program, so I'm applying to schools here for next year, too. I know things were really fucked up the last time we talked about the future, but do you think maybe that changes anything for you?

Is he expecting me to say, *I want to be your girlfriend now*?

I feel like I'm only just climbing out of the way I used to be, and I'll slip backward if I run into his arms.

> That's incredible, I'm so proud of you!
>
> I never thought you were a loser, so it doesn't really change anything, that way.
>
> I'm still trying to figure all the same things out.
>
> I hope you understand. And that you're living your life and not waiting for me.
>
> If you still want to write to me, I'll be here.

And I include my new address, at the apartment above the Eastleigh store.

I get scared he won't.

But a couple weeks after Suzy and I move in, an envelope shows up, with Jay's return address.

Sorry I said that. It was a lapse in judgment.
I hope you don't think that's the only reason I've been writing to you. Waiting for your answer to change.

The letters still come, through the fall and winter. Less frequent, but constant.

He writes to me about his coworkers, how strange it is to be younger than everyone. He writes to me about moving out of Candace's into his own place.

When Mom talks to her brothers for the first time in years, I write to him. Things with her are changing, slowly. Not perfect, backsliding sometimes. But she seems less afraid that being soft with me will make me too soft to survive.

Of course it's painful, a little while later, when Jay says he's seeing someone.

I wouldn't want to keep it from you. I don't want to keep things from you again, like with the college stuff. Our friendship really does mean a lot to me.

It hurts and it's also a relief, because he deserves it. Someone should take care of him for a change. And maybe I can feel less guilty.

The letters slow down, but they still keep coming, every few months, the tide receding and returning.

He writes to me about getting into NYU, and the therapist he's feeling optimistic about, after Candace made him go. I've been seeing one, too, through a program on campus.

He writes to me about an art class he's taking just for fun, and how it helps him feel less like a brain disappearing into a screen.

I write to him about the photo projects I'm dreaming up, the classes I'm taking in sophomore year. How Mom is getting really into plants, taking weekend classes in Eastleigh, making new friends. How Suzy's dad is actually getting the band back together.

When I go on a few dates with a guy from class, and he says something fucked up to me, I remember Jay under the bleachers, saying, *Don't ever let anyone talk to you like that*, and I walk right out of the restaurant.

The months pass, and our moms see each other more than we do. Mom joins Mrs. Jang's book club, and it turns out Jay's mom is already a member. Mom can't stop talking about her famous sandwiches, the next time we catch up on the phone.

But Jay and I see each other impressively little. He has a talent for missing me, somehow.

I save up for my own car, so I can stop relying on rides from Suzy. Jay asks in a letter what color it is, and I'm too embarrassed to tell him it's dark blue.

You can see when you come visit.

But he doesn't. He keeps his distance.

Alex is at Eastleigh, too. I run into him on campus, and he tells me Jay was there. "You just missed him."

I'm almost mad about it, because hasn't enough time passed now that we can see each other in person?

I almost say something. But I'm dating someone now, and if I'm honest with myself, I don't know what I expect Jay to be, or how I might feel, if I saw him again.

So instead, I write:

> It means a lot to me that you're still writing to me after all this time.

The letters keep coming, through the changing seasons. Snow out my window, spring arriving in New York. Months turn into years. I break up with my boyfriend. I cry to Suzy. I drive around for hours looking for locations for this photo project, lose myself in dreaming. Jay's mom graduates from school. Mom plants flowers in the yard.

The summer before senior year, I leave Massachusetts, for once. I get an internship I applied to as a long shot, at a museum in Los Angeles.

When I zip across five lanes of traffic at the 110 junction, I hear Jay's voice in my head, saying, *You're doing good.*

And I kind of wish he could see how different I am now.

But I know he's miles and miles away.

In the fall, I hear from Alex that Jay broke up with his girlfriend. And even though it's been years, now, I immediately get butterflies again.

It surprises me, how quick the longing comes back.

But the letters keep coming, and he never mentions it. I wonder if he's going through something, and maybe I'm not the person he wants to talk to about it.

I'm spending all my free time on this photo project, driving around to in-between places like the ones he used to take me. A lot of the things I like best about myself have little reminders of Jay threaded through them.

Sometimes I'll be driving home in the dark, and the way the street-lights look, the way the moon is—I'm right back in his car, a specific night, a specific conversation we were having, like it just happened. The emotion picks up, a sudden gust of wind, and drops me down again.

Sometimes I think about a world where I'd said yes to him at prom. Maybe we would have stopped talking to each other a long time ago. And I can only be grateful for the extra time.

So I write:

> I'm here if you need me, okay?

But I break my own rule and look at his Instagram. And I notice something in the background of a photo he posted, in his room. I try to make it bigger, *oh so carefully*, so I don't accidentally heart it.

There's my drawing of the fish sauce bottle, taped up at his desk.

FIFTY-EIGHT

"A lot of people came, ha?" Mom does that affectionate pincer thing with two fingers on my arm.

It's the night of my first solo show, at an art gallery off campus. I'm vibrating with nervous energy.

But Mom's right, the room is full, and people are circulating, talking. Perceiving the art I made.

She waves to Mrs. Jang across the room. "You know Bo-ra really does know everyone's business in town? They just tell her *everything*, chatting at the store." Her inner tsismosa finally found someone to talk to.

In the corner, Suzy and her dad are having an irritated back-and-forth. She's trying to be his manager because she's always been the band's biggest fan. But the two of them are also driving each other up the wall.

Suzy crosses the room and touches my shoulder. "We're going to head over to set up." The band is playing in a bar nearby tonight, for old times' sake. She pulls me in for a tight hug. "Congratulations again! See you over there later?"

"I wouldn't miss it." I give her another squeeze before they head out the door.

Mom gestures at an image on the wall, labeled ASWANG (DEROGATORY) / ASWANG (AFFECTIONATE). "I don't understand why you care so much about these strange things."

This would have stung, another day, another time, and I don't blame myself for that. But things are different enough between us now, it's easier to see that she's trying.

"Because I loved your stories growing up."

"All right, well." She's trying not to smile. "If it makes you happy."

Mom's looking around the room, and she stops, like she sees someone she recognizes.

I turn to follow her gaze, and—

There's Jay.

Just *here*, suddenly, even though we've barely seen each other in forever. In this room full of people I know from school, while I'm standing here in a sparkly silver dress and slightly uncomfortable heels.

Same dark eyes, same sardonic smile, hair a bit less messy.

I look away, look back again. He smiles and looks down, shy.

Oh my God, what does this mean?

"There's . . . that boy who was in your room," Mom says. "Thủy's son. Jay?"

She barely remembers my friends from school. She's mixed up the names of all the boys I've introduced her to over the last three-and-a-half years. But of course Jay will always be That Boy Who Was in Your Room.

"That was a long time ago," I say, more forcefully than I mean to. Mom is smiling a little. She looks over at him again.

"Stop looking!" I hiss, shielding the side of my face with my hand.

She raises her eyebrows and glances his way again. "I should get going before it gets too late." She squeezes my shoulder. "Be careful! Call me later!"

I squeeze her arm back. "I will!"

And then she's gone, and he's drifting over, standing in front of me. He dressed up. Collared shirt, blazer. I'm staring.

"Hey. It's Jay, remember?" My face must look blank, because he adds: "From high school?"

I can't cope, oh God, try to say something funny?

"Oh right! Jay from high school. I kind of always had a crush on you."

"Oh yeah?" He laughs and tucks a hand behind his head. "Whatever happened with that?"

"Bad timing, I guess." The strangeness of the situation is messing with my depth perception. "So, uh . . . what are you doing here?"

"I thought . . . you might be hungry?" His other hand comes out from behind his back, holding a little bag of salt-and-vinegar potato chips.

I burst out laughing and mock-punch him in the arm.

"I just heard about this talented artist and couldn't miss it, you know?" He slips a pamphlet from his jacket pocket and reads aloud. "*Liminal spaces, present absences, ghosts.* Sounds like you." He hits me with this wide, completely unselfconscious grin. "I'm so proud of you."

My nose is warming up, and I suddenly need to blink a lot, so I open the bag of chips. Maybe carbs will help me through this.

There's too much motion around us, too many voices.

"Look at this." I lead him over to one wall. "Suzy helped with this one."

"Is she the ghost?"

"Yeah." I laugh. "She was so into it. Like she was getting to be in one of the movies she loves, but less exciting. Actually! Suzy's dad's band is playing tonight, if—" I fumble, searching for the words. "Want to go with me?"

"Are you asking me out?" He's making fun of me. I almost forgot how much I liked it.

I don't answer, just let that sit there.

Mrs. Jang's voice pops into my head, teasing Charlie about the band. *You were always saying you were just ahead of your time. WELL. It's been quite some time!*

And I have to start laughing again.

"What's funny?" Jay smiles uncertainly.

I shake my head and tell him I'm going to say goodbye to some people, and he can wait for me outside.

We're quiet as we walk over to the bar. I feel so exposed and sensitive suddenly, a dozen old feelings ripe under my skin.

I keep wanting to reach out and touch him to see if he's real. But I don't want to mess anything up before it's started.

The moment Suzy sees Jay, she rushes over and yells, "WHAT IS GOING ON HERE?"

I glance at his face for a sign, and he's doing the same to me. We probably both look equally scared, because Suzy starts laughing.

"Oh, you guys," she says. "You poor babies."

I feel like the entire surface of my skin is glowing again.

"I don't know yet," I say, "but I promise you'll be the first to know when I find out."

"Okay, I'll just make sure to shout WHAT THE FUCK ARE YOU TWO DOING every time I see you forever now." Suzy points a threatening finger at Jay. "I'm watching you, buddy!"

We stay for a few songs, and it's truly a delight to see Suzy's dad screaming into the mic. But at a certain point I can't really contain myself anymore, so I lean over and ask Jay, "Do you want to get out of here?"

It's a nice night outside. That spring smell in the air, optimism as a perfume.

"If you could go anywhere right now," he asks, looking up at the sky, "where would you want to go?"

The options run through my mind.

My apartment.

My bed.

But that's too much, probably. This conversation needs some air.

"The roof of the student union building," I say, because Suzy's dad showed us how to get up there.

Jay's trying not to smile too wide. "You know what I like."

It's a little too far back to campus to walk, so we find my car, and Jay laughs when he sees the ghost dangling from my keys.

"I can't believe you still have that." He covers his mouth, smiles into his hand.

"Don't judge me."

"I wouldn't dream of it."

He closes his door, and we're in our own private world again, the air between us vibrating with things unsaid.

The drive passes mostly in silence. There's a stillness to him, sitting beside me. It makes me realize how nervous he used to be, a background hum you don't notice until it goes quiet.

Now there's something unhurried there, sure. Like he doesn't think he's running out of time anymore. Like he thinks we have all the time in the world.

At the student union building, we go up the back stairwell, down a winding hall, up a set of more questionable metal steps. Jay takes my hand and helps me where it gets kind of precarious.

Then we're on the roof, lights of the sleepy college town spread out below us. We go to the low wall at the edge and lean against it, side by side, taking in the view.

"So . . . I heard a rumor that you're single," I say finally. "Does that have anything to do with why you came to see me now? And not before."

"I've been single for a little while, actually. Inspector Deedee's getting rusty." Jay sighs. "I guess . . . I came because I've been feeling pretty good lately. Like I'm a version of myself I like. I kind of wanted to wait for that, before showing up again."

His eyes flicker over to me. "I mean, I didn't come expecting— Honestly, I just wanted to see you. And see your show. It felt right when I saw you post about it, you know? I just wanted to see you doing well." His Adam's apple bobs as he swallows. "It's not like I assumed I'd be showing up to sweep you off your feet."

"So you're saying that might interest you. . . ."

His shoulders shake with suppressed laughter. "Apparently, I still talk about you all the time? Candace kept saying I should do something about it. It's like the two of you are conspiring against me."

"Oh yeah, having women in your life who want you to be happy and work out your issues, that must be hard for you."

He looks at me seriously. "Do you feel closer to who you wanted to be?"

The calm in my chest. The way I talk to myself now. The softness I want, that I carry with me all the time. Things aren't perfect, but—

"Yeah," I say. "Compared to before. Closer than I was."

Neither of us seems to know what to say next, so we stare out at the empty streets, a still life at this hour of night.

And then I work up the nerve to ask: "Where are you staying?"

"With Alex."

"Do you want a ride back to New York? Tomorrow. Or whenever. I mean, I kind of owe you. Since you just drove me there at the drop of a hat."

He huffs out a laugh. "You don't owe me anything."

"What if I want to?"

"Deedee, you . . ." Jay looks down at my hand resting on the wall and covers it with his. "I spent so long thinking I'd never get another chance at this. If you're saying what I think you're saying, I . . . really want to do it right, this time. And it's kind of zero to sixty, jumping right into a road trip." He laughs. "In retrospect, I may have . . . rushed things, last time."

Wow. He said no to me. I'm proud of him.

"Okay." I squeeze his hand. "What do you want to do?"

"Talk. A lot. Get to know each other again. Make some plans." Jay smiles and bites his lip. "And, if it's okay . . . right now, I really want to kiss you."

I pull him close, and when our lips meet, it's like the first time, running through all of me, a rush like the sea. Some things I remember— the softness of his lips, the way he smells. Some of it feels new—the scratch of his stubble, and the way he holds on to me, with the force of how long it's been. The miles we've traveled together and apart, and all the people we've been since the last time we touched. How much I want to meet the people he's going to be.

We stay out there for a while, his hand in mine, the dark sky above us, sleepy college town streets below. Talking until it's the deep blue between night and morning. Knowing we can stay to watch the sun come up.

ACKNOWLEDGMENTS

Midnights With You includes portrayals of painful parent-child relationships. If you've had similar experiences, I hope you can be gentle with yourself as you untangle the ways their impact may be showing up in the rest of your life. For anyone in that situation, I would recommend the following resources: *It Wasn't Your Fault* by Beverly Engel, *Adult Children of Emotionally Immature Parents* by Lindsay C. Gibson, and the work of Sahaj Kaur Kohli (@BrownGirlTherapy on Instagram).

Honestly, there are way too many people to thank, and I feel so incredibly fortunate to be able to say that.

Back before I started taking my own writing seriously, I would read the acknowledgments in books and think, *Damn, I don't even know this many people!* Well, things change, and for this book to make it into your hands, it's really taken a village.

Thank you to my incredible agent, Amy Bishop-Wycisk—I truly couldn't imagine a better partner in my writing career, and I thank my lucky stars every day that I have you in my corner.

Thank you to my editor, Rebecca Kuss, for helping this book become the best version of itself.

Thank you as well to Jim McCarthy, everyone at DG&B, and everyone at Trellis Literary Management for all your help and support.

Thank you to Dana Lédl and Marci Senders for giving me the cover of my dreams. You've captured the essence of this story with such care, and looking at it still gives me butterflies.

Thank you to Ash I. Fields, Sara Liebling, Iris Chen, Guy Cunningham, Andrea Rosen, Vicki Korlishin, Michael Freeman, LeBria Casher, Holly Nagel, Danielle DiMartino, Dina Sherman, Bekka Mills, Maddie Hughes, Crystal McCoy, Daniela Escobar, and the whole team at Hyperion for all of your hard work on this book. Amanda Marie Schlesier, thank you for the note you sent along with the offer email that made me cry.

Thank you to Kate Heceta-Arellano and Teresa Trần for authenticity reading. Any flaws are wholly my own.

Zoulfa Katouh and Molly X. Chang, you taught me so much about story, about voice and character development, and about the grit it takes to revise again and again. Thank you to everyone involved in running Pitch Wars for making all of that possible. Hannah Sawyerr and Olivia Liu, thank you for those early notes that stayed with me and shaped the way I thought about the story. (And Hannah, I'm so glad you moved to L.A.! Let's get KBBQ again soon.)

Nathalie Medina, your belief in this book helped me more than I can express. You're absolutely brilliant, and I can't wait to have your books on my shelf.

Emily Charlotte and S. Z. Ahmed, I'm so incredibly grateful to have you as critique partners and as friends. Thank you for being here through so many stages of this book's life, and for saving my sanity more than once. Can't wait for our next writing date.

To the baddies group chat: I feel so lucky to know all of you, and I can't believe I ended up with so many friends who would read multiple (?!) drafts of this book. Thank you for picking me up off the floor when I was down.

Thank you to Trinity Nguyen for the writing dates and commiserating over Thai noodle soup, for helping me name Jay, and for being down to do my author photo shoot in a giant mall parking lot.

Amanda Khong, thank you for making me feel so seen, for your encouragement and advice, and for everything you do for BIPOC authors on Bookish Brews.

Carolyn Huynh, thank you for all your advice as I've navigated publishing, for the laughs and the gossip, and for writing one of my favorite books of all time.

Lilly Lu, thank you for sharing your brilliance, for trusting me with your words (endlessly obsessed with your books!), and for inviting me to speak to your students.

Gayle Gaviola, thank you for the writing dates and the emails, for reading this book multiple times, and for having my back with publicity advice.

Viviann Do, I'm so in awe of you! Thank you for including me in Little Saigon Book Street and for embracing *MWY*.

Alex Brown, Zoulfa Katouh, Grace Li, Ann Liang, Laura Taylor Namey, Randy Ribay, Hannah Sawyerr, and Trang Thanh Tran: So very grateful that you took the time to read and blurb *MWY* while juggling your own deadlines and commitments! Your books are an inspiration to me, and I'm still floored every time I read your kind words about mine.

Trang: Thank you for your friendship since the early days of my publishing journey, for always being so generous with your time and advice, and for hanging out at Yallfest.

Wen-yi Lee, Jen St. Jude, Page Powars, Birukti Tsige, Sonali Kohli, K. X. Song, Alyssa Villaire, Jade Adia, and Sonora Reyes, thank you for your encouragement and advice, and for keeping me company online during edits. And Skyla Arndt, thank you for sharing your promo wisdom with me!

Maria Dong and Ysabelle Suarez, thank you for reading early drafts of the book, cheering me on, and making me feel seen.

P. H. Low, your prose is so gorgeous! How!! Thank you for reading, for commiserating, and for trusting my driving on L.A. freeways. I'm so glad we get to debut together.

C. L. Montblanc, you are a gem. Thanks for always checking in, for making me laugh, and for being on this wild ride with me.

S. C. Bandreddi, your comments after you finished reading meant so much to me, and I still think about them all the time. Excited for everything you'll do in the future.

D. L. Taylor, Kelsey Epler, Juniper Klein, Elle Taylor, Cassidy Hart, Rosario Martinez, Sarah J., thank you for beta reading before the showcase, and for all the screaming comments in the Google Doc that made my heart grow a size.

Sam Estrella and Jess Gonzalez, thank you for the writing dates, the critiques, and that retreat in the desert in the middle of a huge winter storm.

KT Hoffman, Natalie Sue, Mackenzie Reed, Jamison Shea, Sophie

Clark, Anna Mercier and Lyssa Mia Smith, thank you for keeping me sane through publishing's wild ups and downs.

Thank you to the '21 Pitch Wars class for all your support, especially Megan Davidhizar, K. A. Cobell, S. Hati, Gabriella Buba, Tyler Lawson, Valo Wing, Alexandra Kiley, Crystal Seitz, Sian Gilbert, Tracy Sierra, Aurora Palit, The Mancaruso sisters, Tauri Cox, Evette Williams, Christine Arnold, Hailie Kei, Lily Lai, and R. A. Basu.

Eva Des Lauriers, Sophie Wan, Robin Wasley, and Jill Tew, it's been such a joy to get to know you through the debut group and to get to read your words. To all the 2024-Evers—oh my God lol, what a year! You deserve a long nap.

Thank you to Kat Cho and Claribel Ortega for creating supportive spaces for BIPOC authors and sharing so much knowledge through Write or Die. (Kat, I'll always remember running into you and Rebecca at Yallfest and embarrassingly blurting out, "You helped me become an author!!" 😄 But also: it's true.)

Raillan, Priya, Maddy, Matt and Laura, Luz and Luis—you were really there for this whole damn thing, from the earliest "Uhh so I think I'm actually writing a novel" conversations. Thank you for listening to me complain about publishing for literal years, and for the phone calls and dinners that made me feel like a person again.

Brenda, I still can't believe you read that terrible first draft so fast! Your comments kept me going through many false starts and dead ends. It really means the world to me.

Lauren, thank you for believing in me, and for being so unwaveringly thoughtful and kind (and for the friendship bracelet that matched my book cover!).

Andi, Lilly, Tara, Alexa, Tita, Michele—thank you for getting it and helping me feel less alone. Love you <3